Dylan O'Roarke loved Christmas— and he loved women...

Tall ones, slender ones, plump ones, smart ones, no matter how old, how plain, how naive. Thanks to Grandma Kate, who'd raised him from the age of five and taught him to cherish the female sex. This was her legacy to him, and he'd followed it for all of his thirty-three years.

With one exception.

Beth Winters!

Beth had been his Emergency Medical System instructor at the academy eight years ago, and they'd clashed every time they were together. She'd gone after him repeatedly, criticizing him for what she called his brash, risk-taking personality; he'd responded by needling her about her safety-first, follow-the-rules approach to fire fighting.

Although today he couldn't help noticing how different she looked wearing a graceful dress instead of the conservative Fire Academy uniform. She looked almost fragile. The sprinkling of freckles on her nose added to the illusion of vulnerability.

And it *was* an illusion, he reminded himself.

Dear Reader,

What made me want to write about firefighters? Initially, because it's an exciting profession. The strong, silent, heroic type of guy has always appealed to me, so I thought—wow, perfect heroes. And female firefighters intrigue me, mostly because I admire their desire to break into this traditionally male job.

So, with that in mind, I entered the world of fire fighting. It was then that I realized how little I knew about the job, but I set off on a two-year odyssey to learn about it and the people who did it. AMERICA'S BRAVEST is the result.

The Man Who Loved Christmas takes place at the Fire Academy and gave me a chance to explore one of my personal interests— education. I've been a teacher for twenty-nine years. I thoroughly enjoyed setting up Beth and Dylan to butt heads over their differences in how to instruct the recruits. I also enjoyed bringing together two people who had been enemies for years. And it was a real challenge to write credibly about a woman who dreaded Christmas, as this holiday is my favorite of the year (as it is for Dylan!). I gave her the only reason I could imagine for *not* looking forward to it, and then let the man she loves find a way around this, too.

I think this trilogy is an accurate portrayal of a fire department in upstate New York. The books are, of course, fiction—but I hope I stayed true to the characters of these men and women who are truly America's bravest. They are utterly courageous, often funny, always interesting, kind, sensitive, daring, adventurous and yes, even romantic people. I hope you find that the characters in my books are all these things, too.

Please write and let me know what you think. I answer all reader mail. Send letters to Kathryn Shay, P.O. Box 24288, Rochester, New York, 14624-0288 or e-mail me at Kshay1@AOL.com. Also visit my web sites at http://home.eznet.net/~kshay/ and at http://www.superauthors.com

Sincerely,

Kathryn Shay

THE MAN WHO LOVED CHRISTMAS
Kathryn Shay

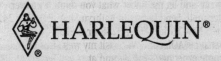

HARLEQUIN®

TORONTO • NEW YORK • LONDON
AMSTERDAM • PARIS • SYDNEY • HAMBURG
STOCKHOLM • ATHENS • TOKYO • MILAN • MADRID
PRAGUE • WARSAW • BUDAPEST • AUCKLAND

ISBN 0-373-70877-7

THE MAN WHO LOVED CHRISTMAS

Copyright © 1999 by Mary Catherine Schaefer.

Visit us at www.romance.net

Printed in U.S.A.

To Pat Ryan, my astute and insightful critique partner,
and my very dear friend. Dylan's book—your favorite
of the trilogy—is for you.

ACKNOWLEDGMENT

There are many people to thank for their help and input in my
AMERICA'S BRAVEST trilogy.

The first group is the Gates Fire Department, particularly their
chief and officers, who invited me to the firehouses and shared their
experiences with me. Thanks also to the many Gates line firefighters
who let me wear their gear, taught me how to hold a hose,
put out a fire with an extinguisher and observe several of their drills,
including live burns.

Next, I had the privilege of working with the 542-person Rochester,
New York, Fire Department. My appreciation goes to many specific
fire stations for allowing me to visit. With meals, tours of their
firehouses and the recounting of many of their experiences, the men
and women at Engine 16, Engine 17, Quint/Midi 5 and Quint/Midi 9
gave me my first feel for the professional life of a city firefighter.
Specifically, I offer deep gratitude to Firefighter Lisa Beth White for
sharing her insights into the life of a female in this predominantly
male department.

The Rochester Fire Academy personnel could not have been more
welcoming. Battalion Chief Russ Valone, in charge of training, allowed
me access to classes, training sessions and practicals, and let me
observe recruits simulating life in a firehouse and putting out fires.
Special appreciation to the 1997 Fall Recruit Class and their trainers.

My warmest gratitude and affection go to the Quint/Midi 8 firefighters.
They were all gracious in letting me ride along on the rigs, wear old
gear and eat several meals with them. These guys spent many
afternoons and evenings sharing their experiences, answering my
questions, giving advice on my story lines and suggesting possible
improvements. From that group, firefighter and paramedic
Joe Giorgione was the best "consultant" an author could ask for.

Any "real feel" these books have is due to all these brave men and
women who told me their stories. Any errors are completely mine.

CHAPTER ONE

DYLAN O'ROARKE loved women—tall ones, slender ones, plump ones, smart ones. no matter how old, how plain, how naive. Thanks to Grandma Katie, who'd practically raised him from the time he was five and taught him to cherish the female sex. This was her legacy to him, and he'd followed it for all his thirty-three years.

With one exception.

Beth Winters.

As he stepped onto the dock, she did the same. But she kept her gaze averted, fixed on the Caribbean sea, sparkling like crystal under the bright Jamaican sun. Dylan figured if Grandma Katie had met the bridesmaid he'd been paired with for his best friend's wedding, she would have understood his inability to adhere to her dictum this time. He glared at Winters, willing her to look at him.

She'd been his Emergency Medical System instructor at the academy eight years ago—all Rockford, New York, firefighters were Certified First Responders, which allowed them to perform basic first aid and medical care—and he and Winters had clashed big-time. She'd gone after him repeatedly, critical of what she called his brash, risk-taking personality. He'd responded by needling her every chance he got and dubbing her Lizzie Borden, for what he saw as her heavy-handed tactics. He'd heard that subsequent classes had continued the name. Ever since his recruit days, whenever he took further EMS training at the academy or was forced to deal with her on department issues, they'd been barely civil with each other. Rotten luck that they'd been matched up for the ceremony.

"I didn't know, Dyl, I'm sorry," the bride, Francey Cordaro, had told him last night at the rehearsal dinner. "Since you two chose lime green, the wedding planner put you together." Because the wedding was taking place in the Caribbean, Francey and her fiancé, Alex Templeton, had chosen sarongs in various bright colors for the women and, for the men, white trousers and gauzy shirts to match the dresses. Furthermore, the bride and groom had insisted they all go to Jamaica three days before the wedding. Chartering an aircraft—Dylan had teasingly called it the Love Plane—Alex had flown the wedding party and the rest of the couple's family members down to enjoy the tropical weather before the big day.

As he watched her, Winters raised her head. The cool aura surrounding her put him off completely. She was the antithesis of everything he considered feminine. Her intense hazel eyes—they had a lot of green in them today—locked on him. The irritation that marred her brow and shadowed her face every time she dealt with him was right there, as always, but today it was accompanied by a wariness he'd never seen before.

She's not on her own turf, he thought with sudden insight. *And not in her usual conservative clothes. So she's uncomfortable.* He considered making some snide remark to add to her discomfort. She probably expected it.

But one of Grandma Katie's truisms, which she got from the many books she read or the sayings she heard, came back to him. He'd been a cocky ninth grader and made the competitive junior varsity high school basketball team. Dylan's arch rival did not. He'd been gloating, and his grandma had said these words as she'd peered at him from under steel-gray hair that had once been as black as his own, her blue eyes, so like his, snapping. *A sharp tongue can cut your own throat.*

So Dylan bit his tongue, but continued to stare at Winters. Truth be told, he was amazed at what the outfit did to her rather ordinary looks. Her slender shoulders, kissed gently by the sun to a golden hue, were bare. The sarong draped over full breasts, indented into a small waist and fell gracefully to just below her knees. He'd never realized she had that kind of body, for he'd only ever seen it in the fire academy uniform. Her cropped auburn hair glinted lusciously in the sun, and when the wind blew it in her face, she brushed it out of her eyes with long, graceful fingers.

Winters looked fragile today, too, so he simply moved up beside her and said nothing. The sprinkling of freckles on her nose added to the illusion of vulnerability. And it *was* an illusion, because Beth Winters was a shark, cold and ruthless as those that swam in the sea. She could take chunks out of a guy's self-esteem before he could blink and dismember every bit of self-confidence he had with well-placed caustic remarks.

Still, Dylan held out his arm for her. She glanced at it as if it were the tentacle of an octopus.

"I don't bite," he whispered irritably.

"Grow up, O'Roarke."

Damn her! Even now she had the ability to reduce him to feeling like a rookie eating his first smoke.

Following the last attendants down the thirty foot dock, she held herself ramrod straight, her hand barely making contact with his arm. Obviously, she didn't want to touch him any more than she had to. The thought made him angry. It also conjured up the little devil that came out in him whenever he got within ten feet of the woman. Casually, he placed his other hand on top of hers, forcing her palm to curl right around his bare forearm, where he'd rolled up the sleeve of the shirt. Her skin felt baby soft and smooth, which took him by surprise and made him subtly draw her closer. He sensed her whole body stiffen, and perversely he winked at her, then held on to her until they reached the end of the dock. She scowled at him, and they parted.

Purposely turning his attention to something more pleasant, he watched the bride's procession down the dock. Despite Winters's annoying presence, he smiled at Francey. He'd witnessed his friend in many situations—caked with smoke and grime and swearing like a trooper; pinned under a fallen timber and moaning in pain; adrenaline-fueled as they headed into a fire together; near tears with ecstasy when she saved a little boy. But he'd never, ever seen her like this.

Her wedding dress was a white sarong embossed with a design of tropical flowers, which highlighted her tan and accented her violet eyes. Eschewing a veil, she wore one white tiger lily tucked in her dark hair.

Dylan's gaze switched to her groom, a few feet away at the end of the dock. The warm Caribbean breeze played havoc with Alex's blond hair. Casual in his white trousers and matching gauzy shirt, he looked utterly happy, obviously besotted with his soon-to-be wife.

Dylan, too, was genuinely happy for them because Francey and Alex had had a long road getting to this point—mostly around Alex's coming to terms with the danger of her job as a firefighter.

The ceremony began, and soon the minister's voice boomed out over the water in the sultry air. "I now pronounce you husband and wife."

Alex Templeton smiled at his bride, then pulled her into his arms and kissed her passionately. When they drew apart, Alex crossed to his groomsmen and Francey to her bridesmaids.

"Congratulations." Dylan grabbed Alex's extended hand and clapped him warmly on the back.

"Thanks for being here for her, Dylan," Alex said. "And for me."

Francey cut between them and threw herself into Dylan's arms. "Oh, Dyl, I'm so happy."

"Yeah, kiddo, I can tell." Dylan hugged her tightly.

After a few minutes the recessional began. He met with Lizzie Borden in the middle of the dock. Again she didn't look at him as he took her arm. Morbidly silent they made it down the dock, without coming to blows.

"Nice talking to you, Winters," Dylan said when they reached the sandy shore.

"Do people really think you're clever, O'Roarke?" Without waiting for an answer, she pivoted and, hips swaying, wound her way through the small crowd.

Dylan scanned the area for his date, Missy. Jake Scarlatta, another groomsman, approached him.

"How's it going, buddy?" Jake asked.

"Great."

"Everybody looks terrific, don't they?"

"Yeah." Dylan still scanned the crowd.

"Even Beth Winters. Did you see her in that sarong?"

"No, I didn't notice."

"You must be blind, buddy," Jake said, shaking his head. "Oh, there's Jessica. I'll catch you later."

Jake hurried to his teenage daughter, who stood to one side, chatting with Francey's friend Chelsea Whitmore. Dressed in peacock blue, which matched Jake's shirt, Chelsea looked very feminine, like she always did, like a woman should, even though she was a highly touted body builder and a more than competent firefighter.

Dylan's gaze strayed beyond Chelsea and landed on Beth Winters. He studied her, considering Jake's comment—until she glanced up and caught him watching her. He shifted his eyes guiltily and continued to search for Missy. Unable to find her, he approached Ben and Diana Cordaro, Francey's father and mother, who were talking with Francey's grand-parents, Gus and Grace.

"Hi, Mom and Dad, Grandma and Grandpa," Dylan said affectionately when he reached them.

Gus and Grace greeted him warmly. They were old friends of his father's, as was Ben.

The grandparents were called for pictures with the bride and groom.

Diana leaned over and kissed Dylan's cheek. "Hello, handsome," she said. "You look terrific today."

"Me? You two almost stole the show from the bride and groom."

It was true. When Diana Cordaro, who was matron of honor, had stepped onto the dock and glided gracefully down the pier in a violet sarong, Dylan's mouth had fallen open. The color of her outfit mirrored her eyes; her bare shoulders were the perfect complement for her blond hair, which fell in waves around her face. Dylan thought he'd never seen a more radiant woman. Ben was a worthy escort. Decked out in white trousers and a deep purple shirt, he looked consid-erably younger than his fifty-three years, despite his salt-and-pepper hair.

After being divorced for almost three decades, the Cor-daros were newly remarried and had come to Jamaica a week ago to celebrate their honeymoon. No one had had a glimpse of them until the rehearsal last night. Dylan liked and ad-mired Ben, and he was glad to see him happy again. Ben, the battalion chief in charge of training, was one of the rea-sons Dylan looked forward to working at the Rockford Fire Academy for the next few months. While Dylan waited for a lieutenant's spot to open up at a station, he'd taken a staff position to help teach the class of the new recruits this fall.

"Wasn't the wedding perfect for them?" Diana asked, beaming proudly at the happy couple.

"It was great. But I thought I saw a few tears there, when Ben brought Francey down the dock."

Diana snuggled into her husband. "Well, it was moving." After a moment she said, "So, you'll be at the Academy now."

"Yep, for a while."

"Are you looking forward to it?"

"Yes, I am." He glanced over to where the bridesmaids were gathering. *Except for working with Lizzie Borden.* Jeez, just being near that woman made his blood boil. He didn't voice the thought, though, because he'd already had a run-in with Ben on the issue.

"Time for pictures of the wedding party," Francey called.

Dylan sauntered over and waited for the photographer to position him, along with the nine other attendants, in front of a garden of tropical flowers; his mind drifted to his first few days at the academy last week and the initial meeting of all the personnel.

Ben Cordaro, always the professional in the white shirt of a Rockford battalion chief with its epaulets, had been friendly and casual with the staff. He'd given a thorough overview of their tasks with the recruits, who would arrive the next Monday, and introduced Dylan and the other two instructors who were new to the academy. He'd ended his talk by acknowledging how the expertise of line firefighters—firefighters like Dylan who worked in the firehouse—would benefit the students.

Out of the corner of his eye, Dylan had seen Beth Winters bristle at the last remark. When Ben asked if any of the academy staff wanted to comment, Eric Scanlon, a veteran captain, welcomed the three of them and joked that he hoped the line guys were in good shape, so they could keep up with the confidence walks—physical-fitness treks required of the recruits to build their stamina. Having been through the walks themselves, the new guys groaned good-naturedly.

Then Winters had extinguished the camaraderie and good mood quicker than a foam blanket on a gasoline fire by angling her pointy chin and leveling her chilly stare on all of them. Wearing the light blue shirt of the RFD—as starched and crisp as she was—and man-tailored pants, she'd addressed the group.

"I'd just like to remind the inexperienced instructors what we expect for the *tone* of the academy. Granted, we'll be more formal at the beginning, and loosen up a bit as we go along, but I hope we all understand the seriousness of what we're doing." Her snooty gaze cut to Dylan. "And about the qualities we need to instill in these recruits—caution, discretion, clear thinking."

The room had grown so quiet that the secretaries' chatter filtered down the hall to them. Everyone present knew about Dylan's recent reprimand—for lack of following procedure. They also knew it had saved a rookie firefighter's life. Ben Cordaro opened his mouth to break the charged silence when Dylan leaned forward in his chair and pinned her with a calculated—and angry—stare. "I'd like to address that, Ben, since everybody knows it was directed at me. I understand the importance of instilling a sense of discipline in the recruits, Ms. Winters. I also know they have to follow orders unequivocally. I can assure you I'll adhere to academy guidelines."

Then Dylan had lazed back in his chair, linked his hands behind his head and propped his booted foot on his knee. "But I also believe in telling it like it is. I think it's valuable to have the three of us who've been in the trenches recently let the recruits know some real-life situations they'll face that aren't in the rule book." The entire time he held Winters's frosty gaze with his smoldering one. She'd said no more, so Ben Cordaro had stood.

"I'm sure there's a happy medium here and that we'll find it. I think you both have valid points." He was quiet for a moment, then added, "And I expect you'll be able to reach some compromise on this issue."

Dylan remembered thinking that at least they'd be working in different areas—Winters in EMS, he in fire suppression. He could probably avoid unnecessary contact with her and get through this without losing too much of his hide in the process....

"Where's the yellow?" the photographer called after he drew Jake and Chelsea together in the middle. Alex's brother and best man, Richard, and Francey's stepsister, Elise, stepped forward. Her hair, a few shades lighter than her yellow sarong, sparkled in the afternoon sun.

Next the photographer placed Francey's brother Tony and sister-in-law Erin to the left; the fuchsia of his shirt and her dress accentuated their light coloring. On the right, he situated Francey's other brother, Nick, and Diana, her mother, both in violet. "All right, we need the green team."

Dylan edged into the group, right up to his partner. Her shoulder brushed his accidentally and she stiffened. She was about five inches shorter than he was, so he could see the sun glisten off her reddish hair. For a long fifteen minutes they held their forced smiles for the camera.

At the end of the session, Alex faced the group and said, "Don't go yet." Seemingly from nowhere, waiters produced glasses of champagne for the wedding party. "I'd like to toast my bride." He tugged Francey close and lifted his glass. "Almost six months ago this gorgeous woman dragged me out of a fire and saved my life." He gazed at her, his eyes so full of love it made Dylan suck in his breath. "But today, by becoming my wife, she gave me an even greater gift." His voice hoarse with emotion, Alex finished, "I love you, Francesca."

Dylan felt choked up. He turned from the scene to look out to sea. As he did so, he noticed Beth Winters watching Francey and Alex blankly, as if she wasn't even seeing them.

Her body was painfully rigid. There was not even a spark of sentimentality on her face.

Jeez, Dylan thought, was the blasted woman made of stone?

IN THE SULTRY Caribbean night, Beth Winters took off her shoes and waded into the warm water, the grainy sand squishing between her toes. She'd left the celebration, held in one of the outdoor restaurants, to try to collect herself.

You're doing all right, she told herself silently. *Just a little while longer.* It hadn't been too bad. During the ceremony, she'd been able to keep her thoughts off her own wedding a lifetime ago, and a young boy who loved the water and hot weather and had dreamed of one day visiting tropical islands. Instead, she'd focused on Francey's absolute delight in joining her life with the man she loved. When that wasn't enough, she'd concentrated on her annoyance at being paired up with Dylan O'Roarke. When she'd left the reception, he'd been dancing with his date—all the attendants had been encouraged to bring a guest, though only Chelsea and O'Roarke had done so. He'd produced another of what his buddies called a Barbie—a tall blonde with seemingly more breast than brains. Though Beth objected to the sexist nature of the comment, the description was apt.

Truthfully, Beth objected to almost everything about O'Roarke—from his too-long black hair which dipped boyishly into his eyes, to his reckless attitude and behavior.

"Want some company?"

Beth turned to find that the bride had joined her in the shallow water. She smiled at her friend. Though the sarong was a little mussed and she'd long since parted company with the lilies in her hair, Francey was still gorgeous in the unorthodox wedding attire.

"Of course, but shouldn't you be back at the reception?"

Francey stood next to Beth and peered over the sea as

waves curled around their ankles. "Yeah, I'll go back in soon. I wanted to look at the water again. I wish we didn't have to go tomorrow." Francey had frantically juggled her schedule to get the week off for their wedding.

Beth smiled. *She* was thinking how good it would be to get back to a routine—a sure remedy for the nostalgia she'd been feeling. This excursion had upset her emotional equilibrium, something Beth didn't like at all.

The breeze ruffled the edges of Francey's sarong as she narrowed her eyes. "You want to go back to Rockford, don't you?"

"No," Beth lied. She'd never let Francey think she wouldn't be there for her.

"You didn't really want to come down here, did you?"

Hesitating, Beth struggled to find truthful words that wouldn't hurt her friend. "I don't…go to weddings and things, France." She reached out and squeezed Francey's arm. "But how could I miss this?"

Francey grinned and didn't probe. That she allowed Beth her privacy was one of the things Beth liked about her and one of the crucial reasons they could be friends.

"Sorry about your getting paired up with Dylan—I just didn't realize…."

"That's okay, it didn't kill me."

"It's been so hectic, you and I haven't had a chance to talk. How did the first few days at the academy go with him?"

Shrugging, Beth said, "Fine. Everyone thinks he'll do a great job."

"I wish you could know him like I do. He's—"

"Francesca!" The male voice came from behind them. Alex materialized out of the darkness in rolled-up trousers, the sleeves of his shirt folded back, looking like some golden Greek god born on the foam of the sea. He banded his arms around Francey's waist. "You left me."

Rolling her eyes, Francey leaned into him and sighed. The chemistry between them almost sizzled. When he began to nuzzle her neck, Beth turned away. Apparently she wasn't out of the woods yet. She took a cleansing breath to banish the ghosts stirred by Alex's embrace of his new wife.

"Bye, Beth," they both sang out.

Pivoting, Beth saw that Alex had scooped Francey up and was carrying her toward the restaurant. Beth breathed deeply again, forcing her shoulders to relax, her mind to empty. For twenty years, ever since she was nineteen, she'd used the technique and become a master at it. When the threat passed, she faced the sea again. And caught a glimpse of a man and woman on the pier. The outline and stature of the woman told her it was O'Roarke's date. A deep masculine laugh and light feminine giggle drifted to her. She watched as the couple slid arms around each other's waists and headed toward the large enclosed hammock for two at the end of the dock. Beth turned and trudged through the water in the opposite direction.

But she was unable to get O'Roarke out of her mind. She still couldn't quite believe he was going to be working at the academy for the next four months. Beth disliked very few people, and the irony of the situation didn't escape her. Usually she didn't let herself feel much either way about most people. But it hadn't taken her long to disapprove of Dylan O'Roarke's whole outlook on life—take every risk you can, beat back every threat and don't let fear ever stop you. He just didn't understand the preciousness of life. She'd found herself calling him on it when he was a new recruit, at the academy and now she felt the white heat of resentment at his becoming a part of the staff.

He'd been so smug last week about his thoughts on training the recruits, so she'd gone after him again as she had in the past. And he'd been good and truly pissed off about it. After the meeting had broken up, she'd returned to her office and was sorting though some files when she heard a noise at the doorway. She looked up to find him leaning against the jamb, his arms crossed defensively over a chest that stretched the blue RFD uniform shirt mercilessly. His eyes were blue diamonds glistening with anger.

"Is this the way my whole time here is going to go?" he asked, ditching his legendary charm. She had to be the only woman in the world he didn't use it on.

"I don't know what you mean."

"The hell you don't." He strode into the room. "You know, when I was a recruit here, I had to take this shit from you. I don't have to take it anymore."

She'd assumed a detached, haughty look, though as always he evoked a furor of response inside her. "Usually instructors at the academy listen to each other and work together. They don't go on the attack and use foul language." She shook her head. "I'd hoped you'd…matured enough to get along out here." She knew that particular criticism had always zinged him. It got the desired reaction.

His face had flushed with anger. "Oh, and Ms. Wise-in-the-Ways-of-the-World knows all about maturity, doesn't she. What are you, anyway, thirty-five? Why do you act eighty?"

The recollection made Beth sigh heavily. Then she glanced around to see how far she'd walked.

Quite far. She could barely see the pier where O'Roarke sat cuddling with his girlfriend. Resolutely she started back. She wished she could go to her room, but Francey and Chelsea, Beth's other close friend, would worry if she didn't return to the reception. She took another deep breath. With any luck this wedding celebration would be her last for a very long time.

"Vrrroom…"

Three little hellions raced past Dylan, their arms held out

at right angles from their sides. Each had dark eyes, olive skin and jet-black hair. Dylan guessed their ages ranged from four to seven. After whizzing by him, they circled a food stall, narrowly missing the sharp edge of one of the carts. They still bumped the back of it, making it teeter precariously.

"Where are their parents?" Dylan wondered aloud, unable to see any adult who might be with them. The Kingston, Jamaica, airport was crowded on Sunday afternoon as the Templeton wedding party waited for their plane to be fueled.

"Their mother's over in the corner, breast-feeding her baby," Missy told him. She reached out and stroked his biceps. He brushed her cheek with his knuckles.

Scanning the room, Dylan saw the woman and smiled at the nurturing sight. Then his gaze was snagged by Beth Winters, sitting alone about three feet from the mother, her nose buried in a book. Now there was a woman who knew nothing about nurturing.

Ben Cordaro appeared and spoke briefly with her. She rose as he headed toward Dylan. "O'Roarke, I'd like to talk to you."

"Sure."

Ben gestured to a small table that butted against a wall behind the food stalls. As Dylan stood to follow him, one of the little boys crashed headlong into him. Dylan bent and scooped him up. "Hey, you guys better settle down. Someone could get hurt."

The boy gave a gap-toothed grin as Dylan set him on his feet. "Okay, mister. I'll tell my brothers. I'm watchin' them for my mom." The kid scampered off.

"Keep them away from those food carts over there. They don't look stable," Dylan called after him, then crossed to Ben, only to find Beth Winters had joined him. She looked quite feminine in a white silky T-shirt and khaki shorts, which revealed tanned slender legs. But she sat down at the table and clasped her hands and once again her posture was so unyielding Dylan wondered if she ever relaxed.

"Both of us?" Dylan asked stupidly.

Ben nodded.

Dylan took a chair at the opposite end of the table from Winters, with Ben between them. Their battalion chief ran his hand through his hair and expelled a heavy breath. "I got a call this morning with some news that concerns both of you. I thought I'd tell you now, instead of springing this on you tomorrow morning at work. We'll all be busy when the recruits arrive."

Beth cocked her head and Dylan waited.

"Tom Jackson slipped last night in the shower. Hurt his bad hip. The doctor told him he'd need the replacement surgery right away." Jackson, the captain in charge of EMS at the academy, had gone off the line because of hip problems. Recently he'd talked of retirement because it bothered him so much.

"Oh, I'm sorry." Winters frowned. Dylan had never noticed how finely etched her eyebrows were. "Is he in pain?"

"A lot. They're hoping to get the operation scheduled this week to keep it from getting worse."

Dylan said, "Good. The healing won't hurt as much."

Wearily Ben drew in another breath. "He'll be out for at least three months—probably till after Christmas."

"For the whole recruit class," Winters said evenly.

"Too bad," Dylan responded.

"I can handle things that long," she said matter-of-factly.

"No, you can't, Beth." Ben frowned. "It would double your teaching load, as well as make you responsible for all the other medical duties at the academy. We've got an EMT course for line firefighters scheduled for November. You'll need help."

"No one else at the academy is trained to teach EMS."

Ben's gaze swung from Winters to Dylan, then to Winters

again. "Dylan's a paramedic as well as a certified instructor. He also has a teaching degree from Cortland State. It's in physical education, but he's had all the methods courses."

Winters clutched a paper napkin and twisted it in her hands. "O'Roarke?" she said weakly.

Dylan shook his head. "No way, Ben. I've already got my assignment for which firefighting classes I'm teaching."

"We'll reassign some of them."

"Ben, this isn't a good idea," Dylan protested. In fact, it was the worst idea in the world.

"I know you two don't exactly see eye to eye," Ben said, "but I don't have much choice." His face hardened. "Look, you're both adults. You'll have to find a way to deal with this…animosity between you." He paused. "Maybe working together is the best thing for you. You'll be forced to deal with whatever it is that turns you into cats and dogs when you're in the same room."

Chastised, neither Winters nor Dylan spoke.

"You'll be sharing the EMS office, too. I'll have Tom's desk cleared temporarily for Dylan." Ben paused. "I expect you to work this out." Giving them his best chief officer look, Ben pushed back his chair, stood and walked away.

Dylan was thrust back twenty-five years, to when he was a Cub Scout and Grandma Katie was his den leader. Their troop had gone camping, and Dylan had been paired with Jeff Miller, the nerdiest kid in the group. He'd griped about it, and his grandma—her cheeks sunburned, her camping clothes grimy—had silenced him with a glare and another saying. *In the middle of difficulty lies opportunity.* He smiled at how right she'd been. He and Jeff had wound up hitting it off and remained best friends through college, until Jeff had moved south after graduation.

Not that this would happen with Beth Winters. It wasn't possible.

Winters watched Ben go. After a moment, she turned to

Dylan. Her eyes, more green than hazel now, were deeply troubled. He stared at her, knowing his own reflected the same turbulence. He opened his mouth to speak, maybe ease her misgivings and his own.

Suddenly there was a loud crash. Followed by screams.

CHAPTER TWO

THE FIREFIGHTERS in the Rockford Fire Department functioned like the parts of a well-oiled machine—even when they were off duty and out of town. Battalion Chief Ben Cordaro raced to the food court, where three little boys had tipped a large serving cart onto themselves. Right behind Ben strode Francey, Jake Scarlatta, Chelsea Whitmore and her date, Billy Milligan, and Nick Cordaro, all part of the squad. Simultaneously Dylan and Beth threw back their chairs and sped over.

Ben Cordaro assumed command. Over the piercing wails of the three victims—though one child, the smallest, was off to the side and not pinned like the other two—Ben yelled, "Nicky and Chelsea, get on the right side. Jake and Billy on the left. Let's lift this sucker off them very carefully."

For a split second Beth watched the firefighters raise the heavy cart that had trapped two boys. Well-toned muscles strained with the weight; their grunts punctuated the still airport gate area. Beth grabbed the black canvas Advanced Life Support bag she always carried and unzipped it as Ben barked, "Beth, you're in charge of the patients. Dylan, you assist. The rest of you wait for instructions from Beth." He scanned the area and saw the boys' mother stumbling toward them, clutching an infant to her chest. "Dee?"

His wife, Diana, came up beside him. "Yes?"

"Intercept the mother. Try to calm her." He took in the people crowding the area, swore under his breath, then ordered, "Billy and Chelsea, keep everybody back."

Beth extricated latex gloves from the bag, donned them, then threw a pair at O'Roarke and one at Jake, who was nearest her. "Put these on." Kneeling, she scrutinized the three boys to assess the situation. The smallest child was gasping for breath but moving around; he didn't appear injured. Beth guessed he was hyperventilating. "Jake, take this little guy over there," she pointed to a nearby chair. "He looks okay, but just check him out. O'Roarke, you handle this one." She pointed to her left, where the second youngest lay kicking his feet and arching off the floor, intermittently yelling for his mama and sobbing. Blood oozed from a nasty gash nearly five inches long on his arm.

The oldest child appeared to be in the worst shape. His knees were curled up to his stomach, and he moaned and clutched his chest. "Shh, it's okay I'm going to help you, fella," Beth said softly.

Behind her, she heard Ben directing the action. Out of the corner of her eye she saw that O'Roarke had taken sterile bandages from the ALS case and was applying pressure on the child's arm. Farther down, Jake Scarlatta was sitting on the chair with the youngest boy on his lap, soothing him.

"Can you tell me where it hurts?" she asked her small charge.

The child whimpered. "Here." He clutched his ribs.

Beth fished in the bag to get scissors. With practiced efficiency, she cut the small T-shirt up the front, right through the decal, "Jamaica, no problem." The boy leaned to his side and cried out. Gently Beth pressed her fingers on his clavicle, then on his sternum above his fifth set of ribs, the one most commonly fractured. The child yelped in pain. Discoloration had already begun.

O'Roarke knelt next to her. She looked at him, wondering why he'd left his patient. His face was calm, but his blue eyes were worried. "Mild bleeding on the other one, slight concussion. Francey can handle it. I thought I could help here.''

She turned away from the boy so he wouldn't hear. ''I think he's got a couple of cracked ribs.''

O'Roarke gave the patient a lopsided grin. ''Hi,'' he said, smoothing the hair from the kid's sunburned brow. The navy blue T-shirt Dylan wore showed bulging muscles tightly under control.

Between shallow breaths, the boy said haltingly, ''Hi, mister.''

''Hurt?'' O'Roarke asked.

Tears fell from brimming black eyes. Eyes that reminded Beth of— She cut off the thought. ''Get the slings from my bag,'' she told O'Roarke while she maintained physical contact with her patient by smoothing her hands down his arms. She knew the most they could do was reduce the pain and provide protection for the child's lungs and the blood vessels located between the ribs.

After handing her the bandages, O'Roarke rested two fingers on the boy's neck. ''Diastolic pulse rapid, but okay.'' He leaned close as Beth unfurled the thick gauze. ''No pallor or dilation.''

''Good.'' Folding the bandage in a triangle, she tied the top together and looped it over the boy's head. When she raised his arm to a sling position, he cried out again.

O'Roarke bent closer. ''Yeah, we know it hurts, buddy.''

Through his tears the boy said, ''I wanna be brave for my mom and little brothers.''

''I cried buckets when I broke my hand two years ago, and I'm a big, tough firefighter.''

The boy's wet eyes widened.

Beth handed O'Roarke one side of the second bandage. ''Help me slip the cloth under him.'' Together, as if they'd been doing it for years, they eased the thin gauze under the child with a minimum of discomfort to him. Beth finished immobilizing the patient by tying the folded bandage across his chest in a swathe. "That feel better?" she asked, smiling tenderly.

He said, "Uh-huh."

Ben Cordaro knelt next to them. "Need anything?"

Beth shook her head. "No, we've done all we can do."

"Nick alerted airport security, and they've called a Jamaican medical team." Ben looked relieved.

Beth nodded to the side. "The other two?"

"One's hyperventilating, so Jake's telling him fishing stories to calm him. His mother's sitting with them, and Diana's got the baby." Ben smiled. "Francey's clucking over the second kid. He's stable."

"Any other injuries on him?" Beth asked.

"None."

The adrenaline rush over, Beth and O'Roarke leaned back on their haunches, gloved hands at their sides, and sighed simultaneously.

"You know," Ben said glibly, his gaze swinging from one to the other, "you two make a pretty good team—when you stop going for each other's jugulars."

Frowning, Beth looked at O'Roarke. His expression matched hers.

It was an unlikely and totally undesirable thought.

"THE FIRE DEPARTMENT is a paramilitary organization." Battalion Chief Ben Cordaro's voice boomed through the academy's arena, a huge gym used for a range of purposes. It housed stations for physical fitness training, a stage, a maze to practice search and rescue, lockers, a kitchen, a classroom off the EMS office and the bays at the far end. In the gym the 1999 Rockford Fire Department fall recruit class lined up at attention. Shoulders back, chest out, chin up and hands clenched at his sides, Hoyt Barnette beamed, proud to be part of the class; he listened attentively to this man everybody in fire fighting idolized. "And your stint here is like boot camp," Cordaro continued.

That was okay with Hoyt. He'd waited seven years after taking the civil-service entrance exam to make it into a class. At twenty-six, he was fit and trim, even though he wasn't as tall or muscular as some of the others. His blond hair was cut short just like the army would require. He was ready for this.

Hoyt noted that none of the twelve recruits groaned at the army comparison. Instead, they focused on the head of the academy, standing at a podium in front of the eight men and women who would be their instructors. The recruits stood at attention in two lines, dressed in the fatigue uniforms of the RFD—long-sleeved light blue shirts, black pants, black ties, hats obscuring their eyes. Hoyt wondered if they felt the same hope and pride he did after waiting a lifetime to get here. He doubted it. No one could feel as thrilled as he was.

"FIRST I'D LIKE to give a brief overview of a typical day," Ben Cordaro told them, the lights gleaming off the gold on the shoulders of his white shirt. "Starting tomorrow, we'll simulate the firehouse routine."

Ace Durwin half listened. He'd been a volunteer firefighter in Beckville, a small town thirty miles from Rockford, so he knew how a firehouse operated and how the academy day would mimic its setup—arrive by seven, check the rigs and start all the equipment, line up for roll call at eight, several hours of classes, sometimes cook lunch or dinner. The day would end with cleaning up the rooms they'd used. Then there would be homework, which was a cinch for him since he'd already read and highlighted key passages in the seven-hundred-page recruit textbook, *Essentials in Fire Fighting*, which he'd gotten from Beckville's fire chief.

Cordaro continued, "Now I'd like to introduce the staff.

These men and women will be working with you for the most important thirteen weeks of your life.''

Keeping his eyes straight ahead, Ace smiled. Yes, these would be important weeks in his life, though he'd had others. In his forty-eight years he'd already started his own business, seen two sons born and off to college and stayed married to a woman who encouraged him to ditch his work to capture his life's dream—to be a career firefighter in Beckville, New York. He very much valued the opportunity to be here.

"First, Captain Chuck Lorenzo," the battalion chief said. "The man in charge of your training. He's the boss of the day-to-day routine. I oversee everything, but he's the guy to please."

Lorenzo, about five-eight and broad-shouldered, looked about Ace's age, his short brown hair receding the same way. Clothed in an officer's white shirt and dark pants, Lorenzo eased forward and waved casually, but didn't smile. He had knowing eyes, though, and Ace decided he liked the man.

"Other members of our staff are Battalion Chief A.J. Rooney, who works with me on training as well as heading up the HazMat Task Force." Rooney came forward, his gray hair also military cut, his stance erect, his uniform mercilessly creased. He wasn't any taller than Ace, either, but was obviously muscular and fit. Thank God Ace had kept himself in shape all these years. When Rooney frowned as he scanned the class of recruits, Ace wondered what he saw that made him scowl. Everything pleased Durwin about being here. Hell, life was just about perfect.

CONNIE CLEARY WATCHED Battalion Chief Rooney scowl at her and Sandy Frank, who stood like a cardboard doll next to her. Damn, another male chauvinist. Just what she needed. Was he going to give her and the only other woman in the class a rough time? She hoped not. She needed all the help she could get.

"Next is Ms. Elizabeth Winters, your emergency medical instructor. She's going to teach you the things you'll need to know outside of fire suppression."

Connie studied the only woman on the academy staff. At East High, where she'd taken the two-year fire fighting course for high school students, rumors about Instructor Winters abounded. They said Winters was just like her name—cold. She looked it today, stepping forward in the crisply pressed and starched traditional RFD uniform—though her shoulder patch read EMS, not RFD. She was about Connie's height, five-seven; she was kind of slight, though, compared to Connie, who had a stocky build. Ms. Winters had an air about her, as her father would say. *Don't get too close,* her body language said. Too bad, Connie thought. She could use a woman to confide in. Since her mother's death ten years ago, there hadn't been any female in her life to help her deal with her father and four brothers, two of whom were firefighters.

"Ms. Winters also runs fitness classes starting promptly at six every other day. Those of you who need to improve your stamina and endurance should plan to be here early Wednesday morning." The chief stared hard at the class. "The first confidence walk is Friday."

Connie bit her lip to keep from groaning. The confidence walks were grueling outdoor hikes, taken in full turnout gear and air pack; the length was only about a mile, but they went up and down hills and three flights of stairs in the training tower. Her heart sank. She'd never make it through the initial walk. She wasn't strong enough yet, and she lacked the endurance to complete one. She feared she wouldn't last the first week in the academy. Oh, God, her father would die of embarrassment.

"CAPTAIN ERIC SCANLON," the chief said gravely, "is in charge of curriculum. He set up your course of study, and he'll be giving you the Question of the Day.''

The blond man who waved from his relaxed pose against a wall looked like a nice guy, but Trevor Tully was shaking in his shoes. He couldn't let anyone know how terrified he was. Oh, it wasn't the thought of walking into fires or treating gunshot wounds that scared him. He'd do that without a qualm, his big basketball-player body and weight-trained muscles serving him in good stead. It was the Question of the Day.

It was just a fluke, his mother had told him—after taking a big swig of Jack Daniels—that he'd scored high enough on the civil service exam to get in to the academy. Oh, maybe he could master the curriculum, as he had in high school four years ago, when he studied all night. But the Question of the Day—that he could never handle, hadn't even known about it until one of his fellow recruits mentioned it to him this morning when they'd all met. The guy had said that every morning the recruits would be expected to answer a question about something in the previous day's lessons. The purpose was to increase retention and to keep the class reviewing the material. Just the thought of it made Trevor want to puke.

"Every Friday you'll be given an RTR, a recruit training report, filled out by the eight instructors. You'll be graded on appearance, attitude, performance and knowledge of firemanics and EMS." Trevor held his breath. "At first, the emphasis will be mostly knowledge and attitude. By the way, the fastest road out of here is a poor attitude. After about seven weeks, the emphasis is on performance."

Well, that was good news. So he only had to sweat bullets for half the stint.

"Though on all tests you'll need at least seventy percent."

Trevor's heart sank.

Ben Cordaro finished the permanent roster list with Lieutenant Drew Sheridan, an instructor who headed the East

High program, where some of the recruits came from. Glancing at that group, Trevor straightened and thought if those kids right out of high school could do it, so could he. He *would*, damn it.

JOHN WANIKYA LISTENED as the battalion chief wound up his introduction of the permanent staff at the academy and went on to the line firefighters who would be working with this recruit class. Older than his twenty-seven years, John had made it a point to find out ahead of time about the instructors. He'd also learned to read people well and recognized that the line guys, the ones in the trenches, were the ones to get the most from. He'd been in the trenches enough himself to know that.

First, there was the legend, Lieutenant Dylan O'Roarke, a certified paramedic and firefighter from Quint/Midi Twelve, one of the busiest fire stations in the department, named for the two trucks it housed. O'Roarke was known as Boy Wonder. He'd effected more daring rescues in the Rockford Fire Department than anyone but Ben Cordaro. John made a note to get on O'Roarke's good side, which shouldn't be hard because he was supposed to be a friendly guy, easy to get along with. He moved the way a man did who was confident in himself and his masculinity. His swagger reminded John of the comments he'd heard about O'Roarke's success with women. Though impressed, John had no time for the fairer sex. Maybe when he got to where O'Roarke was...

Then there was Lieutenant Herb Hanley. His appearance shouted arrogance. His light brown hair was longer than the others, he carried more bulk than they did, and his square-cut features looked bored. He also had a reputation for being cocky and insensitive. John knew how to handle those types—be ingratiating, even if you hated the son of a bitch.

Finally there was Lieutenant Lou Giancarlo, who was fairly well respected, even though he tended to be too macho for most people's taste. Though adverse to stereotyping, John couldn't help but notice Giancarlo looked like a typical Italian hot head—dark hair and eyes, stocky build but shorter than John. He stood with his hands on his hips surveying the class.

"Now I'll turn this over to Captain Lorenzo," Cordaro said. "But I'd like to wish you all good luck. Remember, we're here to help you. We want you to succeed. But you've got to be the best to be a member of the Rockford Fire Department."

Turning his head slightly, John scanned the mixed gender, multi-ethnic group as Cordaro finished. "Regardless of race, creed or sex, you all have to measure up to our high standards."

Some of us more than others, John thought bitterly. Well, he was ready for this. Ready to be the first Native American in the Rockford Fire Department.

OF COURSE he's a slob, Beth thought. *It fits perfectly with his character.* She placed her clipboard on her desk in the EMS office she shared with Tom Jackson. She'd enjoyed working with him these past twelve years and was sorry when she'd heard today that he was retiring as of November first.

She surveyed the office. Painted in neutral beige, with vivid EMS posters on the walls, the room was large, a good thirty feet square, with adequate storage space to keep everything in its place. It was also a formerly tidy area that now looked as if a tornado had swept through it. That's what O'Roarke did to life—wreaked havoc like an uncontrolled storm. For some reason, the thought made her shiver, made her fear what he might do to the neat little world she'd built for herself.

Shaking off the stupid foreboding—and her resentment of his intrusion into her life—Beth eyed Tom's utilitarian steel desk, which matched her own. Piled on it were a black helmet and a black backpack emblazoned Born to Ride in bright yellow letters. It figured that O'Roarke had a motorcycle. And since the late September weather was so mild, he'd still be riding it.

Next to the bag were two boxes with books and other paraphernalia sticking out haphazardly. She saw a couple of model fire trucks peeking out of one. *He even brought his toys with him.* In the other a framed photograph was half visible. She moved for a closer look. It was a picture of a beautiful dalmatian, its healthy, spotted coat shiny, its face friendly. *Of course, a boy had to have a dog.*

Her gaze swung to the six-foot gray bookshelves that had been cleared out for O'Roarke. They were still empty. Pivoting, she saw that behind her, over the computer station chair, he'd draped a black windbreaker. It looked big and male and…dangerous. He'd set a boom box on the worktable under the windows, accompanied by an array of tapes and CDs. Beth wondered what they were for. Surely, he didn't plan to play music during the day. Maybe he intended to use them for class. She had nothing against innovative motivational techniques.

"Sorry I left things in such a mess," said O'Roarke from the doorway. He strode in. Somehow, though dressed in his fire department uniform, he always managed to look rumpled and boyish. His hair seemed perpetually windblown, and his blue shirt and navy pants settled lazily on his body. When he'd reached his desk, she relived the impression she'd had as his partner in the wedding ceremony in Jamaica. It wasn't that he was so big, but just…muscular, giving her the odd sensation—and disadvantage—of feeling slight and small. "I was late getting here this morning," O'Roarke continued, "and just dumped this stuff off."

Stifling her first reaction, which was to make a snide remark about his social life keeping him up late, she said, "Well, clean it up now," and crossed to her desk.

"Yes, Mom," he snapped. She whirled in annoyance. "That's what you sounded like, what you *always* sound like when you talk to me. A scolding mother."

"Perhaps that's because you always need scolding."

His brilliant blue eyes told her that barb could still hit its target. She held his gaze intently.

Before either of them broke the stare, Beth heard another voice from the doorway. "I don't believe it. They really did let the black sheep in here." Reed Macauley, the department psychologist, lounged against the jamb, his hands stuck in his pockets and grinned.

O'Roarke's face lit up like a kid's. "Macauley, you son of a bitch."

Reed pushed off from the doorjamb and came inside. He moved at a slow, relaxed pace, disguising his take-charge reputation. "Morning, Beth," he said to her, then held out his hand to O'Roarke. Instead of shaking it, O'Roarke wrapped Reed in a bear hug. They embraced easily. Discomfited, Beth turned her back. She knew—everybody knew—that O'Roarke had been ordered to spend time with Reed after one of his more brash episodes of breaking SOP—standard operating procedure—late last summer. But she'd heard he'd been angry and resentful about doing it. This obvious connection with Reed told a very different story.

"Yeah, I'm workin' here." O'Roarke's tone was dry. Beth rounded her desk and sat. From under lowered lids she could see the two had pulled apart. "Can you believe it?"

Reed chuckled. "They're lucky to get you, Dylan. I'm glad you're here." The men chatted for a few minutes, then Reed clapped O'Roarke on the shoulder. "Try not to shake things up too much," he said. As he headed for the door, he turned to Beth. "Could you stop by my office sometime today?"

"Sure," she said.

"Good. See you later. Take care, O'Roarke," he called out as he left.

Beth opened a folder.

"Don't tell me Ms. Perfect is in trouble."

She looked up and frowned. "In trouble?"

"Gotta go see the resident shrink?"

"No, of course not. He probably wants to discuss something about one of the recruits." Unable to restrain herself—O'Roarke hadn't exactly been sweet to her—she said, "Only hard-core cases like you are sent to see Reed professionally."

Instead of blowing a fuse, which he was capable of doing without warning, O'Roarke merely said, "Yeah, well, he's one of the few people I really respect."

"Because he was a firefighter before he got into psychology?"

"Partly. He really knows how you feel. But it's more than that. I heard he had some experiences in his past that caused him to leave the line, get his PhD in clinical psychology and come to Rockford to work. God only knows what those experiences were, though."

"The man deserves his privacy," Beth said vehemently.

A little too vehemently, for O'Roarke said, "You're big on that, aren't you, Winters?"

"Not all of us are the touchy-feely type."

"Yeah, you're clearly the—"

"Spare me." Beth stood and held up a folder. "Do you want to go over this outline now? Captain Scanlon's bringing the recruit syllabus down at ten. The first class is after lunch, so we're free to hash this out."

O'Roarke seemed to assess her. "Fine. Give me a second to stow my stuff."

"You'll need more than a second."

His grin was boyish. "Wanna help?"

"No, thanks, Peter Pan. I'm sure you can clean up your room by yourself."

She sat down and extracted the course outline, then fished a yellow marker from her drawer and highlighted the classes Tom Jackson had planned to teach. Hmm, could O'Roarke handle—

Beth jerked when earsplitting music filled the air. "What the hell is that?"

With casual arrogance, O'Roarke turned from shuffling his CDs. "It's Dion and the Belmonts. One of my favorite oldies."

"You don't plan to play music at work, do you?"

"I'll turn it down."

"You'll turn it *off*."

"Why?"

"It's disturbing me."

He crossed his arms and leaned against the desk. "I thought this was my office, too."

Beth waited to compose herself. "For a while."

"Then I have a say in things." He reached over and lowered the music. "That better?"

"It's not enough."

"Look, you aren't doing any lesson plans. When you need quiet, I'll can the music."

"Oh, and *you'll* decide what I need?"

O'Roarke gave her a lazy grin. "Now, there's an idea."

The sexy inflection in his voice disturbed her. Struggling not to look flustered—she'd rather die first—she straightened her shoulders and picked up her clipboard. "What I need right now is to get this course outline in place."

He watched her for a moment, then shrugged and plunked himself down at the worktable, pushing the boom box to the back. "Fine." He motioned to a chair next to him. "Let's do it."

Beth got up and strode to him. With precise movements, she drew a chair out from the table and set it a good two feet from his. "Oh, wait a sec." She retrieved her glasses from her bag and perched them on her nose. When she raised her head, O'Roarke was staring at her. "What?"

"The glasses look cute."

She rolled her eyes. "Cute? I don't think I've ever been called cute in my life." Which wasn't quite true, but those days *were* a lifetime ago, so they didn't count.

"Mm." That was all he said before he shifted his gaze to the papers.

The first thing Dylan noticed when Lizzie Borden got close to him was how she smelled. He hadn't picked it up in Jamaica, but her scent surrounded her here. It was some fresh, subtle fragrance—like the wildflowers that grew in the back of Grandma Katie's yard. In the spring, when they first came out, the scent drifted into the rear of the house. He owned that house now and had converted the entire back to a huge sunroom and bedroom.

"I highlighted what Captain Jackson was going to teach. The rest of the classes are mine."

Dylan peered at the papers she held. He noticed her nails were short and unpolished, yet her hands were very feminine all the same, slender and long-fingered. He forcibly focused on the list. "Most of those topics I can do easily. I've taught some classes at the Red Cross off and on. A few I'll need to study up on."

Her brow furrowed. "No sense in taking those, then. I've done all these lessons before, so I'll teach the ones you're not comfortable with."

"All right." He pointed out four or five he'd skip. "I'd like to be part of the first class."

She raised her head and arched delicate eyebrows. They were the color of cinnamon, a few shades lighter than her hair. "Why?"

"Don't you and Tom usually teach the first class together?" He checked the outline. "On the qualities of a Certified First Responder slash EMT?"

"Well, yes."

"Then so should we."

"Why on earth would we do that?"

"Because I want input into that topic."

She bit her lips. He was surprised to note a touch of pale lipstick on them. "I don't think that's a good idea."

He knew why, but he asked, anyway. "Why?"

She ran a hand through her short wavy hair, mussing it. "It's important to start out right, instill in the recruits the proper demeanor when performing emergency medical care."

"I agree. That's why I want some input."

Carefully she took off her glasses and set them down. "All right, let's get this out in the open. It's no secret I'm worried you'll impress negative traits upon them."

"Like?"

"Too much risk-taking."

He was silent.

"You'll tell them things they shouldn't do."

"I look at it this way—I'll show them choices they'll be forced to make in the field."

She frowned. "Well, that's not bad. As long as you don't tell them the ones you'd make."

His heartbeat sped up. "You're referring to the Roncowsky incident."

"Among others."

"I saved the man's life."

"You got a severe reprimand. From what I hear, you almost lost your card."

A licensed paramedic could be stripped of his card for incautious behavior, and Dylan had come close on more than one occasion. Chief Talbot had been furious this last time. "I'll risk my card any day to save someone's life, particularly another firefighter like that rookie."

"That's precisely what I *don't* want you to convey to the recruits."

There's always a way around things, Dylan. You just have to find it. Grandma Katie's counsel was true.

Swiveling in his seat, he stretched out his legs and hooked his feet on the rungs of her chair. "Let me ask you something. What would you have done? Let the guy bleed to death because you didn't have the proper attire?"

"Well, I wouldn't touch a patient without using universal precautions."

"Really?"

"Yes, really."

Damn, she was telling the truth. "I don't understand that."

"I don't understand *you.*"

He didn't know what to do with her honest reaction. After a moment he asked, "So where do we go from here?"

"You've got to agree to teach the recruits to abide by the rules."

"I can agree to that."

Her eyes widened, their hazel flecked with grass green. "You can?"

"Yep. What I can't promise is to lie to them. If they ask me what I did in a certain situation, or would do, I won't lie."

"That's not enough. They'll learn from example. Eventually they'll come to like you—everybody does—and they'll think you're right."

"It's the best I can do, Ms. Winters."

Her face flushed.

Aw, hell. He wasn't going to back down, but he knew he shouldn't taunt her. "Listen, I'll abide by the rules. I'll emphasize them as much as I can. I do understand their importance. But I won't lie."

She sank back against the straight chair, looking somehow

fragile, the same impression he'd had of her in Jamaica. "All right. We'll drop it for now. Let's divide the curriculum."

For the half hour they worked on the courses, Dylan tried to cooperate. He agreed to let her teach two of the areas he wanted—patient assessment and cardiovascular and respiratory emergencies. After Grandma Katie had died, he'd become a specialist in the latter. He also volunteered to take basic life-support instruction—airway and rescue breathing and oxygen administration—which he found pretty boring. By the time Eric Scanlon knocked on the open door, they'd pretty much divided up the outline and retreated to their desks.

"Hello," Scanlon said. "Are you ready for me, Beth?"

Both of them looked up. Dylan watched Winters greet the captain in charge of curriculum. She gave him a smile, and her shoulders relaxed. Hmm. She obviously felt comfortable around this guy. Must be just *him* who made her as tense as a drum canvas.

Scanlon sauntered into the room, pulled up a chair next to Winters—close—and tilted his head questioningly. From the subdued boom box "Hey Jude" played. "The Beatles? Since when did you start listening to music at work?"

"Since I got a new roommate," she told him dryly.

Scanlon smiled at her and ignored Dylan. "Welcome back," he said with an odd—almost intimate—inflection. His pale eyes sparked with interest.

"Thanks." She picked up her glasses. "Have you got your schedule? O'Roarke was already assigned firefighter classes, wasn't he?"

The captain studied her a moment longer, then opened his butter-soft leather binder. "Yes. He was to be part of the orientation, and scheduled for airpack instruction, extinguishers, Quint/Midi operations, ropes and knots and ground ladders." Scanlon turned the page. He rattled off a few more lessons assigned to Dylan.

After they'd compared notes for several minutes without consulting him—like two parents discussing their child's agenda for the day—Dylan knocked on the desk. "Hey. Will you two quit talking about me as if I wasn't here."

Winters rolled her eyes, and Scanlon smiled indulgently. "Sorry. Beth and I work together a lot, so we're really in tune. Didn't mean to leave you out."

For some reason, the comment irritated Dylan. "How nice for you. Do you want to know which of the fire fighting classes I'd *like* to keep?"

"Of course."

It took thirty more minutes to rearrange the schedule. When they'd finished, Scanlon closed his fancy notebook and leaned back. "Seems all set to me. You'll be there for the orientation this afternoon, right, O'Roarke?"

"Yeah. If I get my room cleaned before lunch."

Winters said nothing. Scanlon laughed. "Speaking of lunch, Jake Scarlatta's upstairs. He wanted me to tell you he was here."

"Jake's *here?*"

"Yeah, seems he hurt his shoulder in the incident you guys had at the Jamaica airport. He got assigned light duty at the academy after he saw the department doctor this morning. He may teach some of the firefighter classes we took away from you."

Terrific. At least I'll have one friend in the place.

"You could go talk to him now," Scanlon suggested, checking his watch. "Take an early lunch."

The hint was obvious, even without the color that crept up Winters's face. He'd never realized her skin was so fair. Like a porcelain doll's.

Dylan stood. "Sure, I'll go see him."

"He's been assigned the desk in the main office, the one originally given to you."

"Fine."

On the way to the door Dylan grabbed his jacket. He jogged about ten feet down the hall before he realized his wallet was in his backpack. Retracing his steps, he reached the office entrance. Someone had half-closed the door. Dylan could see inside but realized they hadn't noticed him. Ms. Prim and Proper was behind her desk. Scanlon sat on the edge, smiling at her, his arms folded. Dylan recalled what he knew about the captain. All the secretaries thought he looked like Robert Redford, with his sun-bleached blond hair and green eyes. Jake, the clotheshorse, said Scanlon really knew how to dress, too. He'd also been divorced for a while.

Dylan had decided to forget about the wallet and leave when he heard a low, feminine laugh. He caught sight of the woman who'd made it and found himself transfixed.

His stomach clenched when he saw the way she was looking at Scanlon and what it did to her face.

It was the same face as before, but different. Her eyes were wide and liquid, simmering with feminine warmth. Her lips were pouty, sensuous, as she gave her undivided attention to the man seated on her desk. Then Dylan's eyes were drawn to the way her uniform shirt pulled tightly across her breasts, which looked very full.

"…good time in Jamaica?" Scanlon finished his question.

"The wedding was great."

Leaning over, Scanlon ran a finger down her nose. "You got some sun."

Winters didn't draw away, only smiled. "Some."

"Looks good."

She blinked.

"It's sexy." Scanlon's voice dripped honey.

"Is it?"

God, Dylan had heard that tone before. From other women. In bed.

"Did you get any tan lines, Beth?"

Her blush was almost virginal.

Only it was clear from Winters's flirtatious manner, to him *and* to Scanlon—given the big bad wolf look on the captain's face—she was no virgin.

"I'd like to see them," he added.

She mumbled something Dylan couldn't hear.

Scanlon gave a sexy laugh and stood.

Quickly Dylan stepped away from the door. But before he was out of earshot, he heard Scanlon say, "Seven. Tonight."

As Dylan hurried down the hall to the stairs to the main office, he was decidedly uncomfortable. Hell, he'd never played Peeping Tom in his life. He didn't know what had possessed him to watch.

But it was more than that. Something else disconcerted him. Taking the steps two at a time, he got to the top and headed down the corridor before it hit him. Even after seeing her in the sarong in Jamaica, he hadn't viewed Beth Winters as a woman. As a sexual being. For God's sake, she'd been his nemesis for eight years. But he couldn't banish the very feminine, very sexy picture she'd created flirting with Eric Scanlon.

It stayed with him a long time.

CHAPTER THREE

"ORGANIZED emergency medical care is thought to have started in the 1790's when the French began to transport soldiers so they could be treated by physicians away from the scene of the battle. During what other war did such care take place in the United States and who initiated it?"

Before she could stop herself, Beth silently answered the question posted on the bulletin board in the common area outside the long private hall that led to Reed Macauley's office. The person who initiated the care was Clara Barton, of course, during the Civil War.

She shook her head at the three other questions, two on fire fighting and a final EMS challenge. What is the National Registry of Emergency Medical Technicians?

Though she couldn't answer the firefighter questions, she knew that the national registry was an agency formed to establish professional standards for local EMS.

"Want to go in on this with me?" She heard a voice behind her. "I don't know the EMS answers, but the name of the city that burned the same night as the Chicago fire was Peshtigo, Wisconsin, and the innovative fire fighting development in Cincinnati in 1852 was the first successful steam fire engine."

Beth looked at Reed Macauley's smiling, craggy face. "Sorry. I don't gamble."

"It's for a good cause," the department psychologist said.

"So I've heard." Everyone knew about O'Roarke's firefighter trivia game. He'd run it at Quint/Midi Twelve for five years. At a dollar a question, a third of the money collected went to whoever got the most right answers and a third to the Christmas party for the School of the Immaculate Conception—an institution for mentally handicapped students and a recipient of a big chunk of the RFD's charitable contributions. "What are they going to do with the last third? They use it for TVs and exercise equipment at O'Roarke's firehouse, don't they?"

"Since Christmas is only a couple of months away," Reed replied, "Ben said Dylan could run the game while he was here if two-thirds went to the school and nothing to the academy."

"Good." She paused. "Do you have a few minutes for me now during the lunch break? I'm afraid I'll be busy until five with the recruits. Or would you rather wait till then?"

"No need. I'm having a late lunch with Ben. I'd like to talk to you now."

Reed stepped around her and motioned for her to follow him to his office. When they entered, he gave her an assessing look. "You don't partake in the Christmas activities here, do you?"

"I'm not much on holidays."

Again, that assessing look. "Have a seat, Beth."

While Reed shut the door, Beth scanned the room and experienced the welcoming feel of the psychologist's office. Its light blue walls coordinated with slate carpeting and muted lighting. His desk was in the corner, a big battered oak piece with a huge comfortable chair, and the rest of the area was filled with overstuffed furniture. As Beth took one chair, her eyes were drawn to the wall directly across from her. Firefighter memorabilia and personal mementos covered the space. Added to them was a Manwaring print she'd never seen in here before. But she recognized the artist because she'd bought one of his paintings for Francey for her thirtieth birthday. The scene depicted an old high-rise building engulfed in flames that shot out from every window in vivid reds and yellows. Two firefighters, looking grimy and exhausted, stood in an aerial ladder bucket, furiously pumping water on the out-of-control blaze.

"Got a new print?" she asked.

"Mmm. From Dylan. He loves Manwaring's work." Reed took a seat on one of the nubby fabric couches. "It was a thank you for helping him."

"He must land in your office frequently."

"No, not really."

"He should."

Lounging, Reed linked his hands behind his head. "He's why I asked you to see me today."

"Oh?"

"Ben wanted me to touch base with both of you. Nothing formal."

She sighed. "I'm not surprised. It's no secret there's animosity between us."

Reed smiled. "No. The mystery is why. Both Ben and I remarked that we don't see any difficulty between you and anyone else, nor with O'Roarke and another person."

Beth shifted in her seat. "That's good, isn't it?"

"Yeah, in a way. Except that it makes it all the more puzzling why you two are at odds all the time."

Leaning forward, Beth clasped her hands between her knees. "Is it so puzzling?" When Reed looked at her, she went on, "Everybody knows what I object to in his behavior."

"True. You made it clear when you tried to block his coming to the academy."

"I said what I thought, is all."

"And then let it go when no one else agreed."

"It wouldn't be fair to the rest of the staff to push my position on them. Or to O'Roarke, either. Besides, I had no idea he'd get assigned to EMS."

"Are you always fair, Beth?"

She straightened her back. "I try to be." She'd learned long ago not to fight the fates. She had become very good at acceptance.

"Are you being fair to O'Roarke now?"

"Look, I know you're trying to help. But this is making me a little angry. I'm not the one who's been formally reprimanded four times in the past two years."

"He's gotten twice as many commendations. There's talk that he's being considered for the *Firehouse* magazine heroism and community service award."

"Which is why he's good to have on staff." Torn by the paradox, she stood and began to pace. "I'm a private person, Reed. I know there are things in my background that O'Roarke triggers. I'm trying to deal with him fairly."

"Is that why you keep everyone at a distance?"

Her heart rate bumped up. "I don't want to discuss this."

He waited a moment. "I can respect that. I've got some experiences of my own I don't like to talk about."

"So the rumor mill has it."

He smiled. "I *do* understand."

She nodded.

"All right. If you can't discuss why, maybe we can talk about tactics you can use to get along with him."

She stopped pacing and sat on the edge of the couch. "I can handle the mess he makes, even the god-awful rock music he brought in. It's his influence on the recruits I'm worried about."

"I think everyone's somewhat worried about that. But he's a fireman's firefighter, Beth. He has a lot to teach the recruits."

She said nothing.

"Think about this. In raising children, do you believe they should be influenced by different people, not just their parents?"

Beth kept her face blank and told herself to breathe evenly. "I don't know much about raising children."

"I think all different kinds of influences are good for kids, recruits and adults."

"Fine, then. You're glad O'Roarke's here."

"Yes. And all Ben wants is for you to be fair with him."

"Has Ben said I haven't been fair?"

"No. He just said you were pretty tough on him. When he was a recruit. And when he came back for EMT training."

"I'm tough on everybody."

"I know, and that's okay. You're highly respected at the academy."

"Yes, I realize that. I'd like to keep it that way." *It's all I have in life.* The thought made her wince.

Reed paused, then said, "You know, if you ever want to talk about anything, I'm here."

She shook her head and surreptitiously wiped her sweaty palms on her pants. "Thanks for the offer. But I don't think so."

"Well, just in case you change your mind I'm here."

"I won't." She stood and headed for the door. For a brief crazy minute, she almost turned back. Almost said, *You're right. I've got things that happened that have made me what I am. Here they are.*

Thankfully, the insanity didn't last. She opened the door and left without giving in to the weakness.

DeLuca's Diner was busy, as always, around lunchtime. Dylan thought again how much he liked the place as he swung into one of its new rough-hewn booths and settled onto the comfortable Indian-print upholstery. The floor sported rectangular terra-cotta tiles, and the walls were cedar-sided. Barbara DeLuca, the owner and the ex-wife of Jake's one-time best friend Danny, had shown him and Jake to the booth and brought them coffee.

"Here you go, handsome," the petite redhead said to Jake, setting steaming mugs in front of each of them.

"No nice words for me, Barb? My ego could use some stroking today."

Barbara peered down her pug nose at Dylan. "Fat chance, lover boy. It's no secret you got women falling at your feet."

Dylan shrugged—it was true, after all—and smiled his killer smile at the owner. "You're heartless, lady."

"You guys know what you want? I'll take the order since we're shorthanded today." Barbara ran her fingers through her pixie cut.

"I'll have the usual." Jake's smile was warm in a brotherly sort of way.

Dylan realized Jake was unaware of the way Barbara was looking at him—the way Beth Winters had looked at Scanlon this morning.

"Club sandwich, hold the mayo," Barbara said.

"I'll have the same, only smother it with mayo."

Laughing, Barbara walked away.

"She doin' okay?" Dylan asked Jake.

His buddy's gunmetal-gray eyes were sober. "The place is making money, if that's what you mean. The remodeling helped."

"It was nice of you and the Cordaros to do the work for her." Dylan surveyed the diner. "A lot of the guys make it a point to eat here."

Jake glanced around the room, too. It was three-quarters filled with RFD personnel. "Firefighters take care of each other."

"When was the last time she heard from Danny?" Dylan knew he was treading on dangerous ground, for Jake never wanted to talk about the friend who'd left town, and the Rockford Fire Department, under a cloud, as Dylan's grandmother used to say.

"Almost a year ago, when he sent money for Derek."

"Derek's graduating from high school this year, isn't he?"

"Yes."

"Will Danny come for that?"

"Who knows?"

"Is he still in Key West?"

"Last I heard." Jake busied himself pouring milk in his coffee, then took a sip without making eye contact with Dylan.

"You ever think about going down there to see him?"

Jake shook his head. "No, I did enough damage, to him and to myself, to last a lifetime."

"You weren't the one who hit bottom with alcohol and drugs."

"No, but I turned a blind eye when I should have done something about it."

"Guilt's a nasty thing." Dylan was assaulted by a specter from his past—Grandma Katie's contorted face, her slack mouth begging him to help her. He'd been only seventeen and hadn't been able to do anything to help her. She'd died in his arms.

"Yeah, well," Jake said, "the situation with Danny taught me a good lesson."

"You run a tight ship at the station."

"As you should, when you're an officer back on the line."

Dylan accepted the change in subject. "Can't be soon enough for me."

"I thought you were looking forward to working at the academy."

"I was, until I got assigned to EMS. That office feels like a fire just waiting to roll."

Jake watched him for a moment. "Did you try to talk Ben out of making you work with her?"

"Yeah, no luck. Not that I blame him. I'm the only qualified medical person there now. Other than Lizzie Borden."

Barbara appeared with their sandwiches. Fast service, Dylan thought. It really paid to come here with Jake.

"Barb, how's Derek?" Jake asked.

She scowled. "Driving me crazy. I'll never get through his eighteenth year, I swear."

"I know what you mean."

"Oh, sure, like that doll of a daughter of yours is hard to contend with."

Jake's smile would have lit up a dreary February dawn. "I know." Then he sobered. "I'll talk to Derek when we go to his high school open house Thursday."

"Thanks. You're the only one he respects these days."

After Barbara left, Dylan chewed his sandwich silently. Always reticent to talk about himself, Jake didn't speak, either. "You take on a lot with that family," Dylan finally said.

Shrugging, Jake shook his head. "Not that much. I'm the kid's father figure—he needs one. Hell, Ben Cordaro did the same for me."

"It's been ten years since Danny took off." Jake didn't respond. "But as I said, everybody's got ghosts." Lazily leaning back, he crossed his arms. "Think Lizzie Borden has any? Or has she just been a bitch from the cradle?"

Jake rested his forearms on the table. "I think she's got them, all right, they're just tucked away tighter than most people's."

Dylan scowled. "How do you know that? Francey tell you?"

"No, Francey says Beth doesn't talk about herself at all. At least her past." Then his eyes danced with amusement. "She's had a lot to say about you, though."

"I heard." Dylan toyed with a French fry. "You know anything about her and Scanlon?"

"Ben told me they've dated for two years, off and on.

Apparently, it was off when Scanlon put the moves on Diana last summer.''

"Brought Ben right to his senses, didn't it?'' Dylan grinned. Everybody in the department knew about the tempestuous reunion of their battalion chief and his one and only love.

"I guess. I'm glad for them.''

"Well, I—''

A chair on the other side of the room clapped to the floor, cutting off Dylan's remark. "I don't have to take this shit.'' A belligerent male voice spat the words out.

Dylan glanced at the commotion. Francey's friend Chelsea Whitmore sat at a table, her pretty face drained of color. Her boyfriend, Billy Milligan, towered over her, clenching his hands.

Chelsea said something quietly.

"Yeah, sure.'' Milligan threw some bills at her and stalked out.

DeLuca's Diner was absolutely silent. Everyone stared at Chelsea. Dylan noted three of her coworkers from Engine Four watching her from a booth. No one approached her. It was odd, as firefighters were notorious about protecting their own.

Jake shook his head. "Poor Chelsea. What's she doing with that guy, anyway? He's a powder keg.''

Dylan scowled. "You know her very well?''

"Just from Francey's wedding. She seems like a decent woman. Great firefighter, I hear.''

Taking another glimpse at Chelsea, Dylan's attention was snagged by the expression on her face. The vulnerability reminded him of Beth Winters. He slid out of the booth. "I'm gonna go talk to her.''

Jake smiled. "You got a thing for protecting women, don't you, O'Roarke?''

"Brings out the caveman in me,'' Dylan joked, thinking

of Beth Winters. Then, wiping Lizzie Borden out of his mind, Dylan strode across the diner. He smiled at Chelsea and took a seat, hoping to make her feel less alone. She smiled back. At least *some* women appreciated his thoughtfulness.

WITH A BRISK, no-nonsense attitude—God forbid learning should be fun—Beth Winters stood ramrod straight at a podium in front of the room to begin the first EMS class. Her shoulders were rigid and her gaze sober. "We won't introduce ourselves again. Battalion Chief Cordaro already did that."

Slumped in a chair to the side, drawing little squiggles on his notepad, Dylan watched her. Though he tried to stop them, he was swamped by a flood of feelings. Primary among them was reliving his recruit days, when he was under this woman's thumb. Thankfully some things had changed.

He surveyed the poor souls in her control. The twelve recruits were as stiff as stretcher boards, sitting at their tables in straight-back chairs. The long, narrow room was only half filled, because they'd kept this fall's recruit class to an unusually small number. Across from him, large rectangular windows let in the September sunlight. He'd opened them for fresh air during his firefighter class. Dylan longed to be out there in that sun, riding his bike, away from Lizzie Borden and her sharp tongue.

Expecting her to start with an overview of the course, he was surprised when she grasped the podium lightly and said, "I started out in EMS as a Certified First Responder, which is the certification you'll all achieve. I worked on an ambulance for years while I attended the University of Rockford. I have a masters in anatomy and physiology."

Dylan stopped doodling. That was a shock. Granted, she'd have to have the training required by the state to teach advanced EMS courses, but he didn't realize she held a higher degree than his. He didn't remember her telling *his* recruit class this, though he wasn't sure he'd have paid much attention if she had.

"Every few months I go back and work with an ambulance crew in town. It's important to experience real-life situations, not just textbook cases."

He was sorry she looked at him at that minute. He knew his mouth was gaping—he had no idea she'd worked regularly in the field. Her smirk said, *Gotcha!*

"Lieutenant O'Roarke will be a bigger help to you with field experience, though, as he's a line firefighter, like some of you will be."

His budding admiration for her fizzled with her last comment. There it was—the subtle message that not all of them would make it. Didn't she realize how that undermined confidence? He could see several recruits squirm.

If possible, her back got even straighter. "Before we go on to content, let's get some rules down. Assignments are expected on time, no excuses. Don't even bother telling me."

Jeez, couldn't there be some leeway? A lot of the recruits were married. What if one of their kids got sick the night before? Man, this woman simply didn't have a heart.

But she did have knowledge. It was evident as she began the lesson. He'd forgotten how easy it was to learn from her.

She was organized. Slapping an overhead on the machine, she pointed to the information neatly typed in columns. "Here's two lists of terms you'll need to know by the end of the class. Open to page fourteen in your textbook for an explanation of the personality traits required of an EMT or CFR."

She discussed each trait thoroughly and gave circumstances where they would be needed. The list included *pleasant, sincere, cooperative, resourceful, self-starter, emotionally stable* and *in control of personal habits*. Well, Dylan joked to himself, the last two cut out half the firefighters *he* knew. She continued with *able to lead* and *neat and clean*—

oh, she'd like that one. He wondered what she'd look like mussed, her hair tousled, sweat on her brow, breathing hard. She ended the list with *good moral character* and *able to listen to others*—shooting him a glance as she discussed the last trait. He smiled, though her silent accusation hurt. He *could* listen to others when needed.

She also kept the students involved. After defining several legal terms, she surveyed the recruits. "I want you to get in groups now and come up with examples of these terms— voluntary consent, involuntary consent, implied consent and informed refusal."

She was precise. On another overhead, she'd written "negligence" and "abandonment." "With your partners, see if you already know the difference." After a few moments she put up the definitions and read them aloud. "Negligence is when something that should have been done was not done or was done incorrectly. Abandonment is leaving the patient before completing care or transferring care to someone who has less training."

And still she was tough. Holding up the book, she zeroed in on a muscular young man in the back row. "Recruit Tully. Would you please read aloud the section from the text on responsibility for possessions, records and reporting and legal implications in special-patient situations."

Looking like he was about to wet his pants, the kid stumbled through the four paragraphs. When he finally finished, she prolonged the agony by asking him, "So, what happens when you find valuables on an injured person?" Dead silence. "Are you responsible for them?" Again, the young man couldn't answer. His face paled. "Better study tonight," she warned. "I'll be sure to ask you again on Wednesday. Or there might be a quiz where you need to score at least seventy percent."

Tully swallowed hard. Winters remained neutral, her look almost robotic.

Watching the new recruit, Dylan's temper flared. He remembered vividly one time Winters had asked him a question from the previous night's reading. When he'd gotten it wrong, she gave him grief about no sick person wanting to be cared for by someone who didn't know the exact location of the sciatic nerve.

He'd never missed a question in her class again.

Three-quarters of the way through their session, she wound up her lesson, assigning fifty pages of reading for Wednesday.

Loosely clutching the podium, her posture still military and her face expressionless, she said, "We'll take a five-minute break, then Lieutenant O'Roarke will talk to you."

Dylan busied himself looking at the few notes he'd jotted, but was distracted by a young female recruit who'd come up to the podium to speak to Winters.

It was Connie Cleary.

"I'm coming to the exercise class Wednesday morning," she said.

Winters turned uninterested eyes on her recruit. "Fine."

"I, um…"

When the poor girl shifted and looked at her feet, Winters stared hard at her. "Recruit Cleary, firefighters need to say what's on their minds with a minimum of words and without stammering. In an emergency situation, it's vital."

The young woman went scarlet. "Yes, ma'am," she mumbled, and fled the room.

Apparently unaffected by the scene, Winters resumed looking at her book.

Dylan told himself to keep quiet. It was none of his business. But as usual, he lost the internal battle to stay quiet where this woman was concerned. At least he managed to wait until all the recruits had left the room to begin the war.

He stalked to her. "You got ice in your veins, lady?"

She peered at him, her eyes wide, her expression surprised. "Excuse me?"

"That girl was terrified when she asked to speak to you. Not that I blame her. You're about as approachable as a porcupine. You scared the hell out of her."

Winters arched an arrogant brow. "That girl might be at your back in less than four months, O'Roarke, at a fire or an accident scene. You want her tongue-tied then?"

She had a point, but he wouldn't let it go. "If you drive recruits like Cleary and Tully out, I'll never have a chance to help them get to the line."

"I don't coddle recruits."

"You don't know the meaning of the word."

"Does all this have a point?"

"Yes. I think you were too harsh on her and Tully."

The discussion was ended by a messenger who brought in a notice about recruits getting tetanus shots.

The students filed back in. Still steaming, Dylan bypassed the lectern Winters had used and sat on a desk, earning a big frown from her before she strode to the back of the room. Well, too bad. She could frown all she wanted. He didn't care what she was thinking.

Oh, great, Beth thought, taking a chair and watching O'Roarke. *He's going to play Mr. Chips.* When all the recruits were seated, he gave them a warm smile. Over the years, she'd heard about that smile and what it could accomplish. "I'm not much on formality," he said. That was news. "As a matter of fact, I'd like to hear *your* input on what you think about the qualities of a CFR/EMT and some of the issues Ms. Winters raised. Okay, everyone take out a sheet of paper." When they were ready, he said, "All right, close your eyes." A little mumbling, but they did as instructed. "Now, visualize this. You're on a rig, racing to an accident." He paused. "You know it's a two-car crash. Several people are hurt. You get there. Two are trapped and one was thrown from the car. Think about what traits you need to have as emergency personnel on the scene.''

Beth didn't participate in the exercise, and though the technique went against her grain, she admitted its validity. It was a good way to spark their thinking.

O'Roarke waited a long minute, his eyes dancing with delight. At what? she wondered. Teaching this group? ''All right, open your eyes and write down the traits that came to mind.''

When they finished, he said, ''Now underneath, ask any questions about EMS that you'd like. Print, if you're worried about handwriting recognition. I'd like you to be honest.''

O'Roarke leaned back and braced his arms on the desk. The pose stretched his shirt across impressive pecs. Line firefighters really stayed in shape, but then, they had to. He gave Beth a challenging glare. She kept her face blank.

Once he'd collected the sheets of paper, he resumed his position on the desk and read off the traits the recruits had suggested. Many were the ones Beth had given. Others were not. When he got to one of the latter, he stopped, raised his eyes to the class and said, ''I guess tact is important, but you need to remember that the patient's well-being overrides that.''

Tapping her pencil on her notebook, Beth waited for him to emphasize that the firefighter's or EMT's safety was paramount.

He didn't.

When the traits were covered, he began to read the questions aloud. Most were the sort of inane things she expected. At a typical station, how many EMS calls are there in comparison to fire calls? What would you do if a person stopped breathing and you didn't know what was wrong? Do firefighters ever get sick on gruesome calls? They were all fairly innocuous, and Beth began to breathe easier, thinking O'Roarke wasn't going to do too much damage the first day.

Smiling at the class, he held up the last sheet of paper. "One more to go, then we can blow this pop stand." He read the question in a confident voice. "If you were at a fire and a victim needed mouth-to-mouth resuscitation, but you didn't have a face guard, what should you do?"

His shoulders tensing, he glanced in her direction. He cleared his throat. "You should find a face guard."

Silence. Then someone from the back—she couldn't see the recruit's name tag—asked, "What would *you* do?"

O'Roarke froze. His eyes scanned the group, but he didn't look at her. "I'd perform the resuscitation without a face guard," he said.

CHAPTER FOUR

BETH BROUGHT no flowers to the graves in Lakeville, an hour's drive from Rockford. She hadn't planned on coming here, but she couldn't go home after she left work at five o'clock. Somehow she'd ended up at the small cemetery with its carefully tended plots, smelling of fall flowers and the rich loam of the earth.

She parked her Honda on the narrow gravel road that snaked through the grass, then trudged down the path that led to a section in the corner, the stones crunching in the stillness. When she reached the familiar spot, she smiled sadly. When she first used to visit, she'd sobbed on every trip. But it had been years since she'd cried about anything. She was older now, more stoic.

Cold, she'd heard the recruits call her year after year. Rubbing her arms on her light navy jacket, she thought, *Well, cold is better than the alternative.*

The plots she sought were marked by a hedge of rose-bushes. She'd have to return soon to cut them back and cover them for winter. She plucked off some dead leaves and let them fall to the ground. Both Mary Mack, her mother, and Leona Winters, her mother-in-law, had loved roses and had planted all different colors, varieties and sizes in a huge garden shared by their two backyards. The flowers had grown just like their twenty-year friendship. The roses had experienced ups and downs, like the women's lives—tender loving, nurturing, health problems and death. Once in a while, Beth wondered if that garden was still there, between the two houses that nestled thirty feet from Camden Lake. She'd never once gone to see.

There were many graves here in her little family area. Too many. She visited each one, brushing the autumn leaves from Mary's and her father Bill's, whisking the dirt from Leona and her father-in-law Mike's. At another, she ran her hand over the delicate angel statue perched on top of the smooth cool marble. When her eyes began to sting, she knelt at the grave she always saved for last.

How many times had she sat on the grass in front of its headstone? Slowly, she reached out and fingered the beautiful script she didn't even remember deciding upon, she'd been so overwrought after the accident. Lovingly, she traced the carved lettering—''Timothy W. Winters, Beloved Husband and…''

She bit back the emotion and removed her hand. Sighing, she closed her eyes and composed herself.

You've gotten pretty good at shutting down, sweetheart.

Beth shook her head. She was at it again. She understood that having these imaginary discussions with the only man she'd ever loved would seem crazy to anyone who knew about them—thank God no one did—but she also understood they helped her work out things in her head, as well as relieving the loneliness she rarely gave in to. After Tim had died, the psychologist she'd been urged to see told her these kinds of dialogues could be healthy as long as she didn't get dependent on them. So, carefully, as she'd done everything else for the past twenty years, she weaned herself away from them. In fact, she couldn't remember the last time she'd had one with him.

Sweetheart?

I know I shut down, Tim. I need to be in control.

You only think you need that.

Smiling indulgently, she shook her head. *You always did think you knew what was best for me.*

I always did know, Bethy, baby. She could still see his lopsided grin and his dark brown hair falling into his beloved brown eyes when he teased her. And the nickname. It transported her back almost twenty-three years.

"Tim," she'd giggled as he unbuttoned her blouse with sure hands. "What if I get pregnant?"

"We're gonna get married, anyway, Bethy, baby," he'd whispered as he'd touched her. "So we'll have a kid, too. What's life without a little risk?"

So, tell me about it, Beth thought now, her gaze on Tim's gravestone.

There's a person at work I'm having trouble with.

Dylan O'Roarke?

Sometimes, talking with your alter ego had its drawbacks.

Yes, of course.

Silence.

He's just so incautious. He takes so many risks.

You know how I feel about that.

Yes, love, and look where it got you.

Touché. You always were a good arguer.

As if she'd ever really argued with Tim in their short time together. They'd been so in tune since she was fourteen they'd only disagreed over his recklessness with his safety, and whenever she started to cry about it, he'd promise her he'd be better.

Being around O'Roarke... Beth searched for the words, trying to diagnose her feelings.

Spit it out, sweetheart.

It's hard.

He reminds you of me.

No! Absolutely not!

I see.

He's shallow...and selfish.

Ah.

Anyway, the point is, he's going to be a bad influence on

the recruits, and I can't let him do it. Today was a prime example.

Recruits, adults and children need all kinds of influences.

You sound like Reed Macauley.

Hey, this is your fantasy.

She smiled. Tim could always do that to her, coax her out of the worst mood.

What should I do? He can't say those things in class. The recruits will think it's okay for them to take the outrageous risks he does.

Talk to him.

It's like talking to a brick wall.

Pot calling the kettle black, Bethy?

I'm more reasonable than I was before you died.

I know. You're too reasonable and too serious.

No, Tim, don't say that. It's the only way I've been able to... She broke off, not wanting to finish the comment.

The only way you could survive without us.

Yes.

I wonder...

What?

Nothing. Let's discuss what you can handle.

I need to be able to handle Dylan O'Roarke.

Hey, my girl can do anything once she sets her mind to it.

Forty-five minutes later, Beth felt better. As she trekked down the gravel path to her car, her step a little lighter, she enumerated the strategies she'd figured out to deal with O'Roarke, particularly around what he'd said to the class today.

If only he didn't do anything else to upset her equilibrium, she might just be able to get over this particular hump.

DYLAN BLEW the whistle and stopped running alongside the two four-man teams. Like him, they were covered with sweat, and the academy arena was redolent with it. Although only one other teacher had been able to make it on such short notice this had been a good idea, getting the recruits and instructors to play basketball together.

He remembered Grandma Katie's maxim clearly. *Leading others to happiness is the greatest triumph.* She'd lived by it. Before she'd quit to help raise Dylan after his mother had died when he was five, Grandma Katie had been a volunteer at a recreation center in the city and had dealt with troubled boys. At ten, Dylan had gone with her to the college graduation of one of her former charges. Her blue eyes had sparkled with motherly pride when the graduate sought her out after the ceremony to thank her. Dylan had been bursting with pride for her.

He turned his attention to his charges. He'd see them through their graduation. "Good job, guys." Dylan jogged to center court. "But you fouled, Tully."

"Fouled?" Recruit Tully slapped his hands on his thighs with playful male bravado. "You need glasses?"

Dylan grinned. "No, but you need to control that hot dog streak. Okay, white team gets the ball."

Play resumed, and Dylan followed the recruits up and down the court, his heart thumping a good healthy rhythm in his chest. He made a few more calls but let most of the infractions slide. This was, after all, a game with a purpose. The guys needed to let off steam after a grueling first day. And they needed to feel like part of a team. When more instructors could participate, it'd be even better. Dylan smiled, smug, satisfied with himself.

He was about to signal the end of the game when he felt cool air on his bare legs. Someone must have opened the door. He pivoted to see who it was.

And came face to stony face with Lizzie Borden.

She stood stock-still by the doorway. With avid interest, he watched the emotions play across her face. First confusion, next surprise. Then—low and behold—disapproval. Reserved just for him. She dragged a hand through her hair, mussing it into a pleasing disarray.

Scanning her rigid form, he wondered why she was still dressed in her uniform at eight o'clock at night. For an uncomfortably long moment, her gaze stayed on him. It spiked his heart rate more than the running he'd done.

He let the play go on and crossed to where she stood. "Hi."

"What's going on here?"

"What does it look like?" he asked mildly.

"The recruits should be home studying for tomorrow's lessons!"

Shrugging, he glanced at his watch. "Well, it's only eight. We're almost done."

For a few seconds she watched the players move up and down the court. Seven guys and Eric Scanlon. He'd gotten more than half the class here. And was proud of it, damn her.

"How did you set this up?" Her voice was cut-glass cold.

He couldn't believe it. She was making him feel like a schoolboy caught playing hooky. "I posted notices in the men's locker room and john."

"I see."

"Oh, good. I thought for a minute you might disapprove." She gave him a merciless stare, which he ignored.

"What are you doing here?" He took in her clothes. "You even been home yet?"

Briefly she closed her eyes, shook her head and started for the office without answering him. Her carriage was impossibly tense, her stride angry. He thought about calling after her but didn't want to create a scene. Out of the corner of his eye, he could see play had slowed and several recruits were snatching curious glances at them.

When she was out of sight, he blew the whistle. "All right, looks like we're done for the night." He didn't know why he added, "Now, go home and study." Good-natured groans all around, then the guys headed for the showers.

Dylan glanced toward the office. Begrudgingly he started for it. He knew he couldn't leave the academy wondering what kind of hissy fit Lizzie Borden was going to throw over this.

The office was eerily still, smelling of coffee and a subtle hint of Winters. She was seated at her desk, head down, glasses on, staring at some files. For a second he was bombarded by the isolation of the image—her in work clothes, here at eight o'clock at night, no one else around. "Hi," he said softly.

Her head snapped up. The look in her eyes stopped him momentarily. She really didn't like him. Not that he thought he was so irresistible. It was just that he couldn't fathom—

"What do you want?" She sounded like a classic irritated mother.

Slowly he came into the room. He thought about sitting on the edge of her desk like Scanlon had, but her sour expression made him change his mind. Besides, his white T-shirt was soaked through, and his gym shorts were damp, too. He had a feeling she didn't like sweaty men. Halting a few feet from her, he held the long chain and swirled the whistle in a circle, making it whir.

"Don't do that," she chided. "You could hurt someone."

He looked dramatically to the side and behind him. "No one's here."

"It's a dangerous habit."

He stopped the motion and crossed his arms. "Did you never, even once in your life, do anything dangerous?"

Her face blanked. She did that a lot—closed down, wiped away all reaction. It made him goad her, like the patients did Nurse Ratched in *One Flew over the Cuckoo's Nest*. "Well, did you?"

"My habits are none of your business."

"They are when they intrude on my life."

"O'Roarke, why did you come in here?"

He edged close enough to see that her eyes were sad. He wondered why. "We may as well have it out now."

She eased back in her chair, folded her arms and crossed her legs. "Have what out?"

Sweat ran off his brow. He lifted his shirt and mopped his forehead. Her gaze dropped to his bare stomach—and she flushed.

He was embarrassed, which surprised him. Quickly he let the shirt fall.

"Take your pick," he said belligerently. "The basketball game or what happened in class today."

Looking at the ceiling, she shook her head. "You haven't got the sense of a two-year old."

"What do you mean?"

"Dragging those guys out here at night when they should be preparing for tomorrow. They need to study."

"They need to unwind. And stay in shape."

Her eyes narrowed. "Hmm. I thought I was in charge of physical fitness for the recruits."

"Is that what this is all about? That I stepped on your professional toes?"

"No, this is about poor judgment—something you've honed to a science."

"For cripe's sake, it's a simple basketball game."

"All right, hotshot, think about this one. There's only male recruits here tonight."

"Huh?"

"Where were the two women recruits?"

Dylan got the point right away. "Um..."

"Since the notices were in the men's room, Cleary and Frank didn't know about the game, did they?"

He shook his head.

"Were you aware that Sandy Frank was center forward on the East High School women's basketball team?"

That took the wind out of his sails. "No, I wasn't." After a moment he added, "You're right, I was being sexist."

"And you could get us a big fat lawsuit out of this."

"How?"

"The fire department has been an all-male organization for decades. We're just now coming out of the Dark Ages as far as women are concerned. The personnel here can't afford to slight them or treat them unfairly in any way."

"I wasn't thinking."

"You never think."

He sighed in exasperation. The woman didn't give an inch. "It was just a game."

Her gaze was glacial. "Tell me, O'Roarke, is everything a game to you?"

That did it. "Just because life's a Greek tragedy to you, full of accidents lurking around the corner and fatalities waiting everywhere you turn, don't let it—" He stopped his tirade when he saw her pale. Her eyes were so bleak he caught his breath. Uncomfortably he muttered, "Look, I—"

She stood abruptly. "Forget it."

She circled her desk and tried to brush past him, but he caught her arm. "Wait a sec. I didn't mean..."

Immediately she stilled and stared at his hand on her arm. When she looked at him, he could see the gold and green flecks sparkle within the hazel of her irises. "I don't appreciate being manhandled."

It was the last thing he expected—he'd never been accused of such a thing in his life. He dropped his hand as if he'd been scalded. And got mad.

"This isn't about my grabbing you or the game. It's about this afternoon in class, isn't it?"

She angled her chin and nodded.

Her honesty called forth the same reaction in him. "I told you I wouldn't lie to them."

"You misled them. You'll hurt them by doing that."

"No, I won't."

"Yes, you will. You just don't understand."

He cocked his head. "What don't I understand?"

She swallowed hard. Her eyes got a faraway look for moment, as if she was remembering something. "How precious life is."

Dylan inhaled sharply. An image of his grandmother came into his mind, like a television flickering on, then off. Naked pain sliced through him, and he tried to keep it from his face. "I do understand that."

She shook her head. "How can you, when you behave as you do?"

"Because I've learned that you have to live life to the fullest."

"No, you have to take precautions to make sure nothing bad happens." Gone was the frigidity of her gaze. Her eyes were furnace hot.

For the first time in the eight years since he'd known her, he felt as if they were communicating. It made him step forward. This time, he reached for her arm and stroked it. She started, then watched as his big hand closed over her biceps. When she looked up, there was a different kind of heat in her eyes. Or was it just his imagination?

"Am I interrupting?"

Winters spun away from him like a woman caught with an illicit lover. She turned to the doorway, where Eric Scanlon stood. Dylan faced him, too. Scanlon had showered and looked good in his pressed jeans and what appeared to be a designer T-shirt. His thick hair was slicked back. He seemed older, and sophisticated.

"Eric." Winters barely breathed the word.

"Captain," Dylan said formally.

Scanlon smiled. "I saw you come in, Beth. I stopped by to see if you wanted to go for a drink."

"A drink?"

He gave her a sexy grin. "Yes, as in your favorite Chardonnay? We could stop by the club."

The club? Shit, did the guy think this place was Harvard?

Winters seemed to shake off whatever odd mood she'd gotten into. "Of course. I'd love to."

Without glancing at Dylan, she retrieved her purse, then preceded Scanlon out the door. Scanlon peered over his shoulder and gave Dylan a very male grin. "Lock up the office, will you, O'Roarke?"

Mutely Dylan nodded. He stared after the couple, even when he heard the front door to the academy whoosh closed.

He swore, vaguely angry. Now why the hell was that? Probably because they hadn't had a chance to finish their fight. What did she know about what *he* knew of the preciousness of life?

And why did she make that statement? What was in *her* past that caused her to know—and fear for—the preciousness of life?

As he headed for the shower, he was shocked to realize he had every intention of finding out the answer to that question.

PUMPERS WAS a firefighter hangout located two blocks from the academy, and at seven the following Friday night, the end of the first week of the new recruit class, it was hopping. Beth loved the place because of its fire fighting motif, the shelf space and walls covered with firefighter memorabilia. She didn't allow herself to come here too often, but Ben Cordaro had asked her to make a special effort to show up tonight—a sort of instructor bonding, she guessed—and since Francey and Chelsea said they'd meet her here, she'd agreed.

She socialized with the other teachers for a while, then sought out her friends.

"You look pretty spiffy tonight," Chelsea told her as Beth slid into a corner booth that had a clear view of the goings-on. "The shirt looks great."

Beth fingered the silk, leaf-green blouse Chelsea had talked her into buying. The girl nosed into everybody's closet, she thought fondly. If the material hadn't felt so good against her skin, Beth would have resented its exorbitant price tag. "I love it, Chels."

"You should. It looks like a million bucks on you," Francey said. "But why'd you go home to change before you came here?"

"We had our first confidence walk at the end of the day. I looked like something the cat dragged in."

"You don't have to go on them, you know."

"It's a good example for the recruits."

"Who else took the walk today?"

Beth smiled. "Your dad."

Shooting a glance to where her father stood at the bar, Francey grinned. "Jeez, ever since he remarried my mother, he thinks he's twenty again."

"He kept up just fine. Let's see, Lorenzo went, too, and Rooney and Sheridan. And all the guys from the line, of course."

"Well, it didn't slow Dylan down." Francey nodded towards the side of the room.

Sipping her Chardonnay, Beth glanced over. O'Roarke stood with his blond bombshell, about ten feet away, leaning against the wall. She was all over him, and he wasn't trying to curb the public display. Beth bit her lip to keep from commenting. One of the strategies she'd worked out with Tim in her crazy conversation Monday was to focus on O'Roarke's good traits.

"Melanie's going in for the kill," Chelsea said.

"Yeah." Francey laughed. "She's gotta work tonight at Minx's and is leaving in a few minutes. Looks like she's saying a fond goodbye."

Beth gave Francey a half-smile and tried not to stare at O'Roarke. But she couldn't help observe his white-kneed beltless jeans that fit him indecently enough to make even *her* notice them. Tucked into the denims was a navy fire department T-shirt that outlined his world-class muscles. Seeing him relaxed and mellow made something warm flicker inside her.

"Beth," Francey said, "how's it going with Dylan at the academy?"

Beth rolled her eyes. "We survived the first week without any scars. Only twelve to go."

"I see. How about your sanity?"

"Well, the first day was pretty bad, but after that we settled into some routines."

"What happened Monday?"

Beth recounted the run-ins—the office mess, the music, the face guard question and the basketball game.

"Wow, all in one day. I'll bet Dad had a fit about the basketball thing."

"He's supportive of the game, but O'Roarke's neglect of the women didn't sit well. To give Boy Wonder credit, though, as soon as I pointed out the inequity to him, he took care of it."

Beth shook her head as she recalled O'Roarke apologizing to recruits Cleary and Frank. He'd oozed charm as he told them what a stupid sexist he was for leaving them out, gave them a Boy Scout grin and promised not to do it again, then coaxed Sandy into attending the next game. Despite her antipathy toward him, Beth had to admit he handled the potentially difficult situation well.

Her eyes strayed to him again. His big hand was on his

date's waist and squeezed her gently. Beth remembered the heat of that hand closing around her arm Monday night.

"The office seemed pretty livable when I was there yesterday," Chelsea observed. "He's messier than you are, Beth, but then, everybody is."

"It's fine. Once he got his toys all in place, and turned his music down, he was bearable."

"His toys?" Chelsea asked.

"Model fire trucks."

Francey waited before she spoke. "Uh, about his trucks…"

"Yes?" Beth took a sip of wine, tension creeping into her at Francey's tone.

"He started that collection with his grandfather."

Beth didn't want to hear this. It reminded her too much of things she tried hard to forget.

"Dylan was close to his grandparents, especially Grandma Katie after his grandpa died. I think he continues collecting them as a means of keeping his grandparents alive."

In spite of her desire not to, Beth pictured her dolls.

"Anyway, I thought you might like to know the facts."

Sighing, Beth admitted, "I'm trying to understand him better so we can coexist. That *does* help, France. Thanks."

To defuse the moment, she scanned the bar for something else to think about. Her gaze snagged on O'Roarke, his arm hanging on Melanie's shoulder as he walked her to the door. His lazy smile was very male. Again, she warmed at the sight.

Just as they reached it, the door swung open. "Chelsea," Beth said, "Billy's here."

Chelsea's face darkened, and she narrowed her eyes. "Yeah, well, he better behave himself tonight or I'm outta here. I've just about had it with his immature behavior."

"What happened?" Francey asked.

"Monday lunch happened. But I already told Beth about it."

"Go ahead and fill Francey in. I don't mind hearing it again."

As her friend launched into a description of Billy's temper tantrum at DeLuca's Diner—and O'Roarke's friendly support—Beth surveyed the room. The guy was everywhere. Now he was talking to his cronies at the bar. He drank beer from a bottle and smiled as he joked with them. Every once in a while, he reached out and touched Ben's arm, socked Jake on the shoulder or clapped Lorenzo on the back.

O'Roarke was a toucher. That was the first thing she'd noticed last week when she'd watched him teach the recruit lesson on fire extinguishers.

When she'd returned from lunch, he'd been outside with the fourteen potential firefighters in full goods gathered in a circle around him.

"I need a volunteer," he'd said easily.

Recruit Griffith raised his hand. "I'll do it."

O'Roarke motioned him forward. "All right, Griffith, you're the guinea pig." He handed the man some equipment. "But the rest of you aren't off the hook. Abbott, what did your reading give you as a mnemonic device to remember how to operate an extinguisher?"

"Mnemonic device?"

Beth had rolled her eyes. Part of O'Roarke's problem was that he was so smart he didn't see others' limitations.

Ace Durwin bailed Abbott out. "A mnemonic device is a memory jogger. Something to help you remember."

"Oh," Abbott said. "It's PASS."

O'Roarke said, "And—together, class—what does PASS stand for?"

In unison, the recruits recited, "Pull the pin. Aim at the base of the fire. Squeeze the handle and use a Sweeping motion."

"Very good." O'Roarke's praise was genuine, and the students responded to it. He handed Griffith the extinguisher. "Okay, Jeff, let's do it."

Griffith stepped to the fire O'Roarke had lit with a blowtorch in a three-foot-square iron ring. "I want to walk you through it aloud for reinforcement. First, hold the extinguisher in your left hand." The recruit did so. "Discharge the pin." Again Griffith did as he was told. "Aim at the base." Griffith pointed the nozzle at the fire. "Squeeze the lever."

When Griffith got a little too close, O'Roarke said, "Walk into the fire, but stay back a ways." The recruit did. "Now, remember to back away from the beast, never turn your back on it or it'll bite you in the ass."

The recruits chuckled.

O'Roarke reached out and covered Griffith's hand with his. "Now spray like this, with one big, sweeping motion. What you're doing is providing a sustained, concentrated supply to the base of the fire. A little lower, Jeff." O'Roarke clapped him on the shoulder and, still covering his hand, lowered the nozzle. "That's it, buddy. Real good. You got it on the first pass."

Beth had watched him lead three more recruits through the use of the extinguisher. She could still picture him brushing one of their sleeves, adjusting their hands, slapping them on the arm or the back. The physical connection, which worked wonders, was foreign to her. She'd thought about it all the way to her office—

"Hi, ladies."

Beth gave a start and looked up.

It was Dylan. With a poster in his hand. "Mind if I put this behind your booth?"

All three nodded.

"What is it?" Francey asked, as he leaned over their table and tacked up the sign. Beth caught a dark, spicy scent from him. For a moment he all but obscured her vision, and she felt enveloped by his presence.

"A playmate pinup."

Chelsea and Francey laughed. "Oh, sure," Francey said.

"Can I join you?" he asked.

Chelsea smiled. "Of course."

Beth was alone on one side and Francey and Chelsea were crowded into the other. She was certain O'Roarke would pull up a chair. He didn't. Instead, he scooted in next to her, forcing her to move over. Since she couldn't go far, she was uncomfortably close to him. Again, she was assaulted by how he smelled. Potently male and musky. And he seemed bigger this close, more male.

O'Roarke nodded at the wall. "The poster's for the Christmas shindig at the School of the Immaculate Conception." Dylan referred to the annual firefighter's day-long Christmas party for the students. It was a huge affair, with a parade of fire trucks, a funny program using the Shriner clowns, a visit from Santa, of course, and lunch with firefighters and their kids.

"Oh, I love that day," Chelsea said.

"Me, too, that's why I'm in charge of it now, as well as playing emcee and Santa, like I usually do."

"Since when?"

"Since Tom got hurt."

"Ah."

"You're all going, right?"

Francey and Chelsea nodded, both taking quick glances at Beth. O'Roarke turned inquisitive eyes on her.

"I, um, donate money," she said circling her finger around the rim of her wineglass.

"But you're coming to the party, right?"

She shook her head.

"Why not?"

Beth swallowed hard and felt her pulse rate quicken. Damn

him. Nobody questioned her about her choices. "I'm just not, O'Roarke."

"That's not an answer." The disapproval in his eyes singed her already raw nerves.

Just then Billy came to their table "Chelsea, can I see you a minute? In private?"

Chelsea peered up, hesitated, then shrugged. "Okay."

As she rose, Beth said, "I need to use the ladies' room."

O'Roarke slid out and Beth followed, then headed for the john. She could feel his eyes on her back.

Dylan watched until she disappeared into the bathroom.

"Why do you do that?" Francey asked as he sidled into the booth. Her violet eyes were clouded with concern.

"Do what?"

"Push her like that."

"I just asked her a freakin' question."

"Dylan, you must have felt the tension. Why didn't you just drop it?"

"Tension? Over a simple question?"

Francey sighed. "Not to betray a confidence or anything, but you might want to know that Beth doesn't celebrate holidays."

"That's ridiculous." His brow furrowed. "Unless it's for religious reasons."

"I don't think so. She just doesn't."

"Why?"

"We don't know. She doesn't talk about it, and we respect her privacy. The past couple of years she's done birthdays with us, but nothing else."

Dylan stared in the direction Winters had gone. Her retreating back had given him a nice view of the way her jeans molded her curves. And that blouse. It was the kind of material that made a man's hands itch to touch it. Her arm muscles were firm, he knew. Was her waist, too? Frowning at the direction of his thoughts, he groused. "Why am I surprised at this? She's so uptight."

Francey frowned. "This is unlike you."

"What is?"

"Being mean-spirited."

"Just where Lizzie Borden is concerned."

Francey's frown deepened.

"Oh, all right, I know. I...lose a little bit of my sanity where she's concerned."

"Maybe you should try to concentrate on her good points."

"What good points?" When Francey glowered, he said, "Okay." Dylan pictured her during the confidence walk. "She did the walk today like a pro."

"How far'd you go?"

"Only a mile, and the stairs twice, but no air packs."

"Not too bad."

"Winters wasn't even breathing hard." He could still see her jaunty steps as she ran circles around some of the recruits.

"How'd the recruits look?"

"Okay. A couple had trouble wearing their turnout gear in the heat." Connie Cleary had been one of them. Now that he thought about it, Winters had hung back to talk to the girl. She'd pointed to Cleary's coat and headgear, and Connie had unsnapped the coat and taken off her helmet. The sensitivity of the gesture had shocked him, given Winters's treatment of Cleary the other day. But then the good instructor walked away and made the rest of the hike without talking to anybody.

"Dyl?"

"Hmm?"

"Try to get along with Beth, would you? She's not as tough as she pretends."

He doubted that. Her veneer of ice was glacier thick. But he shrugged and stood. "All right. The best way to do it is avoidance. I'll get out of here before she comes back. Take care, kid,'' he said, mussing Francey's hair.

Dylan settled on a bar stool just as Winters came out of the john. He watched her shoulders relax when she saw he was gone from the table. She glanced around the room, her gaze landing on him. As if to confirm his earlier thought, the look she gave him was intentionally cool. He let her know she'd been caught looking for him—been caught being *glad* he was gone—by raising his beer and saluting her. She averted her eyes.

Swiveling, Dylan sighed and rested his elbows on the smooth mahogany surface. Francey was right. He goaded the woman. All the time. He knew she'd hate his sitting next to her, but he'd done it anyway.

And she *had* tried to get along with him this week, he could tell. Though he had no idea why. Monday night, when she'd left with Scanlon, he knew she was furious at him. But she'd come in Tuesday morning and been quite civil. Who the hell knew why. Maybe she was mellow from a night in the sack with Scanlon.

Rather than smiling at the thought, he frowned. The idea of her in bed with Robert Redford did not please him, and— Damn. He must really be losing it. Maybe it wasn't such a hot idea to concentrate on her good points. Maybe it would be best to remember their clash over the recruit training reports this morning.

They'd begun with a checklist that rated the recruits in several categories, giving scores. One was unacceptable, four was acceptable and seven was superior. Dylan remembered the assessments from his own academy days, where he'd gotten almost all superior scores except for two categories— acceptance of feedback and firefighter safety. He didn't have to ask who'd knocked him down there.

The discussion of each recruit had been grueling, beginning at eight that morning and ending at noon. Meanwhile the recruits underwent weekly testing in content and physical endurance conducted by Ben Cordaro and some of his personnel. The instructors had been in surprising agreement until the last two came up.

"Recruit Tully has missed every Question of the Day," Winters had said, "and his test scores are low." She had her glasses on, reminding him she could look cute.

"He's struggling," Scanlon had said.

Captain Lorenzo had asked, "Should we tag him as one to watch?"

"Tagging" meant they'd keep an eye on him for a while, then actively intervene if necessary.

"Absolutely," Beth said when no one else spoke up.

"I don't think so," Dylan interjected.

She raised a brow. "Why?"

"I think it's a mistake to pigeonhole somebody so quickly." As he stared at her, he wondered, *Is this what you did to me?*

She held his gaze. "We only have thirteen weeks, O'Roarke. Maybe you should stop distracting Tully from his studies with your basketball games." She'd dismissed him with a twist of her slender neck. "What do the rest of you think?"

The line firefighters had sided with Dylan, the staff with Winters. Tully was tagged.

When Connie Cleary's name came up, Beth also wanted her watched. "She's out of shape. She'll never be able to carry the hoses in the evolutions." In a few weeks the recruits would practice lugging heavy equipment into buildings and up flights of stairs.

They'd batted that one around until Dylan had thrown up his hands in dispair and exasperation. "You know, Winters, instead of bitching about her, maybe you ought to help her get into shape."

Winters hadn't responded—but Recruit Cleary had been tagged.

As Dylan sat on the stool, he considered his last remark to her. Maybe she had been trying to help Cleary on the confidence walk.

He stood abruptly, tired of trying to figure out a woman he didn't even like. Deciding to go to Minx's to get something to eat, he said goodbye to his colleagues and headed out of the bar. Though he tried not to, he glanced to where Francey and Winters had been standing. His buddy was still there, talking with Chelsea, but Lizzie Borden was gone. Once in the evening air, he felt better. Late-September nights were generally mild, but nippy for riding. He shrugged into a blue windbreaker when he reached his bike, then donned his helmet and he started up the motorcycle. He shot out of the space and circled the parking lot.

His headlight skimmed a dark blue Honda Accord—and a woman kneeling next to it. The light caught the shiny auburn mane of none other than Beth Winters. Reluctantly he switched off the bike's ignition, removed his helmet, left the headlight on and walked to her.

"Got a problem?"

She looked up. Several emotions crossed her face—irritation, frustration and disgust. "I dropped my purse and now I can't find my keys. They must have fallen out and slid under the car." She made a move to flatten herself on the ground.

Before she could, he bent and grasped her arm. "Don't. You'll get that pretty blouse all dirty." The blouse that he'd wondered how it felt to touch. Now he knew—like the hot, smooth skin on the inside of a woman's thigh.

She halted, surprised.

"Let me do it. Washing my dirty clothes won't cost what it'll take to dry-clean this." Against his will, his fingers fondled the material of her sleeve.

Winters was nothing if not practical. "Oh, sure, I guess."

Still she stayed on her knees, staring at him, her eyes wide and luminous. From his angle, the open vee of her shirt revealed an alluring glimpse of cleavage. He coughed and unzipped his jacket to lower his suddenly elevated temperature. She scooted back, then rose. He dropped onto the blacktop, ducked his face under the car and fished around with his hand. It connected with cold metal. "Got 'em," he said, and slid out. He rolled easily onto his feet.

From under lowered lids, she looked up and smiled at him. "Thanks."

His stomach clenched the way it had that day he'd watched her smile at Scanlon. "You're welcome." Purposefully he tore his gaze from her and glanced at his body. "See, just a little dirt on my knees and elbows. No big deal."

She scrutinized his face. "You've got a smudge on your cheek." She reached up and brushed her fingertips over his cheekbone several times. He swallowed hard at the smoky look in her eyes when she touched him. Her touch was feminine and soft. "There, it's gone."

Stepping back, she busied herself with her purse. He stared at her, squelching the absurd urge to seize her hand and bring it to his face again. Then she was watching him once more.

He jammed his hands in his pockets. "You're, um, leaving early."

She nodded.

"Got plans?"

She shook her head, sending waves of touch-me hair into her eyes.

"Not tonight. This is my ambulance weekend, and my shift starts at seven."

"Ah."

"You?" At his puzzled look, she asked, "Do you have plans?"

"I'm getting something to eat."

He bit his tongue to keep from asking her to go with him. God, what had gotten into him?

"Well, enjoy your meal." She unlocked the car door, and opened it. Still, he stayed where he was. She hesitated behind the door, her hand clasped on top of it.

He smiled. "Be careful tomorrow. On the ambulance."

She frowned with quick, hot annoyance. "Are you mocking me, O'Roarke?"

"No. I've worked on a lot of ambulances. It can be dangerous, is all. Just…take care."

Man, he had to get out of here. Before he said something else stupid. Or touched her again.

Without another word, he turned and mounted his bike. He flicked on the ignition, but waited until she'd closed her door, started the engine and pulled out.

Shaking his head, he watched her taillights until they disappeared.

CHAPTER FIVE

"It's eight-thirty."

Dylan raised his eyebrows at Jake. "Yeah?"

"Only a few minutes since the last time you checked your watch. What's up?" Jake lifted his cup, which said, EMS... Trauma Is My Business, and sipped his coffee. He and Dylan were shooting the breeze in the EMS office on Monday morning before the first firefighter class at nine. They'd already had roll call for the recruits, who were getting some special instruction on air pack use from the battalion chiefs.

"Nothing's up."

Jake surveyed the room, his gray eyes mischievous. "Where's your partner?" he asked.

Dylan gave him what he hoped was a scathing look. Obviously Jake had guessed that his *partner* was causing his clock watching. "I don't know."

"Scanlon said at roll call that he'd never known her to be late."

"Well, he should know." Dylan paused. "Did he call her?"

"Yeah, while you were giving Recruit Nicodemus a hard time about his shoes."

"And?"

"No answer."

It slipped out before he could stop it. "I hope she's all right."

"Maybe she spent the night with someone and...got tied up."

The notion of Beth Winters in kinky sex play was more than Dylan could handle. "Maybe. But it doesn't sound like Lizzie Borden's style."

"What doesn't sound like my style?"

Dylan closed his eyes, embarrassed big-time at having been caught discussing her and hearing him call her Lizzie Borden. Had she also heard the comment about her sex life? Shit! Slowly he swiveled the chair, but when he got a glimpse of her, he lost all chagrin. "What the hell happened to you?"

Winters reached up and fingered the four-inch bandage on her temple. There were deep smudges beneath her eyes and a bruise on her cheek and another on the underside of her chin. Her hair was still a little damp. "An accident."

For a minute Jake's comment came back with new meaning. Had some guy done this to her? Battered women often covered with so-called accidents.

"What kind of accident?" Dylan asked tightly.

At her desk, she looked up. Dylan noticed her uniform wasn't quite as starched and ironed as usual. "I had a run-in with a patient yesterday."

Jake frowned. "A patient?"

"I worked on a city ambulance crew this weekend."

"How'd you get hurt?"

"Some jerk who'd been beating up his wife threw a testosterone-induced tantrum when she called nine-one-one."

"My God, Winters," Dylan said. "Don't you know better than to walk into situations like that?"

Her mouth fell open and she stared at him as if he'd just taken a bite out of her arm. "You've got gall, O'Roarke, warning *me* about dangerous situations."

Jake stood and hitched up his uniform trousers. "I'm heading for the classroom." His gaze swung from Dylan to Winters. "If you two are going to yell at each other, close the door."

"Shut it on your way out," Dylan snapped.

After Jake had gone, Dylan strode purposefully across the room to Winters and tipped her chin. It felt small and delicate in his fingers. She winced, but didn't stop him. "Bruises aren't too bad. What's underneath the bandage?"

"Six stitches."

"Stitches?"

"From his broken beer bottle." She rubbed her arm. "The tetanus shot hurt more."

Letting her go, Dylan sagged onto her desktop. He couldn't understand why this upset him so much. He'd been hurt a lot worse, and her bruises weren't all that bad.

Women are meant to be cherished, Grandma Katie had often told him. Maybe that was why. He'd had a rotten weekend, too. He'd felt restless and out of sorts for two days. He'd taken his dog, Quint, on several runs, and even that hadn't helped. Every time he'd heard a siren, he thought of this woman. And for the life of him, he didn't know why. He was on a short fuse today—and Winters's attitude was really tripping it.

"O'Roarke, it's no big deal. The worst thing is how hard it is to wash my hair. I'll be glad for Friday when I can take the stitches out."

"You shouldn't perform medical procedures on yourself. A hard and fast rule of EMS, Instructor Winters."

She rolled her eyes. "Whatever."

"I'll take them out for you."

"Fine."

"Why'd you come in today?"

"Because I have to work."

"You should have taken some time off."

Impatiently she glanced at the clock. "Don't you have a class to teach?"

That infuriated him. He shook his head and injected a shot of sarcasm in his voice. "Sorry I was concerned about you."

When she just stared, owl-eyed, at him, he said, "Forget it," and left the room.

Beth sank onto her chair and let out a deep breath. Her entire body ached. What the hell had brought that on? It was the last thing she'd expected. It was bad enough she'd been up half the night with the pain from her bruises and the itching from the stitches. She didn't expect to take on O'Roarke the minute she walked in.

Granted, she'd been prickly. But he'd been talking to Jake Scarlatta about her, using his favorite insulting nickname. It got her mad, so she'd struck out at him. She slapped her hand down on the desk, wincing with pain. When Manson had come at her with a bottle, she'd automatically raised her arms to protect her face. He'd gotten a good swipe at her before the others restrained him, and her hand was cut, too.

She closed her eyes and shook her head. Man, she'd gotten into a dicey situation, and it had had harmful results. She'd like to talk about it in the EMS class today, but O'Roarke was conducting the session. She might be able to talk to the recruits, anyway. Maybe some good would come out of yesterday's debacle. Given her fatigue and aches, she certainly hoped so.

At three she left the all-day meetings she'd been in with Ben and Reed, and, despite the drum beating in her head, strode to the EMS classroom. She walked in just as O'Roarke told the class to be quiet.

"Would it be all right," she asked, "if I spoke with the recruits for about ten minutes? You could go get coffee."

He scowled, but said, "All right."

As she went down the aisle to the front desk, she heard the tiny gasps of shock at her appearance. Yes, this definitely needed to be discussed. O'Roarke ambled to the back of the room and sat at a table. He obviously wasn't going out for coffee. Damn.

She scanned the students, who were all watching her with

interest. "I thought we should talk about this before there are any rumors. I know I look like I was hit by a Mack truck. I was attacked while responding to an ambulance call last night. I obviously handled it inadequately or this wouldn't have happened. I'd like to describe what took place and have you brainstorm some things that could have been done to prevent my getting hurt. In other words," she said, focusing on O'Roarke, "let's talk about the safety of the EMT or firefighter—which, though I don't feel it's been emphasized enough yet to this recruit class, is primary in any rescue operation."

O'Roarke reddened at the direct hit. He remained maddeningly silent the entire time she and the recruits analyzed the situation, his face granite, his arms crossed. He didn't stop her when they went over the ten minutes. It was only when she grasped the end of the table with fatigue—she hadn't realized how whipped she was—that he spoke. "Half the class is over, Ms. Winters. And you look tired. Perhaps this is enough of a lesson on safety for one day."

"Yes, it is." She kept her expression a cool mask. "Thank you, Lientenant O'Roarke, for your class time." She nodded to the recruits. "You came up with some good suggestions. Remember them." Her gaze leveled on O'Roarke. "All of you." And she walked out.

Dylan knew why he was so pissed off at her—most of her remarks had been clearly aimed at him. But he couldn't figure out why he was concerned about her. He taught his lesson on the anatomy of breathing passages almost by rote, all the while picturing Hulk Hogan attacking the indomitable Ms. Winters. It made him wince.

After class, he took care of some paperwork at the desk, then went to the locker room, where he'd stowed his gym clothes instead of leaving them in the EMS office. He hadn't wanted to flaunt, in front of Winters, the fact of the basketball game tonight.

He spent a good ninety minutes burning off his frustrations, returned to the locker room at eight soaked with sweat and breathing hard from exertion, showered and changed and headed to his office to get his duffle bag and jacket and go home. He was surprised to see a light on under the door. He eased it open and stepped inside. No one was there. He surveyed the room. Winters's desk had papers spread over it, and a half-filled cup of coffee sat near the phone. Her lamp was switched on. Hmm. Very unlike her to leave the place so disheveled. He noted her duffel bag on the floor where she'd dropped it earlier. He checked the closet in the corner by the storeroom. Her coat was there. Jeez, the fool woman was still here? She didn't have any sense. She should have gone home early, not stayed late tonight.

Dylan heard a moan. He glanced toward the storeroom, which held myriad medical supplies. And a cot. Which, through the half-open door, he could see was occupied. By her.

She moaned again.

The small storage area was in shadow, but he could see that she lay curled up on the cot fully dressed. Her head was nestled on one hand, and her chest rose and fell in an even rhythm.

Widening the door to let in light, he eased into the room. His heart rate sped up. She must be feverish. Bending down, he felt her cheek and forehead. She was cool, but the room was warm, so that could account for the flush. He scowled. She lay on her right side, as the left was swollen and probably hurt. Her fingers were curled around a pill bottle. Gently he removed it from her hand and studied it. Percocet. She'd probably taken one and—

Another moan. He squatted next to her. Close up, he took the opportunity to study her. In repose, her features were soft and feminine, her body all slender curves. After a moment he squeezed her shoulder. It felt surprisingly slight, given how bravely she faced everybody. "Hey," he whispered, "wake up."

She reached up and covered his hand with hers. And smiled. "Mmm."

Dylan froze.

He'd heard lots of *mmm's* in his lifetime. This one was decidedly sexual.

"Come on. You need to wake up."

Again, the smile. She slid the hand she covered to her breast and pressed. Full, womanly flesh filled his palm. Dylan's heart leapfrogged. "Mmm," she said once more.

Without his conscious consent, he grew hard. His hand instinctively flexed on her breast. He was assaulted by the sensuality of the moment.

"Mmm. Tim."

Tim?

His ardor was instantly doused. He snatched his hand away and rose. He took several deep breaths before he felt in enough control to shake her shoulder. "Winters, you need to wake up!"

After a few seconds her hazel eyes opened. They were cloudy with...desire. She'd obviously been dreaming. About this Tim.

He cleared his throat. "You fell asleep here in the storeroom." He held up the pills. "My guess is you took one of these and it knocked you out."

She stared at him, and all the softness left her face when she recognized him. Or rather, when she recognized that he wasn't Tim.

She pushed herself on her elbows. Locks of auburn hair fell over her forehead. "I, um... What time is it?"

"Almost nine."

"At night?"

"Yeah."

"Wow."

"What time did you come in here?"

She scanned the storeroom, clearly disoriented. "About six. I was looking for some cups—I'd used the last in the bathroom. I remember seeing the cot and..." Her voice trailed off. "I must have lain down just for a minute."

In spite of his pique—at what, he wasn't sure—he smiled. "More like three hours."

"Yeah."

She took in his jeans and T-shirt. "Why are you here?"

"Basketball."

"Oh."

"Are you all right to drive home?"

"I think so." She scooted into a sitting position and swung her legs to the floor.

"Do you want to call someone to come and get you?" He stuck his hands in his back pockets. "Maybe Tim?"

He'd never seen eyes turn so bleak so fast; he immediately wanted to take back his words.

"There's no Tim in my life," she said, and stood. Giving her head a shake, as if to clear it, she circled him, then went out of the storage room and into the office.

He crossed to the door and watched her. "Have some of the coffee—the pot's still on. It'll be kind of strong, but I'm not letting you drive until I'm sure you're all right."

Silently she did as he asked. He thought about making small talk, but instead he went to his desk and made a pretense of examining papers. She got out a couple of folders and busied herself, too.

Fifteen minutes and two cups of coffee later, she closed the folders, put on her jacket, and picked up her bag. They hadn't spoken a word.

"I'm fine now. I can drive."

He nodded.

He watched her as she left the office. One thought assailed him. Who the hell was Tim?

BY WEDNESDAY MORNING'S fitness class, Beth felt almost normal. She stood in front of the recruits, led the warm-up exercises and studied each one of them. Hoyt Barnette was all bright-eyed and bushy-tailed, as usual. Ace Durwin stretched and strained as well as the kids who were ten—or twenty—years younger. Sandy Frank was in top form, in contrast to her buddy, Connie Cleary, who had struggled through the last class and the confidence walk.

"All right, let's get the hand weights. We'll do the rest of the stretching with them. Some of you need to build up your flexibility. Firefighters get in all kinds of crazy situations where they contort their bodies."

For fifteen minutes they stretched. Cleary moved fluidly in those exercises.

"Next is cardiovascular fitness. Fifteen laps around the arena. I'm going to randomly time some of you."

She began with John Wanikya. Piece of cake. He started slow and built up just right. So did Durwin.

Sandy Frank beat all the guys with her long, coltish strides. Beth loved to see women do well; it tickled her fancy when they outdid the men. She thought fondly of Chelsea and Francey, who'd been a joy to have as recruits.

Near the end of the aerobic training, she timed Cleary. As she rounded the corners, she gasped for breath and flushed much too quickly. "Cleary, c'mon. You've got to make these laps." Cleary was winded early and by the time she'd finished, the others had already gone to the weight room. Beth let Cleary catch her breath.

"You're out of shape," Beth said simply.

"I know."

"Why?"

"I...um..."

Beth waited, hugging the clipboard to her chest.

Her hands on her thighs, Cleary bent and sucked in air as if she'd run a marathon instead of a few laps. Her face was red, and her chest was heaving. After a few moments, Cleary stood straight and sighed. "You might as well know. After I graduated from the East High firefighter program, before this class started, I was in a car accident. I pulled something in my back. The doctors said with complete bed rest for a month, I'd be as good as new."

"How's your back now? In firefighting, a healthy back is essential."

"I know. That's why the doctors insisted on the bed rest. It's fine. But I lost a lot of wind capacity. And I gained twenty pounds that I *haven't* lost."

Beth frowned. "The latest research shows that in a study of elite runners, twenty-one days of bed rest took forty-two days to recoup full capacity."

Cleary stared at her.

"Was all this reported to the fire department?"

The woman shook her head.

"I'll have to tell Battalion Chief Cordaro."

"Does it matter? I'm not going to make the grade, anyway, with this lack of stamina, am I?"

"No."

Beth's message settled around them like noxious black smoke.

Cleary turned away and started toward the locker room, her head down, her stride plodding. Her shoulders were shaking.

You know, Winters, instead of bitching about her, maybe you ought to help her get into shape.

"Cleary, go to my office," Beth called sharply.

After taking a few minutes to check on the weight training and put Durwin in charge, Beth went into her office. It was early and no one was around, but she'd rather not be overheard.

The recruit was staring out the window.

"Cleary?"

The young woman faced her. Tears streamed down her cheeks. Her lips trembled.

"You'll never make it in fire fighting unless you toughen up physically and emotionally."

"I know."

"Why don't you join a gym, get a fitness trainer and have him or her get you into shape? I could recommend someone."

Cleary shook her head. "I can't. I don't have the money. My dad's laid off and two of my brothers are in college. I was supposed to go to work to help support everybody, but when I got into the academy, my dad said I had one chance to make something of myself, if I failed, I'd have to get a job someplace else."

"I see. What does your mother say?"

"My mother's dead. I take care of the house, so I really don't have time to go to a gym, anyway."

Beth had the picture. "You won't make it without help."

The tears came again, though Clearly wiped them away fast. "I...I know."

Beth squelched the foreign impulse to go to the girl and hug her. God, what was happening to her? She didn't do warm fuzzies. Well, not in a long time, anyway.

Action and firm plans were more her style. "All right, stop crying. Here's what we'll do. I'll set up a program for you. Threefold—flexibility, weight training and cardiovascular. I'll make charts for you to follow. You can use the equipment here at the academy—I'll even supervise. And a diet is in order. I'll figure that out, too. You come *every* day at six, instead of just three days a week. We'll start tomorrow."

Cleary gaped and swiped again at her cheeks. "Why?"

"Why what?"

"Why would you do this for me? Everybody knows you don't give any special consideration to anybody. It's either measure up or you're out."

Beth paled at the stark description of herself. Stark, but true. Why the hell *was* she doing this? *Maybe because Connie's just nineteen, the same age—*

Beth cut off the thought. Who *cared* why she was doing this?

At the prolonged silence, Cleary's face reddened. "I'm sorry, ma'am. I didn't mean...."

"Never mind, Cleary. Just leave before you say something else that may make me change my mind."

"Okay."

Cleary spun past her on her way to the door, then stopped short as she ran into O'Roarke.

He caught Cleary by the shoulders. "Connie?" he said, then nodded to Beth. "Shouldn't you say thanks to Ms. Winters for her kind offer?"

Beth glowered at him. At the devilment in his eyes.

Turning, Cleary said, "Thanks, Ms. Winters. So much," then darted out.

O'Roarke raised his arm and leaned against the jamb, the gesture accenting those damn muscles of his.

"What are you doing here so early?" Beth asked, trying to infuse a frigid note into her tone. Inside she was as rattled as a rookie facing a veteran.

"Had some things to do before class. I sure am glad I came in, though. It's amazing what you find out by comin' in early." He meandered into the room, over to his desk. "Just amazing."

DYLAN WAS STILL chuckling at the end of his lunch hour about the inimitable Ms. Winters softening that morning. He sat in his office grading the recruit pretest papers on breathing passages. He tapped his foot to "Mustang Sally" and checked off the answers on John Wanikya's test. Perfect score. Wanikya was intense, serious, his coal-black eyes always sober. Like Winters, he thought, but then frowned.

Sometimes that type was a tinderbox that could explode un-expectedly. Dylan wished he could lighten Wanikya up, but none of his efforts so far had succeeded.

Next was Trevor Tully's paper. Poor Tully. He'd blow the big exam Friday if this was any indication of what he knew.

We only have thirteen weeks, O'Roarke. Maybe you should stop distracting him from his studies with your basketball games.

Dylan traipsed across the office and peeked out. Several guys emerged from the kitchen where they'd been sharing pizza for lunch. "Tully, come in here a minute, will you?"

Tully hustled over. "Yeah, Lieutenant?"

Dylan motioned the young man into the office and into a chair at the table, then joined him. His back to the door, he purposely affected a casual posture, feet on the table, arms linked behind his head. "I graded your pretest just now, kid."

Tully's boyish smile slipped, and his gray-blue eyes clouded. "Didn't do so good, did I?"

Dylan shook his head.

"It's just like my ma said. I don't have the brains for this."

Dylan cringed, recalling Grandma Katie's constant assurances of his self-worth. "You know, Tully, I had this terrific grandma. She told me once that people don't fail, they give up."

Frowning, Tully cocked his head.

"You want some help in not giving up?"

"Sure."

"I've got some extra time Thursday, about six. I've got this hot date at eight," he said, and winked, "but I can meet with you for a couple of hours and go over this stuff with you, if you like."

"You'd do that for me?"

Dylan nodded, thinking of all the kids his grandma had helped in her volunteer work.

"Why?"

"Who knows? Maybe so I can have one worthy adversary in basketball around."

"I can't believe you'd do this for me." Tully frowned again. "I hope I don't let you down."

"You won't." Dylan smiled and socked the recruit in the arm. "Now get out of here."

Tully rose and squeezed Dylan's shoulder. "Thanks, man."

And he was gone.

Dylan leaned his head back and closed his eyes. He hoped it was enough. The kid seemed really slow. Still, though Dylan couldn't name exactly what it was, he thought Tully had the right stuff to make a hell of a smoke eater—if he could make it through the curriculum.

Singing along with his CD player, Dylan reached for the rest of the test papers. Over his off-key rendition of the Turtles singing "Happy Together," he heard someone speak. "I hope you're a better tutor than you are a singer, O'Roarke."

He winced as he slanted a glance over his shoulder and found Winters, jacket on, car keys in hand, back from lunch.

Just a mite too early, it looked like.

THE BATHROOM in the EMS office was long and narrow. There was just enough space between the sink and the shower stall to fit two bodies. Dylan's backside was pressed up against the shower, her cute little rear against the sink. Her breasts practically brushed his chest. A cool breeze drifted through the window, but Dylan sweltered with her nearness.

"Shut up, Winters. I can't do this with you raggin' on me."

"I can do it myself."

"No, you can't. What if the recruits found out you broke with procedure? Medical personnel aren't supposed to treat themselves."

"Oh, shut up, O'Roarke, and put the gloves on."

He didn't want to. Right then, her chin felt velvet soft between his fingers, and her hair was by far the silkiest thing he'd ever touched. He decided to compromise. "I'll put one on—the hand I'm cutting with."

Quickly he slipped on the latex. Again, he finger-combed her bangs from her face. Who would have guessed she would smell so great? Like lilacs. "Okay, darlin', close your eyes and let me do my thing."

He saw a grin tug at her full lips. "Your usual line, O'Roarke?"

Holding back a chuckle, he said, "Since I'm the one with the scissors, I wouldn't press my luck if I were you."

She tried unsuccessfully to stifle another grin.

Truth be told, he wasn't in any hurry to remove the stitches, because she'd shoot out of the bathroom like a rabbit from a foxhole as soon as it was done. He'd had a hell of a time getting her to agree to let him play doctor to begin with. And he liked being so close to her.

"O'Roarke, you've got ten seconds to do this."

"Jeez, Winters, never tell that to a guy."

A soft laugh escaped her lips.

A chuckle escaped his and he nudged even closer to her. "All right, here goes."

Snip, snip, snip.

He tugged at the threads and dropped them in the basket next to the sink, then set down the scissors.

But he didn't let her go. With his gloved index finger, he traced the small scar. "This will fade soon," he said, his voice whispery. He kept rubbing.

It was a moment before she said, "Oh, yeah, sure." Her voice was husky.

His gaze slipped from her temple to her eyes. They seemed huge this morning, shades of amber and green. Watching her closely, he slid his hand from her forehead to her crown. Her bangs tumbled in place. As he caressed her scalp, she gave a slight gasp.

"Hurt?"

She swallowed hard and shook her head.

A lazy smile spread across his face, though his temperature kicked up several degrees. "Good."

His fingers moved again, tracing her skull, massaging as they went. He glanced down and saw both of their chests rising and falling a little faster than a minute ago. His eyes returned to hers. They were full of emotion—deep, dark and desperate. Because of him? He let his hand fall to her nape, then burrowed his fingers under the silken strands of her hair to the tender skin there.

She swallowed hard again, but didn't move.

Her lips parted slightly.

So did his.

Unconsciously, he was sure, she leaned toward him.

Consciously, he did the same.

"What are you two doing in here?"

Ben Cordaro's voice from the doorway was like a bomb explosion. Winters gave a start and bumped her head on the medicine cabinet. Dylan jumped back and banged into the shower door.

It would have been funny if their battalion chief hadn't been wearing his General Patton look.

"I was, um, taking out Winters's stitches."

Ben nodded. "I see."

She cleared her throat. "What's up?"

"Come out here," Ben told them gruffly.

Without meeting Dylan's eyes, Winters ducked out of the room, and he followed.

In the office, Ben slapped his thigh with a rolled-up magazine. Winters and Dylan stood like two teenagers caught skinny-dipping.

"Ben?" Winters asked.

"*Firehouse* magazine just arrived."

"Not exactly earthshaking news."

"It's what's inside." He looked at Dylan. "You've been chosen for the *Firehouse* magazine heroism and community service award."

Joy shot through Dylan. "Really? That's great." At Ben's pained look he asked, "Isn't it?"

"Yes, it is. Congratulations."

"Something's wrong, though," Winters said.

Ben unfolded the magazine and opened it. He handed it to them so they could read it together. Each took a side and held it up. Next to a grinning picture of Dylan was the text.

On July 17, 1999, Lieutenant Dylan O'Roarke of the Rockford Fire Department responded with Quint/Midi Twelve to the site of a multialarm, four-story structure fire. With two fellow firefighters, one a first-year probie named Robbie Roncowsky, O'Roarke rushed into the blaze with a fully charged hose line. Once inside, glass shattered, and the rookie's femoral artery was slashed. Lieutenant O'Roarke promptly staunched the flow of blood by whipping off his turnout coat, tearing off his shirt and using it as a makeshift tourniquet. With conditions excruciatingly hot and fire all around, O'Roarke dragged Roncowsky out of the blaze, sustaining second-degree burns. When he learned that three other firefighters were trapped, O'Roarke accompanied rescuers into the blaze—with no regard to his own safety or injuries, nor with the knowledge of the incident commander. The three trapped firefighters were rescued, and O'Roarke was rushed to Rockford Memorial Hospital burn unit.

As they read, Dylan felt his face redden. He also felt the woman beside him stiffen by degrees. The stiffening escalated as she digested each paragraph.

To add insult to injury, there was a sidebar with a list of Dylan's other exploits in years past. It was titled, Hero of the Year or Hero of the Decade?

Dylan O'Roarke, chosen for this year's Heroism and Community Service Award, has had a track record of daring rescues. Take a look.

January 1992—During a fully involved fire, O'Roarke dove through a glass window to save a baby trapped in the house.

March 1993—On his birthday, O'Roarke was ventilating a roof when cracking was heard under the firefighters' feet. Though ordered to come down, O'Roarke stayed on the roof until the ventilation was complete; officials recognized that the firefighters inside would not have survived without the ventilation O'Roarke single-handedly provided.

April 1995—On a routine rescue call on the Erie Canal in Rockford, O'Roarke plunged into the cold waters of the lake to rescue a twelve-year-old boy who'd fallen into the canal while riding his bicycle. Fighting the icy water and the encumbrance of the SCBA, O'Roarke surfaced with the boy, and hauled him onto dry land. Both suffered serious cuts from the jagged rocks in the water.

May 1997—When he was off duty and on a date, O'Roarke gave mouth-to-mouth resuscitation to a baby who'd stopped breathing in the entryway of a restaurant.

September 1998—On an accident call, O'Roarke crawled under a piece of blacktopping machinery to do CPR on a man trapped beneath, with no regard to the danger of the vehicle falling on them both. The victim survived.

When she was done skimming the article, Winters raised her eyes to Ben.

He nodded. ''The recruits have seen the extra copies we get. They were buzzing about it on their break.''

Ignoring Dylan, Beth said, ''Well, how are we going to undo this latest damage Boy Wonder has caused?''

CHAPTER SIX

BETH SLAPPED Ben's desk. She could feel her face and her pulse hammer. "Implicit in every one of these heroic acts is a total disregard for firefighter safety."

Ben crossed his arms over his chest and frowned. "Isn't that a bit of an exaggeration?"

She snatched the magazine from his desk and yanked it open to the smiling face of Dylan O'Roarke. "Number one—jumping into a fully involved fire, through a glass window, no less. Number two—ignoring an official command to vacate a roof. Number three—unless he's unusually fastidious, he didn't bring a mouth guard on a date. Certainly he performed the respiration without one. Number four—we don't carry the needed props for a paving machine. You know damn well he didn't wait until the vehicle was secured."

O'Roarke shot to his feet, his fury evident in the darkened blue of his eyes and the thin line of his mouth. "The man would have died if I'd waited for the right chocks. The baby in the theater was blue. And those firefighters inside the warehouse could have bought it if I hadn't taken the few extra minutes on the roof."

"*You* could have bought it, O'Roarke, any one of those times. Even that baby could have been HIV positive and could have contaminated you."

"It's a risk I'm willing to take."

"Fine. For you. But I won't have our recruits thinking this is the way firefighters are supposed to operate."

"All right, you two. This isn't helping." Frustrated, Ben

ran a hand through his hair. He turned to Reed Macauley, who sat in the corner quietly observing the scene. "Want to help me out here, Macauley?"

Reed's eyes sharpened. "I can't say this isn't going to be a problem with the recruits. They *will* get a mixed message from it. I can't say I condone Dylan's total disregard for his own safety, as well as dismissing standard operating procedure." The psychologist edged forward in his seat and linked his hands between his knees. "But I also won't sit here and condemn a man for some of the most courageous acts I've ever heard of in fire fighting."

Beth took a deep breath. "I'm not condemning him."

"The hell you aren't." Dylan's eyes blazed blue fire.

"I'm not. My sole concern is the effect this has on our recruits."

"Why is this such a big deal? It'll die down in a few days."

"It's a big deal because I just stood up on Monday in front of the entire class and highlighted the academy's emphasis on safety, on following SOP." She waved the magazine in front of him. "This litany of your exploits contradicts everything I said."

O'Roarke crossed to her and they stood face-to-face, much as they'd been earlier in the bathroom. Now, however, he seemed to tower over her. He said, "You really hate me, don't you?"

She drew back.

"Dylan," Reed intervened.

"Let her answer. You do, don't you?"

Her breath hitching, Beth shook her head. "No, I don't hate you. But what you do is totally objectionable to me."

"Then *I* am totally objectionable to you. Because what I do is who I am. If you despise that, you despise me."

Beth swallowed hard.

Dylan glared at her, his hands fisted at his sides; anger simmered hotly between them. Then he headed for the door.

"Dylan?" Ben said. "Don't leave yet. There's something else."

His back to them, O'Roarke stopped. Shoulders rigid, he seemed to struggle to control himself. "What?"

"The governor wants to present this award to you."

No one had to point out that this would garner more publicity.

"Next weekend."

Again the charged silence.

"At the National EMS Firefighter Convention in New York City."

Beth threw up her hands. "Oh, for God's sake."

Ben nodded. "You want to tell him?"

Shaking her head, she walked to the bulletin board, tore down a brochure and flipped the pages until she found what she wanted. She crossed to O'Roarke and handed it to him.

He skimmed the list of presenters at the conference. "Shit."

"Did you note the topic of my workshop?" she asked sweetly.

He read aloud from between clenched teeth. "Safety on the rescue scene, with special emphasis on recruit training." He was silent for a moment. Then he said, "I won't go to the ceremony."

"You don't have a choice. Chief Talbot delivered the news about the governor this morning. He loves the idea. As a matter of fact, he wants you to attend the whole conference. Says it's good PR." Ben shrugged. "What's more, he wants someone at the ceremony with you to officially represent the Rockford Fire Department, and since Beth is already going, he's named her. He says it's perfect."

"I say it sucks," O'Roarke said.

Reed expelled a heavy breath. "Maybe we should table this for now. Give us all a chance to calm down."

O'Roarke rounded on his friend. "I'm calm, Macauley. I'm just truly pissed off." With that, he turned and walked out of the office.

IN THE EMS CLASSROOM, Trevor Tully approached the front desk, and several other recruits crowded around. "So, Lieutenant, what does it feel like to be a hero?" he asked.

O'Roarke smiled but didn't seem happy. Trevor knew he'd been holed up in the battalion chief's office for an hour, but he thought they were celebrating. Instead, O'Roarke looked like he'd gone to a funeral. "I'm not a hero, Tully. I did what I thought was best at the time." He hesitated. "You know, you guys—" he smiled at Sandy and Connie "—and gals, there's another side to this you should look at. I broke the rules in some of those instances."

"Yeah, man," Brady Abbott said, "and saved lives."

"Right." O'Roarke crossed his arms. "But a firefighter's safety is more important than the victim's."

Sure, Tully thought. *No way is that true. The guy's just being modest.*

"Lieutenant?" Hoyt Barnett asked. "If you had to do it over again, would you do it like you did? Or would you follow SOP?"

O'Roarke seemed to struggle with that. As far as Tully was concerned, his hesitation said it all.

Their lieutenant opened his mouth to answer when from behind Tully came an exaggerated cough. "All right, people, we've lost enough time today. Let's get in your seats." Trevor turned to see Lizzie Borden calling the troops in line. Mega vibes shot from her to O'Roarke.

What a bitch, Tully thought. *How can the lieutenant stand to work with her?*

POISED in the front of the training maze, already in his heavy turnout goods, John Wanikya blinked when O'Roarke placed the headgear on him. It was covered with brown paper, and he couldn't see a thing.

He heard the lieutenant say, "There's a person trapped in there. The house is full of smoke." A pause. "You can lift that off while we talk, Wanikya." John pushed back the helmet, breathed a sigh of relief. "Mr. Wanikya will be our first firefighter to enter the maze, aka the burning building. His face mask is covered to simulate the density of smoke. You won't be able to see your hand in front of your face in a real rolling fire. But you'll have to perform."

From the other side of him, John heard Winters add, "EMS is often required under adverse circumstances. We want you to get used to this, since it's your third week of training. You haven't seen the maze yet, so we thought we'd start out with a simple search and rescue. Find the injured person and bring her out. Perform whatever emergency medicine is necessary out here."

"Her?" Cleary asked. She shifted nervously from one foot to the other.

"Yes, our dummy Harriet is in there suffering from smoke inhalation. She's the size and weight of an average grown female. For each of you, we'll place her in a different location."

Winters turned steely eyes on O'Roarke. The current arcing between the two had been high voltage since the article on the lieutenant had come out last Friday. Wanikya wondered briefly if he should take sides in whatever was going on between them, if it would help him in any way.

"Would you like to be inside to watch their progress or should I?" Winters's tone was cold, as usual.

"Your choice," O'Roarke said curtly.

"I'll go inside."

Winters headed into the maze, and Wanikya saw Tully and

Abbott exchange disgusted looks. So, some of the kiddies were already choosing sides. Interesting.

"Go ahead, John." O'Roarke's tone was encouraging. "See if you can get Harriet out of there without losing her." Almost as an afterthought, he added, "And without hurting yourself."

Someone in the back mumbled, "As if O'Roarke would think twice about that."

Wanikya cleared the opening of the maze and dropped down on his knees. He knew the drill. Crawl. Feel your way. The boards on the floor were rough. He inched in about two feet before he encountered the first obstacle. Stairs. He ascended them, groping for each one. Suddenly they stopped. He probed to his right. A wall. To his left was an opening. This time it was narrow. He slugged down it, his air pack knocking on the sides. His breathing escalated due to the confined space and heat—they must have a way to kick up the temperature. He ran smack into a door. Knowing Winters was watching from above, he took off his glove and tested the door with the back of his hand, then opened it and edged through. There was a series of rungs. He descended the ladder. Blind as he was, it was scary. At the bottom, his feet connected with something. Ah, Harriet. He reached down and outlined her body with his hands.

Knowing he had to get her out, he calculated the distance he'd already come. Could she make it without air? Were they expecting him to consider this? Every day they told the recruits to think on their feet. Should he give Harriet some of his air?

What would O'Roarke do?

CONNIE CLEARY shrank into the shadows as Brady Abbott faced Ms. Winters at seven on Tuesday of week four. She and the instructor had just finished their workout, and Connie was cooling down on the other side of the room divider in the arena. When she realized they didn't know she was there, she stayed very still.

"Ms. Winters, can I talk to you?"

"What is it, Abbott?"

"You said on Friday if we had any questions on our weekly RTR to wait until Monday or Tuesday to think it over, assess it, then come to you."

"All right. But make it quick." Ms. Winters was often curt, but today even more so.

"I got a one in EMS safety."

"Yes, you did."

"Is it because of what happened in the maze?"

Uh-oh, Connie thought. In the debriefing after the maze work last Thursday, Ms. Winters had reamed Brady out for getting both himself and the victim stuck. He'd stood there stoically and taken the criticism; apparently, he'd decided to deal with it today.

"I don't understand the one. I got stuck trying to save a victim's life."

"I intentionally put up that impediment so you'd have to choose between saving yourself or risking your safety to get the victim out. You made the wrong choice."

"Did Lieutenant O'Roarke agree with the one?" Brady asked.

"An RTR is consensus."

Connie knew that wasn't an answer.

"If you have a problem with my response, Abbott, you can go see Battalion Chief Cordaro."

"No, ma'am," Brady answered, "I don't. I just wanted clarification."

Ms. Winters turned from him and headed into her office.

When Brady passed Connie, she called out to him. "Brady?"

He stopped, and when he saw her, his face reddened.

"I'm sorry. I overheard."

Brady looked down and smiled sadly. "It doesn't matter."

"Want to talk about it?"

"Sure." He plunked down on the mat. "She knows damn well O'Roarke would have done the same thing."

Connie watched Brady as she finished stretching. Lieutenant O'Roarke was a doll, but he was wrong this time. She'd studied the textbook thoroughly—she'd always been good in school, and Ms. Winters had told her to capitalize on her assets—and it warned against jeopardizing your safety for the victim's. In this instance, Connie would side with the woman who'd come in at six in the morning for the past three weeks to help her out.

Brady looked at her with eyes that were confused. "I can't figure it out, Connie. O'Roarke and Winters are contradicting each other. How are we supposed to know what to do?"

Even Connie couldn't defend her new idol on that one.

ACE DURWIN halfheartedly listened to the other recruits chatter until they got into the latest happening in the academy. Then he paid attention. Durwin hadn't expected so much intrigue.

"They're both going to be gone Thursday and Friday." Austyn Myers dropped the bomb as they sat around the lunch table munching hamburgers and French fries from a fast-food joint.

"Yeah? Why?" Ryan Quinn, Myers's best buddy, asked with a mouthful of chocolate shake.

The two eighteen-year-old recruits had graduated from the East High School firefighter program together and were by far the youngest, in many ways, of the recruits. Ace felt like their father most of the time. Like a good parent, he let them talk before intervening.

"They're going to a conference together."

"You're shittin' me," Quinn said.

"Nope. Get this. O'Roarke's getting his *Firehouse* magazine award at the same conference Winters is presenting a workshop on firefighting safety.''

"They call that irony," Al Battisti, a rather quiet young man, put in.

Durwin shook his head. The recruits had been buzzing about Winters and O'Roarke's difference of opinion ever since O'Roarke's exploits had been published the same week Winters had given her spiel on EMT safety. Durwin was torn on the issue. He could see O'Roarke's point about saving people. But he sided more with Winters. Maybe it was his age, but Durwin wouldn't have wanted one of his sons to risk his own life any more than necessary to save a victim, so he didn't plan to do it himself.

"I'd hate to be on that plane with them," Tully said. "Poor O'Roarke."

Cleary said, "I feel bad for Ms. Winters. She's just trying to protect us."

"You're defending her because she's helping you get in shape," Tully said.

Cleary bristled. "You're defending him because he's helping you with your schoolwork."

Ace shook his head. This kind of dissension wasn't good. No matter who was right or wrong, the recruits were suffering.

"We're paying the price." Brady Abbott echoed Ace's thoughts. "I got a one because of the maze stuff on Friday's RTR."

Everybody immediately fell silent. Recruit training reports were crucial to making it through the academy.

"You should have opted for safety," Wanikya said at last. "I did."

The younger recruits were amazed. John Wanikya rarely talked to them. Hmm, maybe this feud was having some positive effects, too, Durwin thought.

"I was thinking about sharing my air pack with Harriet,"

Wanikya continued. "I even contemplated what O'Roarke would do. I went the other way."

"Why?"

"Because it was safer."

Sandy Frank spoke for the first time. "Could you live with it, John, if somebody dies and you could've saved him?"

Wanikya's dark eyes narrowed. "It'd bother me."

Durwin sighed. Things were sure more interesting here than they'd been in Beckville.

IN THE ACADEMY weight room, Beth sucked in air as she flicked the treadmill's pace switch up to seven. She didn't always run this fast, but she was trying to work off her frustration. Wiping the sweat from her forehead, she swore softly. Damn, how had things gotten to this point?

Though she'd stayed aloof from everybody all week, she was churning inside. Primary among her chaotic emotions was the fact that she felt bad for O'Roarke. She shook her head and ran faster. No one knew how much she loved the fire department—or why. Firefighters were truly "America's Bravest" to her. To be chosen for the award O'Roarke had been given was a coveted honor.

And she'd spoiled it for him. She hadn't meant to. But she'd been so shocked by the magazine's account of his dangerous rescues. All her initial fears about O'Roarke coming to the academy had been validated. The article's effect on the recruits had been borne out this week. There had been odd questions, contradictory statements made, even infighting. It had been like picking through a minefield the past week and a half.

"I didn't know you were in here."

Beth slowed down and shot a glance over her shoulder. In black nylon running shorts and a gray T-shirt, O'Roarke scowled at her from the doorway of the exercise room. "I'm working out," she said, stating the obvious.

"I see." He nodded to the treadmill next to her, a shock of black hair falling into his turbulent eyes. "I could wait, if you'd prefer."

"I don't care if you use it now."

His scowl deepened. He'd been so angry at her all week he'd barely been civil. As if to reinforce his animosity, he strode to the stereo system and turned it on full volume. Rolling Stones music blared out. The first song to play was "Rip This Joint." Beth said nothing. She imagined that was how O'Roarke felt about working at the academy right now.

He crossed the room, mounted the treadmill next to her and switched it on—and up to five.

She bit her tongue. He notched it higher a few minutes later. Over the music, she said, "You should warm up on this equipment." When he ignored her, she asked, "Why are you here, anyway? Aren't you and the recruits playing basketball tonight?"

"I canceled the game because we're leaving tomorrow. I wanted to run outside, but it's raining." He increased the speed again.

Trying to block him out, she closed her eyes and listened to the Stones. She hadn't heard them in years. Their sexual beat thrummed in her head, and after several minutes, when she started to feel uncomfortable, she decided to slow down and get out of there.

So, twenty-five minutes after O'Roarke had come in, Beth got off her treadmill. She took about five minutes to stretch on the mat. He abruptly shut off his machine and dismounted.

Her mouth dropped. "Aren't you going to cool down on that thing?"

"Get off my back, Winters," he snapped, wiping his face with a towel. He looped it around his neck.

She thought about joking that "Get Off My Cloud" would be a better retort, but she decided to play it straight. "I was just…"

O'Roarke made a move toward her, his eyes filled with scalding anger. Halfway to her, he stopped short and gasped, doubled over to reach for his left calf.

Her heart in her throat, Beth sprang toward him.

"What is it?"

"My calf. A cramp."

She dragged his sweat-slicked body to the mat. "Lie down."

"Goddamn son of a bitch," he said as he sank to the floor.

Flat on his back, he spread his legs apart and Beth knelt between them. She reached for his calf and began to knead it. She could feel the muscle roped in tension.

He moaned. "That hurts more."

"Shut up, O'Roarke." She kept kneading.

The massage went on for minutes. Each second she touched him, Beth became more aware of O'Roarke, lying on his back in front of her, his legs spread. There was that smell again—spicy cologne mixed with male sweat. His legs were corded with muscles and dusted with soft black hair all the way up to the hem of his black shorts. The Stones yelped about getting their rocks off and she closed her eyes, but the rhythm pulsed hotly in her blood.

When the pain began to subside, Dylan started to focus on Winters. He was startled to see her kneeling between his legs. Suddenly he became more attuned to her, her strong, supple fingers on his sore calf. She eased the pressure bit by bit and gently worked the muscle. The beat of the music abruptly changed when "I Can't Get No Satisfaction," came on. He was distracted from the soreness by the intimacy of their positions and the song's sexy implication. She was about a foot from his groin. She was breathing fast. Her hair was damp from her workout and curled a little around her face. Desire flickered and burned low inside him.

Then he noticed her clothes. A black leotard that outlined

very full breasts. Which he'd touched a few nights ago. Sweat glistened on her bare skin above the neckline.

She looked at him. Her hands stilled but stayed on his leg; then they slid along his skin behind his knee. She stared for a minute into his eyes—something kindling in hers—then swept his body from chin to crotch. He'd worn a jock strap, but his reaction to her nearness, the flicker turning into roaring flames, was obvious, particularly from her vantage point. She looked away. When the Stones' harmonica signaled their ''Sweet Black Angel,'' his gaze fell to her leotard again. Against the revealing spandex, he could see her nipples pucker.

Damn! What was he doing?

''Get off me now, will you?'' he snapped.

Her eyes narrowed and turned cool; she dropped her hands. ''Well, I wasn't going to say I told you so, but since you're being so sweet and all...''

He sat up fast and grabbed her wrist. ''You know, too bad you don't have any kids. You'd make a perfect nagging mother.''

Her whole body froze. Her face went completely blank. The vacuousness he saw there stunned him. Just like the other night when he'd asked about Tim.

Abruptly the music switched off.

''Look, I...''

She flung off his hand, stood and fled to the door. Hampered because of his cramp, he got to his feet and caught up with her before she made it out.

He grasped her arm. ''I didn't mean that the way it came out. But I'm so angry at you, I can't control myself.''

Her back to him, she said, ''You can never control yourself. That's part of the problem.'' She jerked her shoulder, forcing him to drop her arm. ''Leave me alone, hero.'' And then she was gone.

Dylan sank to the floor and rubbed his sore leg.

Looked like a great weekend ahead.

CHAPTER SEVEN

AS DYLAN RODE the glass-enclosed elevator to the eighteenth floor of the Marquis Marriott, he stuck his hands in the pockets of his black Nike nylon jacket and stared at the flash and glitter of Times Square. New York was a great city and a fun place, but he'd hate to do his job down here.

Exiting the car, he walked down the hallway and found his room—the one that adjoined Winters's room. He shook his head. Nothing went right with that woman. He could still see the young desk clerk beaming proudly. "We've given you and your fellow RFD attendee connecting rooms. We were able to do that with our new computer system for all the fire departments."

Dylan thought about telling the clerk they might need the homicide squad when Winters found out she was sleeping so close to him, but he kept his mouth shut. Of course, Winters would have known by now if she'd taken the plane to New York with him. Instead, she was driving. Dylan had stopped at the academy this morning on his way to the airport and Ben had dropped that little bomb—something to do with the leaves being pretty and wanting to be alone.

She never did anything he expected, so Dylan had made up his mind not to worry about her. Who knew—maybe her car would break down and she'd never get to the conference at all. It would sure make things easier.

Then he frowned. What would she do if it *did* break down—on one of those long stretches with no gas stations?

Oh, hell, she probably belonged to an auto club. Did she have a cell phone in her car?

He unlocked the door and he entered the hotel room. Nice. Striped wall paper. Spacious for New York City, with a king-size bed, dressers in deep mahogany and a sitting area with a couch and chair. Too bad he wasn't looking forward to his stay here.

Stowing his gear, which had been delivered by a bellboy earlier, his ire increased, like fire did when the building was ventilated. This should have been a happy time for him. Truth be told, he was ecstatic to be getting the *Firehouse* award. Being honored like this should have been one of the best times in his life. Even after he took a quick shower, he couldn't let it go. It was *her* fault. She'd spoiled it for him.

Suddenly Dylan saw Grandma Katie's face before him. He'd been inducted into the National Honor Society and elected the next president. His father missed the ceremony because he'd made captain and had to go to a training course required of all new officers. Sulking, Dylan had told his grandma before the ceremony that his father not being there spoiled it for him. He could still see her in a pink satiny dress, with the strand of pearls she always wore around her neck, frowning disappointedly at him. *If you think someone can spoil things for you, young man, then they can.*

Drying off and dressing in casual gray slacks and a black silk shirt that a woman had once told him made him look dangerous, he said aloud, "Okay, so I won't let her spoil it."

He was in a better frame of mind when he registered for the conference, then hit the welcome reception at seven that night. Grabbing a beer from the bar in the corner, he surveyed the attendees. There were about a hundred people here. Three hundred were booked for the conference. Must be a lot of them got in late, like Winters. He checked his watch. Where was she?

An hour later, as he munched on hors d'oeuvres and chatted with a group of firefighters from Buffalo, she came through the door.

She looked whipped. Her slender shoulders sagged. The long white shirt she wore over black jeans made her look paler than usual, and smudges marred the porcelain skin beneath her eyes. Those eyes scanned the room.

He excused himself from his colleagues and headed toward her.

Her brows arched as he approached her. Did she expect they'd ignore each other the whole time?

"Hi." His tone was conciliatory. He really didn't want to fight this weekend.

She hesitated, then said, "Hi."

"You made it okay?"

"As it turns out, yes." She raked a hand through her hair, mussing it. "I hit construction on Route Seventeen and was delayed for hours."

"Why didn't you fly? The fire department can afford it."

"I like driving. I enjoy the scenery. Being alone." She shrugged. "Look, it's not for everybody, but—"

He held up his hand. "I wasn't arguing. Why are you always ready to go off on me like fireworks?"

"Your tone was critical."

"Is this how the whole weekend's going to be?"

She blew her bangs off her forehead with a heavy sigh. "Why don't we just stay away from each other until Saturday night?"

"With connecting rooms that might be impossible."

"Who has connecting rooms?"

"You and I do."

"No one told me that when I registered."

He shrugged.

Pique sizzled in her eyes. "Well, I'll make sure I keep my side locked."

Without thinking, he grasped her arm. "Come on, Winters, I'm not going to jump you during the night."

"Not your style, O'Roarke?"

"I've never had to resort to it, no."

She opened her mouth to comment when a good-looking older man came up behind them. "Beth, I was wondering when you'd get here."

Winters turned and smiled brightly. "Josh." She held out her hand. "How nice to see you."

Bypassing the handshake, Josh enveloped her in a hug. She appeared to stiffen for a moment, then accept it. Dylan took the opportunity to study him—about six-two, broad-shouldered, with thick salt-and-pepper hair and a dynamite set of muscles.

When they drew apart, Josh perused her face intimately. "You look tired. Long trip?"

She glanced at O'Roarke. "No, it was fine."

Josh finally noticed him. "Hi. I'm Josh Carrington." He honed in on Dylan's badge, which in addition to giving his name and department had an insignia from *Firehouse* magazine that indicated his award. "So you're the hero of the day. Congratulations."

Dylan took in the other man's badge. FDNY—Fire Department of New York. "Actually I was just thinking that you guys are the real heroes. Been a firefighter here long?"

Carrington smiled. "I was on the line for twenty years. I'm in our training program now." He gave Winters a sideways glance. "Just like Beth here."

Winters rewarded him with another smile—a blood-sizzling one this time. For the life of him, Dylan couldn't figure out why that smile wreaked havoc with his stomach.

She turned cool eyes on him. "Josh is giving a workshop on fire ground safety tomorrow at..." She transferred her gaze to Carrington, and it warmed twenty degrees. "What time?"

"Ten o'clock."

"You should attend, O'Roarke," she added pointedly.

"Can I get you a drink?" Carrington asked her. "I was hoping to spend some time with you this weekend. We still have to plan those exchange visits between our departments."

"Of course. I brought my calendar so we could set that up." She threw a dismissing glance at Dylan. "You'll excuse us, O'Roarke."

Dylan bristled but said sweetly, "Sure. Have a nice night."

But *he* didn't. He mingled, ate some more and tried not to keep track of the two trainers—who both obviously valued safety above all else. When they disappeared out a side door, he ordered his third beer and asked himself why the hell he cared that she'd taken off with the guy.

He went to his room about eleven. Falling into bed naked, he thought about Winters. Somewhere between sleep and wakefulness, he wondered why she seemed to prefer older men. Carrington had to be fifty. So did Scanlon. Winters looked like she was in her middle thirties, only two or three years older than he was. What was her fascination with older men?

He turned in his bed, punching the pillows. What the hell did *he* care, anyway?

BETH SIPPED her coffee and glanced at the clock. She should get out of here and go to Josh's workshop. Instead of getting up, she stared at the door. The *connecting* door. God really did have a sense of humor. Not only was she O'Roarke's date for the big shindig with the governor tomorrow night—black tie, no less—but they had damn connecting rooms.

It'll work out, she told herself. *Stay cool.* She'd gotten through last night okay, though she hadn't slept well. She'd had wild dreams about a faceless man caressing her. Her body had ignited under his incendiary touch. She shook off the feeling of arousal she'd awakened with. No, the man wasn't faceless. It was Tim. Had to be.

Pushing away the reflections, she rose, found her bag and checked her appearance in the mirror. Nice navy slacks and a striped top. Not too casual or too dressy. She shook her head. When was the last time she cared what she looked like? she thought as she headed past the connecting door. Should she wake O'Roarke? Nah, he was the sleep-till-noon type. He wouldn't take advantage of any of the workshops.

It fit his know-it-all image.

Not fair. It was common knowledge that he loved everything about the fire department and consumed firemanics material. He was a voracious reader, filing away new information in that sharp brain of his.

As she descended in the elevator and found the room for Josh's workshop, she wondered how any man could be such a study in contradictions. O'Roarke was brave to a fault, brash and self-absorbed. But he really listened when the recruits talked, and he was unaccountably sensitive to their needs. Look at what he'd done for Tully. He was a hard worker. She'd seen him doing his lesson plans in their first four weeks of instruction.

Josh, standing at the lectern wearing a light blue oxford shirt and khaki pants, smiled at her as she walked in. Beth took a seat near the front, fished out her notebook and waited for the session to begin.

Her friend's presentation on fire ground safety was organized, chock-full of information and very important. The delivery was a little flat, though. Josh was relaxed enough, she thought as she watched him. But he was missing something.

Something she saw every time O'Roarke instructed the recruits. What was it?

Warmth.

After the hour-long presentation, Josh fielded questions

from the audience. The session was just ending when Josh nodded to someone in the back. "Okay. One last question."

"Captain Carrington—"

Beth snapped her head around at the familiar husky voice. O'Roarke lounged in his chair, dressed disreputably in jeans and a red polo shirt, looking like he'd just rolled out of bed. He hadn't even shaved.

"—how do you live with yourself if you implement all those safety guidelines and people die in a fire when you might have been able to save them?"

Beth's heartbeat escalated. There was no answer to that question. It was something she privately wrestled with all the time. She thought of the Lakeville firefighters who'd dragged her out of frigid water while ice cracked beneath their feet. Had they followed SOP, she wouldn't be here today.

Josh smiled at O'Roarke. "I don't live with it very easily. It's harder for some people than others. But I guess I'd rather lose someone and live to save others at some future point."

As answers went, it was pretty good. Beth watched Josh end his talk. She stayed in her seat when several people stopped to chat with him. As Josh approached her, O'Roarke came from behind. He extended his hand to Josh. "Good presentation."

"I saw you taking notes."

O'Roarke glanced at Beth. "Contrary to popular opinion, I know I have a lot to learn."

Beth brushed off the gibe and stood. The action brought her too close to O'Roarke. He smelled clean, like strong, masculine soap. "Well, I'm off to a session on EMS and terrorism," she said, her voice a bit shaky.

Josh nodded. "In case I don't catch up with you, where are we meeting later?"

"In the seventh-floor lobby?" She smiled. "About six?"

"Sure."

O'Roarke raised his brows. "Got plans for tonight?"

"Josh is going to show me his favorite haunts in the city."

"How nice."

"It is."

"Thanks for coming, Beth. I'll be at your workshop tomorrow." He turned to O'Roarke. "How about you, Dylan?"

O'Roarke grinned. "I wouldn't miss it for the world."

THE NEXT AFTERNOON Dylan lounged in the back of the Grange Room in jeans and T-shirt and watched Winters get ready for her presentation. He wasn't sure why he was here. It would probably make her nervous. He'd wanted to talk to her to see if it really was okay by her if he attended, but she'd put in another late night with Carrington, and Dylan had once again fallen asleep alone in his bed wondering where she was.

Was she sleeping with the guy? It didn't seem so. She didn't act like she did with Scanlon. Beside, Winters wouldn't be the promiscuous type. She was way too cautious. Was she a one-man woman? What would those long legs feel like wrapped around his waist?

Today, they were encased in wine-colored slacks, which she wore with a matching tunic, but he could still see the curves that were so visible in the black leotard Wednesday night, that he'd felt Monday in the storeroom. His hand flexed spontaneously.

How could he feel this attraction to her? He didn't even like the woman. Yet she aroused him. Just her nearness and that damn flowery smell of hers sent him into overdrive. He thought of her in sexual ways. Specific, graphic sexual ways.

Ninety minutes later he wasn't thinking of her sexually. He was thinking of her dead—by his own hands around her neck.

Her entire workshop had been a personal indictment of him. She'd begun by saying, "Training recruits in safety is crucial. Not to do so—or to present contradictory standards—is negligence in its purest form.'' And that was the good part.

She'd made veiled references to things he'd done since he'd come to the academy, using them as poor examples, and to his track record at the station, saying the fire department was giving mixed messages. She'd alluded to the turmoil among the recruits these past two weeks—only in general terms, but he recognized them—as the harmful result of not instilling the importance of following SOP.

Dylan was so angry he stalked out when she finished the formal part of her talk.

He was still seething as he dressed for the governor's dinner. ''Who the hell does she think she is?'' he asked aloud, as he stared in the free-standing, full-length oval oak mirror in his room, trying to knot his tie. Shit, he never could get one of these things right by himself.

Using examples of his *exploits.* Oh, she was clever, he thought, ripping the two ends of the tie apart for the fiftieth time. No one else would know who she meant. Damn her. *Damn* her.

As he struggled with the tie, he heard a knock on the connecting door. The one that had been locked for almost two full days. He knew they had to go down to dinner together, but he let her knock twice more, trying to control his anger. Barely composed, he whipped open the door.

And almost swallowed his tongue.

She was dressed in the gown she'd worn to the firemen's ball in early September. But he didn't remember it being so clingy. The soft material shimmered around her curves, the color of wet grass in the morning. Since the dress was strapless, she'd draped a matching shawl around her sleek shoulders; the wispy covering fell halfway down her arms. Things didn't get any better when he looked at her face. She wore makeup that made her skin and eyes glow. The word *stunning* came to mind.

"What's the matter? Is my mascara smudged?"

"What?"

"You're staring at me like I have two heads."

No, one is enough. "Sorry."

"You're not ready."

He flipped the ends of the tie. "I can't get this damn thing done up. I never can."

Turning away from her, he strode to the mirror again to fight with the tie. It was a minute before she appeared beside him in the glass. Tonight her scent was subtle, sexy, reminding him of messy sheets and a darkened bedroom. "We're going to be late."

He scowled and continued to wrestle with the noose around his neck. "You know, I can bandage a bleeding limb quick as a flash, fix up a sling in seconds, secure a splint in minutes. Why can't I get this friggin' thing tied?"

A smile breached her rouged, kiss-me lips. It didn't help his mood one bit. She stepped in front of him and batted his hands away. "I'll do it."

"I don't need help getting dressed."

"Yes, Peter Pan, you do."

Dylan stared down at her head. With the light reflecting off her hair, he could see several different shades of red. He fisted his hands when they itched to bury themselves in it. He noted the eye makeup she'd applied. It thickened her already lush lashes, darkening them to inky black.

Expertly her fingers moved on the tie.

"How the hell do you know how to do this?"

"Let's just say I've had practice."

"I'll bet."

"What's that supposed to mean?"

He thought about Eric Scanlon and Josh Carrington. "Nothing."

As she finished with the tie, he swung his eyes to the mirror and drank in the reflection of her dress. It bared the upper half of her back. Was she wearing a bra? He wondered what color it was. The mirror also revealed how the material hugged her fanny. God, those hips. He wanted to—

"All done!"

He continued to scrutinize her reflection.

She didn't move away.

The air crackled around them.

"O'Roarke?"

"What?"

"Why don't we declare a truce for tonight?"

He looked into her eyes. The browns and greens were like a fall forest. "Why?"

"Because this award is an honor. Because it means a lot to you." She bit off some of her rum-colored lipstick with even white teeth. "Because I hate the knowledge that I'm spoiling it."

"Thanks for being so concerned about me," he said unpleasantly.

Startled, she drew back. He grasped her wrist. His fingers encircled it completely. He was shocked at how slight she was, given how she went head-to-head with him all the time. "I'm sorry. You make me crazy, you know that?"

"Yes, I know." She smiled. "If it's any consolation, you do the same to me." The soft look she gave him melted his insides. "I meant what I said. Let's enjoy tonight."

"All right." He released her, and she scooted away fast. He wondered briefly why she always did that. She was at the door waiting for him when he turned. "Thanks," he said.

"For the tie?"

"Yeah, that, too." And he crossed to her.

IT WAS A MISTAKE, Beth thought as she sat next to him at dinner. A colossal mistake. How could she have known the effect O'Roarke at his most charming would have on her?

Now she understood why so many women went gaga over him.

Just his presence in the black tux was overpowering. He outdid even Chelsea's favorite male cover model. The raven color complimented his near-black hair, which fell rakishly over bright blue eyes. And his grin, when aimed at her, caught her behind the knees.

All night long he'd been unbearably attentive. He'd held her chair, settled his palm at her back, adjusted the damn shawl around her shoulders when it slipped. More than once, contact with his hand, or even brushing a bulging muscle, had given her goose bumps. When he solicitously asked if she was cold, she'd lied and said yes. He was so close for so long, all she could smell was his woodsy cologne and the special scent she hadn't even realized she'd come to associate with him.

He watched out for her all evening—making sure she had a drink, directing chitchat to her, just as a damn date would. By the time dinner arrived, she was furious at herself that she'd suggested the truce.

Furious and aroused. How, *how* could she feel that sexual pull to him? And how on earth could it be so strong? She'd been a virgin when she'd met Tim, of course, and the sweetness of his lovemaking stayed with her even today, like a precious old photograph. She'd also had good, sometimes passionate sex with a few well-chosen men in her adult life. Now, however, she felt a potent, attraction she'd never experienced before. For O'Roarke!

But she did her part, as she'd promised. When he was called to accept his award, she accompanied him as a representative of the RFD. Throughout the presentation, she smiled like a woman who cared about him. She forgot he was getting this honor for reasons she hated. She forgot she disliked him so much. Instead, she grinned into the cameras with him and didn't balk when he slid his arm around her for a shot by some reporter. She smiled like his girlfriend would have, leaned into him—against her will, but her body wasn't listening—and tried to ignore the thrill of his hand resting intimately on her waist. If it stayed there longer than necessary, she didn't complain.

When the festivities finally ended, she was a churning mass of conflicting emotions.

And she was relieved when Josh Carrington approached them.

"Congratulations, O'Roarke," he said congenially.

"Thanks." O'Roarke's color was high, as were his spirits. Beth was glad he'd enjoyed himself.

"What time are you leaving tomorrow, Beth?"

"Early."

"Too early to have a nightcap with me?"

Still too close to O'Roarke, she felt him stiffen and his hand go possessively to her back.

"No, not that early."

"You don't mind if I steal Beth for an hour or so, do you, O'Roarke? You've had her to yourself all night."

"As a matter of fact, I—"

"He doesn't mind," Beth interrupted quickly. She needed to get away from him. From this man she didn't even like.

Slipping her arm through Josh's, she threw a glance over her shoulder at O'Roarke. His face was thunderous, his eyes deep blue—and churning with an emotion she refused to identify.

"Good night, O'Roarke."

The hero just jammed his hands into his pockets and watched her walk away with another man.

ONE O'CLOCK. The awards ceremony had ended at eleven. Dylan berated himself for rejecting the invitations of two rough Poughkeepsie firefighters to go out on the town and the suggestion of a statuesque blond EMT for a lot more.

Why was he here, pacing the floor of his room like a caged tiger? He hadn't even changed out of his evening clothes, just shed the jacket and tie and rolled up his sleeves.

Where was Winters?

Restless, he ended up at the door to her room, still open from earlier in the evening. He frowned, but stepped inside.

It smelled like her. Unique. Womanly. Alluring. He prowled around, noting that not a thing was out of place. No surprise in that. He went into the bathroom and switched on a light. On the vanity sat a hairbrush, perfume, a cosmetic bag. He picked up the perfume and took a sniff, remembering how she'd smelled. He picked up her hairbrush and pulled a few strands from the bristles. He recalled how shiny and full that auburn hair had been tonight, how it felt in his hands last Friday.

Disgusted with himself, he left the bathroom and crossed to the bed, king-size like his. All night she'd smiled at him, listened to him, paid attention to him—and he'd loved it. She'd only been pretending, but somewhere along the way he'd forgotten that, so when Carrington stole her away, he'd been furious.

A nightgown had been laid out on the end of the bed. He picked it up and let the diaphanous material slide between his fingers like the caress of a waterfall. Against his will, he brought the garment to his nose and breathed in the subtle scent. A pang of longing shot through him.

How many men had taken this garment off her? Was Carrington slipping the sexy green gown from her body right now?

The idea drove him crazy.

He threw the nightgown down and stalked to his room, then crossed to the window and picked up the bottle of champagne that had been waiting for him on his return from the ceremony. "Congratulations," the card read. "Reed."

He'd already uncorked it and drunk two glasses; he poured

another. Sipping the bubbly wine, he stared out the window at Times Square and thought of what Reed would say to him now. *Why are you upset, O'Roarke? What are you feeling? Where does Beth Winters fit in all of this?*

By the time he heard the outer door to her room open and close, Dylan was completely disgusted with himself and his ruminations. When he turned, she was at the connecting doors.

"Still up?"

He nodded, not trusting himself to speak. Her hair was mussed, her cheeks flushed, as if she'd been kissed and touched. Her bare shoulders looked so smooth, they made his fist curl with a need to touch them. He gripped the stem of the glass so hard he was afraid it might snap. He knew the look he gave her was full of feeling, because her eyes widened and she stepped into the shadows of her room.

"I, um, I'm going to turn in."

Staring hard at her, he said simply, "No."

Beth sensed O'Roarke's mood and started to turn away when his hand clasped her arm. She stilled. *Please, God, make him let me go. I don't want this.*

Liar. She knew it as sure as she knew her name.

"Have some champagne with me."

"Champagne?"

"From Reed." He motioned to the other side of the room where a bottle chilled in a fancy steel stand. "To celebrate the award."

Not letting go of her, O'Roarke led her to it, poured a glass for her and held it out it to her—all one handed. She felt claimed by his strong fingers. He released her when she took the champagne. Raising his glass, his eyes locked on hers. "To tonight," he said huskily.

She sipped the champagne but glanced away.

He grasped her chin, forcing her to look at him. "Was it all an act?"

"An act?"

"The smiles. The interest. The…response when I touched you?" When she didn't answer, his fingers tensed on her jaw. "Was it?"

Holding his gaze, she lied boldly. "Yes, it was."

His brow furrowed, and his blue eyes went smoky with anger. "Did you sleep with him?"

"Who?"

"Carrington."

She jerked her chin away. "That's none of your business."

"Isn't it?"

"Look, O'Roarke, don't get carried away with our truce. It's over." Panicky, she slammed the glass on the bureau and tore away from him, from the intimacy of the darkened room, from the feelings bubbling inside her like a geyser about to erupt. She fled to the connecting door, knowing if she could just make it there, get to the other side, lock it and—

His hand closed on her shoulder before she reached it. "Beth," he whispered, using her given name for the very first time.

Feeling nearer to tears than she had been in a lifetime, Beth turned slowly to face him. She raised her fingers to his lips. "Shh, don't talk. Please, don't talk."

As agreements went, it wasn't much, she knew, but he seized on it. He lowered his mouth. His lips were soft but incredibly demanding. Like every one of their contacts, he drew from her a response she was helpless to control. Tracing her mouth with his tongue, he prodded at the seam of her lips, and she opened to him. He invaded her mouth like he'd invaded her life—brashly and with fiery intensity. To fan the flames, she moved closer to him so that her breasts flattened against his chest. He gripped her bottom and ground against her.

His lips left hers and traveled to her ear, then the side of her neck.

She bit her tongue to keep from crying out, from saying something she'd regret. An inferno raged inside her, but she allowed herself only to tell him, "Touch me, more."

His mouth found its way to her throat, then worked down to the cleavage revealed by her dress. His hands sought the zipper at the back. She felt him fumble, and then the dress fell to the floor. Her bra was next, and the scrap of pink lace soon joined the dress. His mouth closed over her, ravaging each breast, and her whole body bucked with her response.

He knelt to tear off her panty hose and pink lace panties, to bury his face in her stomach, her curls. She wanted to protest the intimacy of the gesture, but her mind blanked when he nuzzled her, igniting a response so hot she was scorched from the inside out.

He stood again, ripped at his shirt. She helped, yanked at the studs, tore at the buttons. Her hands clawed at his chest when it was finally naked. Her mouth sought the hard buds of his nipples. He moaned, and his fingers clenched again on her bottom.

Passion burst out of them both like fire through a roof. She plucked at his belt; he yanked on his zipper. Her nails dug into him as she pushed down his trousers and briefs. She knelt, too, removing his shoes and socks with hands shaking with the urgency of her passion.

When she took his aroused flesh into her palms, he started as if seared. "No," he growled, and dragged her upright. "I...can't. I'll never last."

She moaned incoherently and wrapped herself around him.

He clasped her to him and backed up toward the bed. But they were at the bathroom door, so he inched inside, never letting her go.

Fumbling in the drawer with one hand while securing her with the other, he drew something out. He said, "I need to protect you, sweetheart."

The endearment sucked all the air from her lungs like a fire in backdraft. "No, no," she said. "Please, no words."

"Shh. It's okay."

Then he swung her into his arms and strode to the bed.

Dylan was incoherent with need. His last bit of sanity made him seek protection, but when he put her on the bed and rolled on a condom, he knew he was near lunacy. His control vanished liked thin, white smoke. All he could think about was possessing her. She was so many beautiful angles and curves, and she was his, at least for tonight. He covered her with his body, pushing her legs apart so he could fit himself between them. His temperature skyrocketed at the intimate contact. She was hot and wet, and she arched and pulled him closer. He bit her neck, suckled her breasts again, but he couldn't wait any longer. Inching his hands down, he grasped her hips and lifted her. "Open your eyes," he said thickly.

She did as she was bid. Her eyes were almost all green and glazed.

"Lizzie." With one urgent thrust, he was inside her.

"Oh, O'Roarke."

He wanted to tell her to call him Dylan, to say his name, but he couldn't get the words out. She spiraled so fast, just one more thrust, that he was senseless with her clenching spasms. He plunged deeper, with no finesse, only a miasma of feeling, only a driving need to have her, take her as his own.

Utter blackness enveloped him as she cried out and he matched her release.

Beth had to get out from under him. His weight felt too good. He was still deeply embedded in her, and it felt too right.

But it was all wrong.

She'd had sex with a man she didn't even like.

He came up on his elbows and smiled at her. "Beth."

"You called me Lizzie."

He grinned and kissed her nose.

"I want to get up."

"Why?"

"I just do."

He frowned. "Only if you promise to talk about this."

Terror flashed through her. It must have shown in her eyes.

"I mean it."

Sucking in a breath, she thought, *All right.* Maybe she could effect some damage control, perform some salvage and overhaul on her emotions. She nodded.

Before he pulled out of her, he jammed his hips forward, sending a wave of aftershocks through her so intense she closed her eyes with the pleasure. To a lesser degree, she felt it again when he pulled out of her.

He lounged back into the pillows when she got up, tugging the sheet up so it barely covered his hips. Hips she'd clawed at, clung to.

She found his white shirt by the side of the bed, where one of them had flung it—she couldn't recall who. She struggled into it, then secured what buttons were left. She sank onto the end of the bed with her legs tucked under her. The light he'd left on cast them both in an intimate glow.

"Look at me," he said.

She did.

"What happened here?"

"I don't know. I'm shocked."

"Are you?"

She frowned. "Yes, aren't you?"

"No, not really. Not after the past few weeks."

"What do you mean?"

"Beth, I've felt this attraction for a while now." He hesitated, as if unsure of himself. "Haven't you?" When she still didn't say anything, he added, "Please, be honest."

"All right, yes, I have. But I don't understand it. We don't even like each other."

O'Roarke ran his hand through hair that had been disheveled by her fingers. Lying back against the sheets, he looked so sexy she wanted to cry. "Well," he said hoarsely, "something just clicked here. It's never happened to me before."

They were both quiet.

"You?"

Damn. He was bridging all her defenses. But she couldn't lie again. "No. Not like this. It was so…primitive."

"What are we going to do about it?"

"Do?"

"Yes."

"Nothing. We're going to forget about it."

"Hmm."

"What?"

"Do you think that's realistic?"

"What do you mean?" She sounded like an idiot, repeating herself.

"It's been building up for weeks, Beth. And I think it's caused some of the tension between us, along with our other differences."

She didn't say anything.

"I don't think we can afford to ignore it."

"Why?"

"For one thing, it'll take over again. Explode on us like this again."

"I suppose it could."

"And, in the meantime, it could eat away at us. Manifest itself in other ways."

"With the recruits."

"Well, you have to admit, we're really blowing it now. They're so confused, they don't know which end is up."

"What do you suggest? So it doesn't make things worse. So it doesn't eat away at us."

"Maybe we should feed it periodically."

She shook her head. "I don't know."

He asked, "Aren't you usually nicer to someone you're sleeping with?"

"I guess."

"Me, too. It might make us more willing to compromise, work at a solution to our differences."

"It could."

"I always thought that was why God gave sex to Adam and Eve."

Her answering smile was very weak.

"If it'll make us get along better, what'll it hurt?"

Beth tried to look horrified, but she didn't feel that way. Instead, she felt the embers of excitement kindle inside her. "Maybe. If there are parameters."

"Like?"

"Well, it's just sex, right?"

"Right."

"No caring, no romance."

"God forbid."

She scowled at him.

"All right. As you said, we don't even like each other."

She angled her chin. "Okay. How often?"

His look was sexually potent. "How often do you want it?"

Too often, I'm afraid. Without censoring her reaction—what difference did it make now, anyway?—she came up on her knees and moved closer.

He reached out and grasped a handful of his shirt and pulled her to him.

CHAPTER EIGHT

THE PHONE RANG on O'Roarke's desk Tuesday morning at seven-thirty. Beth had showered after her workout with the recruits, dressed in a crisply pressed uniform and was towel-drying her hair and sipping badly needed coffee when she came out of the bathroom. It took her a split second to decide to answer it. Like one buddy would do for another.

Yeah, right. As she sank into his chair, she tried not to remember that buddy driving into her like a man crazed, caressing her like a man in love.

"EMS office. Winters speaking."

A long pause. Then, "I, um, was looking for Dylan. I mean, Lieutenant O'Roarke." The soft feminine voice dripped with sexy southern honey. "Isn't this his number?"

"This is his extension, yes." Beth ignored the anginalike tightness in her chest. "He's not in yet."

"Oh, well, can I leave him a message?"

Beth closed her eyes, telling herself she was only angry at the inconvenience of having to act as O'Roarke's social secretary. But she couldn't block the images of him above her, beneath her, on his knees. Loving her.

No, it was just sex.

"Ma'am?"

"Oh, yes. Of course. A message. Go ahead."

Retrieving a pencil from a mug that said, Firefighters Are Always in Heat, she thought, *Tell me about it.* In her distraction she knocked over a photo. As she righted it, she looked at the old picture. It was black and white, of a man and woman, arm and arm, in front of a firehouse.

Dylan was close to his grandparents. He started the fire truck collection with them. Her eyes drifted from the photo to the rows of Quantum Pumpers, American LaFrance replicas, even a HazMat vehicle. In spite of her inner turmoil, Beth smiled.

"...if we're on for tonight?"

"Excuse me?"

"I said—" the Georgia drawl became irritated "—ask him if we're on for tonight. I tried to call him before my grave-yard shift at the diner, but I couldn't get him. And I'm going to bed now, so he shouldn't call me until...well, he knows when."

"Fine." The word was clipped.

"Or," the woman said, her voice perking up, "is his calendar there? On his desk. You could see if he penciled me in."

Penciled you in? Oh, for God's sake. What kind of idiot would put up with that treatment?

But as she searched for O'Roarke's calendar, she answered her own question. The kind of idiot who'd been subjected to his drugging kisses and mind-bending caresses until she'd do anything to feel them again, to feel him again, inside her.

Beth swallowed the bonfire of emotion that threatened to consume her. "I found it," she said, opening the swimsuit edition of the *Sports Illustrated* calendar with shaky fingers. "What did you say your name was?"

"Melanie."

Ah, the Barbie who'd had her hands all over O'Roarke's chest at Pumpers that Friday night. The chest that Beth had traced in exquisite detail with her own mouth and fingers last weekend.

"Why, yes, I see Melanie penciled in here. For eight o'clock tonight."

"Does it say where?"

"No," Beth told her. Exasperation finally won out over decorum. "Look. I've got a class in fifteen minutes. I'll leave him the message."

Hanging up, Beth bit her lip and sank into O'Roarke's chair. Her lids fluttered down out of fatigue and disgust. What did she care what he did? Or who he screwed? He was a paramedic, he'd take precautions, so it wouldn't affect her. The utterly sick feeling in her stomach was simply due to exhaustion and the stress of her weekend with O'Roarke. Anyway, she was glad she'd taken the phone call because it reinforced one thought. She *would not* become another of O'Roarke's groupies.

When she opened her eyes, he was slouched in the doorway. Her traitorous mind took in every detail of him—damp hair that looked inky black, shoulders encased in light blue that almost spanned the archway, the long, lean lines of his legs—before he said, in a husky voice, "You left me Sunday morning. Without even a word."

He wasn't going to give her any quarter, that was obvious. Setting the right tone was vital. Crucial to the health and wellness of her emotional life. She raised her eyebrows in an intentionally condescending gesture. "Yes, I did."

"Why?"

"You were sound asleep."

"That didn't stop you at dawn from, ah, getting me up."

Remembering how she'd kissed her way down his body when she'd awakened the first time with the sun, she felt the telltale blush start in her chest and sweep its way up to the roots of her hair.

The pencil she'd used to take the message from his girl-friend snapped in her hand. It sobered her. She picked up the pink slip. "You had a call before you got in."

"Leave it on my desk. I want to talk."

"No, really, you should take it. Barbie needs to talk to you, and she's going to bed in a few minutes."

"Barbie?"

"I mean Melanie." Beth shot an exaggerated glance at the clock. "But you could probably catch her before she goes night-night, if you try now."

O'Roarke scrutinized Beth until her throat felt parched and her skin prickly. Seriously shaken—by just seeing him, damn it—she rose unsteadily and crossed to her desk. She was in the chair before he pushed away from the doorjamb and sauntered over to her. The big steel desk offered little protection from his Schwarzenegger muscles. He braced his arms on its surface and bent close to her.

"We need to talk, Beth." His voice was gravelly, like it had been when he was inside her.

"O'Roarke, we're at work. This isn't the place for personal business."

"You're right. Let's do it tonight. About eight."

Her brows arched. "You have a date. Remember, you *penciled* her in." In spite of her vow to remain neutral, Beth snapped, "Why would anyone put up with that shit, anyway? Is she just *penciled* in until something better comes along?"

"I made that date before you and I..." His words purposefully trailed off. Her mind filled with snapshots of "you and I" all on its own. *More like an X-rated video. Oh, God.*

"It's fine with me," she said waspishly. "I'm having dinner with Eric tonight, anyway."

O'Roarke's hands fisted on the desk. After a long stare, he drew back.

Dylan watched her for several seconds. *Play it right, buddy, or you'll be out of the game before you even have a chance to score.* Well, he'd scored, so to speak, but he wanted to win the game, go on to the playoffs and take the whole damn tournament. Obviously, though, *she* was choking. Which maybe was a good sign.

Noting the smudges under her eyes and the pale cheeks—the instructor was definitely not herself today—he drew back and crossed to his desk. He set down his backpack and pulled out some notes. He would have preferred to bring her roses this morning—delicate peach buds—but he knew that would be a big mistake. So he planned to give her something she'd accept. If he was going to break down her defenses, which he had every intention of doing, he'd have to be sneaky about it.

He'd been pissed off when he'd awakened at ten Sunday morning to find her gone, not only from his bed, but her entire hotel room swept clean of all evidence of her. If his body hadn't borne the signs of their lovemaking, what she insisted was just sex, he'd have thought he dreamed it. But she'd left her mark on him—long scratches on his hip, teeth imprints on his shoulder, even a bruise from hands that gripped him with a passion he'd been shocked to discover in her. His body hardened just thinking about it.

He strolled to the computer, flicked it on and waited for it to boot up, watching her surreptitiously. She looked exhausted. Yesterday he'd made himself crazy with worry about her driving back from New York City, six hours all alone, in what had turned out to be drizzly weather. He remembered thinking just before he fell into a comalike sleep the night before that he'd ride back with her the next day.

She hadn't given him the opportunity to suggest it. She was determined to keep things strictly sexual between them. Her attitude called for drastic measures, one of which he'd implement today.

On the short flight home yesterday, he'd asked himself if it *was* just sex, as she'd insisted. The answer was clear. Not for him. They'd made a powerful connection with their bodies, one that had knocked his socks off as no other lovemaking had. And he'd never been able to separate his body from his emotions. He didn't want to. What he *wanted* was to get close to her, physically and emotionally, and he was going to do it. Why? He was intrigued by her, probably had been for years and had disguised it with anger. Was the same true for her? He'd also had a premonition that if he didn't pursue this relationship, he'd regret it for the rest of his life.

Full of those surprising thoughts, he focused on the computer, typed his sheet, printed it and swiveled to face her. She was reading some reports, her head down.

"Want first shot at this week's trivia game?"

"Not particularly." She didn't raise her head.

He checked the clock. "We've got time before roll call. How about if I read them to you?"

"No, thanks."

"Hey, I need somebody to tell me if they're worded right."

She threw the folder down and yanked off her cute glasses. "Fine, if it will stop your wheedling."

Ah, there it was again, the attempt to make him feel like a little boy. Well, she knew—first hand, he thought, chuckling—he wasn't a little boy.

"I've changed the format a bit this week. All the questions relate to one topic and they're true or false."

"How clever."

He cocked his head and gave her a searing look. "Sleeping together was supposed to make us nicer to each other."

Her lips thinning, she glanced at his phone.

Oh, so she was steamed about Melanie's call. Well, hell, that made his day.

"You're right." She gave him a poor imitation of a smile. "Read."

He flashed her a let's-go-to-bed grin. She squirmed in her chair. *Good, good.*

"Number one. Though scores of firefighters still die in blazes, the U.S. Fire Administration states that after peaking at 171 in 1978, the latest stats show a continuing downward trend in line-of-duty fatalities.''

Her jaw tightened and she didn't speak.

''Since you don't play, I'll give you the answers. It's true.''

Still the stony response.

''Number two. Recent reports indicate that firefighters are being killed and injured during the initial stages of the fire.'' He spared her a quick glance and could see her temper simmering. ''Also true. Number three. Considering the four factors contributing to these deaths—lightweight wood truss construction, energy-efficient windows, older buildings and lack of survival training—little can be done to rectify the situation.''

She was scowling, that lovely brow striped with pique.

''The answer to that is false. Fire departments can hone in on survival training.''

''What are you trying to pull, O'Roarke?''

He gave her a look of little-boy innocence. ''I went to a few workshops in New York on safety issues, besides yours and Carrington's.'' He let the message sink in. ''This one guy from Dunkirk gave a great talk that I really related to.''

In spite of her obvious determination to remain aloof, the hazel eyes that had haunted him for twenty-four hours warmed to the topic. She leaned over and clasped her hands in front of her. ''I'm sorry I missed it.''

''I think you were off cavorting with your boyfriend,'' he said with a little more edge than he intended. ''Anyway, the guy's point was that firefighters, like me, will inevitably get themselves in dangerous situations. It's the nature of the beast. Therefore, the training of recruits, as well as experienced firefighters, should be on staying alive in tight situations.'' He grinned again. ''As a matter of fact, that was the name of the workshop—Stayin' Alive.''

He wanted to kiss the surprise off her face. Then it narrowed into suspicion. ''Why are you taking a sudden interest in this topic?''

That burned his buns. There was nothing sudden about his concern for fire fighting safety. But he quelled his irritation and leaned back in his chair, mimicking a nonchalance he didn't feel. ''Well, we agreed to try to get along better, right?''

Warily, she nodded.

''That was the purpose of continuing our sexual relationship, right?'' When he got no response, he cocked his head. ''You haven't forgotten about that, have you?''

Her nod was accompanied by a blush.

''So, I thought this might be a good thing for me to explore.'' He sobered. ''It fits in with my MO—getting into tight spots.''

''What do you mean?''

He stood. ''Just that I think I can help teach myself, and others, better ways to get out of them since I can't seem to keep from getting into them.''

''What are you going to do?''

He held up the trivia game. ''Increase awareness first.''

''Then?''

He swaggered to her desk and leaned near her face. ''I guess you'll have to wait and see. Just remember, I'm keeping my part of the bargain.'' He hesitated for effect, then gave her a meaningful look and said with all the subtly of a fire truck blaring its siren, ''You better keep yours, *Lizzie*.''

LIZZIE. O'Roarke had called her that only once before, the first time he'd thrust inside her. The way he'd said the nickname—a crazy, affectionate combination of teasing and intimacy—conjured a vivid image of that one moment in time; for her, it evoked the sight, sound, smell and feel of him.

It stayed with her most of Monday and into the dinner she shared with Eric at his country club. The sexy, handsome

Scanlon bored her to tears. When she'd yawned her way through dinner, he took her home early.

She hadn't seen O'Roarke much Tuesday, and for that she was grateful. Connie Cleary had asked to switch their workout to the evening, and Beth had just finished with the recruit and was heading to the office to shower when she heard the commotion behind the maze. There was a large storage room, and light spilled from it. Several male voices could be heard arguing. Tugging a knee-length T-shirt that said, EMS: When Seconds Count over her leotard—she'd done weights, too, and was grungy with sweat—she went to investigate.

The entire twenty-by-twenty room had been cleared and scrubbed clean of cobwebs and dirt. There were no windows, but the overhead lighting kept it from resembling a cave.

Ben Cordaro, his father Gus, and an older man Beth didn't recognize pored over some plans spread on a table made of sawhorses and a slab of plywood. Jake Scarlatta measured a far wall. "If we section this off, it can house the consumable material that will need to be replaced after every training session."

"Is that the best location?" Alex Templeton's handsome head popped up from behind a stack of Plexiglas squares.

The older man talking with Ben and Gus circled. "Yes, young man, it is. I owned a construction company for years before you were born. It's best there."

Alex shot Jake a befuddled frown; Jake threw an indulgent look at the older man and shrugged at Alex.

Beth's presence in the doorway went unnoticed, and she watched the guys confer, measure and trade suggestions. Then she felt a hand squeeze her shoulder; the instant prickle on her neck told her who it was before he spoke. "Nice outfit, Winters. But Sergio Oliva has a weak heart, and I don't think his seeing what that spandex does to your legs is a good idea."

She spun, and the wise retort died on her lips. O'Roarke

hovered behind her, sexy as sin and as dangerous as those fires he loved to fight. His hair was damp with sweat, his face animated with high color. He wore the blue jeans that ought to be illegal and a white T-shirt that was just as criminal. Tearing her gaze away from him, she nodded to the room. "Who's Sergio?"

"A friend of ours from Dutch Towers." At her quizzical look, he added, "you know, the senior citizens' apartment complex around the corner from Quint/Midi Twelve."

Beth remembered that Francey had told her Dylan spent a lot of free time there with the older people. "What's he doing here?"

"Helping out."

"With what? What's going on?"

"Part two of my plan."

"Your plan?"

"For stayin' alive, babe."

"Hey, O'Roarke, quit flirting and give us a hand." Sergio's booming voice didn't indicate a weak heart. "We're marking off where we're gonna divide the interior wall section and the window section."

Squeezing her arm, O'Roarke said, "Oops, gotta go. Sergio is a hard taskmaster."

He entered the consultation as Jake and Alex crossed to the older men. Beth watched them gesture and argue for another few minutes, then she left.

It wasn't until ten o'clock the next morning that she found out what was going on. O'Roarke was teaching a firefighter class in the EMS classroom because the firefighter classroom was being used for confined space training for station house personnel. Since the EMS room was connected to Beth's office, she was disturbed by the CD blaring through the open door. It played a disco song from some movie, she thought distractedly. She was trying to order supplies for the upcoming recruit practicals. She rose to shut the door.

But stopped at the entrance.

And couldn't believe her eyes. The front tables had been moved back, and O'Roarke was standing in the midst of the recruits. On the boom box, "Stayin' Alive," from the 1970s film *Saturday Night Fever,* blasted out. O'Roarke addressed the class. "I was just playin' the song to make a point, wise guys. I wasn't plannin' a demonstration."

"Come on, Lieutenant," Austyn Myers called. "We've never seen live disco. We don't believe you can do it."

"Oh, ye of little faith," he said, faking insult. "All right, just one time."

Beth watched openmouthed as he executed the dance, stabbing his finger in the air in the fashion of John Travolta's character. The recruits howled. Sandy Frank laughed so hard she doubled over.

Unexpectedly Beth's eyes stung, but not from mirth. She'd been seventeen when the movie came out, and she could still see her and Tim at the drive-in movie theater, laughing about the new dance craze.

The song ended. O'Roarke switched off the music and raised his head. His eyes narrowed on her. She shook off the sadness, but the look on his face told her he'd misunderstood it.

"I was just focusing the recruits on my lesson for today." His voice was curt, and something else. Hurt, maybe.

She arched her brows. "Oh, you're going to dance your way out of fires?"

Several of the recruits turned and gaped at her. So she *could* make a joke.

O'Roarke gave her a grin that said, *Good job, little girl. You'll get your reward later.*

Beth coughed to cover her response to him. He asked, "Care to watch the initial lesson on stayin' alive, Ms. Winters?"

Don't stay, an inner mechanism that had kept her sane for twenty years warned her. *He's pulling you in.*

But how could she ignore this…this peacemaking effort? Anyway, the standoff between them wasn't good for the recruits. She and O'Roarke had agreed to compromise. So she sank into a chair at the back. "Yes, I would."

The recruits moved the tables back and were seated. Dylan's face sobered as he addressed the class. "We've added a part in your curriculum under firefighter safety. Handouts are being prepared now, but we want to get some instruction in this week, and for the next two weeks, before evolutions and practicals begin."

Beth watched with interest as he put an overhead on the screen. It read, Remember The Three Stay's. He asked, "Who can repeat the three Stay's of firefighter safety?"

Ace Durwin replied. "Stay low, stay oriented and stay calm."

"I get it," Tully blurted. "Stayin' alive."

"Very good, buddy." O'Roarke smiled at his protégé. "This new program is going to teach you some skills to do that—stay alive. You'll be the first recruit class to get this training, so you'll be ahead of the experienced smoke eaters. However, Chief Cordaro is thinking of recommending this course as required training for all RFD personnel."

No one asked why.

"Now, let's look at the program. It consists of these seven elements." He traded one overhead for another. "In order to get out of dicey situations, you need to learn and practice the following: rapid location of windows and doors, window removal, breaking down interior walls, emergency SCBA realignment, forcible entry, following a hose line, escape via windows." He shrugged. "Some of this isn't new. We've already instructed you on three of these. But at this conference I went to, it was packaged a little differently and emphasized the practice part. It's also coupled with some new stuff even *I* haven't done.''

"Oh, yeah," someone called out. "Like what?"

O'Roarke gave a self-effacing grin. "Like interior wall breaching. So we're going to learn pieces of this together. We managed to get plans from the workshop guy to build a simulator room, and they were okayed yesterday morning by the brass. Donations of time and money have come from firefighter personnel and local businesses. The room should be ready next week, but we can start the instruction today.''

Beth remembered that Alex Templeton was here last night and guessed his local business had provided funds—partly to help keep his wife safe. Jake, Ben and O'Roarke, and probably other firefighters, were giving up their free time to build the room.

O'Roarke watched the silent recruits for a minute, then set his hands on his hips. "Yeah, yeah, I can see it in your faces. Why me? Why do I want to do this?" His brief glance at Beth was sheepish. "I've recently been touted as a hero by *Firehouse* magazine, but it's been called to my attention that my actions could be a negative example to you. If that's the case, I'm publicly stating that you should follow SOP. However, even that's gonna get you in deep doo-doo with the red devil, so I'm gonna show you—and myself—how to get out of tight spots.''

Beth closed her eyes, terror streaking through her. He was playing dirty. Attacking her animosity at its core—like he'd attack the base of a fire. What would she ever do without that barrier between them?

Become one of O'Roarke's groupies?

IT HAD BEEN a terrific week, Dylan thought. Cleary had lost five pounds and regained fifty percent of her aerobic capacity, Tully had squeaked by on his EMS exam with a seventy, and there had been no real run-ins at the RTR meeting this morning. Now, if he could just get Lizzie Borden into the sack tonight, life would be perfect.

He was in the office storeroom at about five o'clock, after a not too grueling confidence walk, replacing some gauze he'd used with the recruits, when Beth came in, all sweaty and grubby like he was.

"Oh. I didn't know you were here. I needed a Band-Aid." Stepping back from him, she knocked her arm against a box, which crashed to the floor. They both bent and reached for it.

"What the hell are these?" Dylan held up a handful of foil packets.

Beth bit back a grin. "We should throw those out."

As awareness dawned, Dylan chuckled. "Mind if I ask why you've got a box of—" he peeked inside "—hundreds of condoms in here?"

She stashed them in the box as he held it. "The pharmaceutical companies we order from send us free samples of new products on the market. For some reason, Ramses and Trojans have put us on their mailing lists." She grinned. "Tom Jackson was fascinated by the…variety of styles and colors of these things and kept them all. It's been a joke around here for a while." She stood. He matched the action, clutching the box in front of him. He fished inside and drew out a handful.

"Mmm," he said suggestively. "French ticklers. This one has little curlicues on the end."

Beth blushed.

"And lookee here. Scented ones and flavored ones." He dropped his voice. "You prefer raspberry or banana, Winters?"

She choked. "Banana?"

"Well, it's an appropriate image, isn't it?"

She chuckled.

Without touching her—he swore he wouldn't compromise

her at work, even though his fingers curled with need—he leaned close to her ear. "Why don't you pick out three or four and bring them over to my place tonight?"

She swallowed hard. In her beautiful eyes, he could see the struggle. He stifled a spurt of exasperation.

But he pushed. "I thought we agreed to work at the animosity between us. To have sex from time to time in order to get along better." When she remained maddeningly silent, he said, "I'm exceeding my part in this compromise, Beth."

She looked at him with more than a business agreement in her eyes. They were deep and wide with fear. Damn, why couldn't she just admit she wanted this, too?

"You're right. I did agree. Give me your address."

BETH ARRIVED at O'Roarke's house exactly at eight o'clock. In the intervening three hours, she'd taken a long bath to calm herself, rationalized all her reactions to O'Roarke and felt in control once again.

He lived near Ellison Park. She was surprised to find his home was a log cabin, nestled by itself on a back road and surrounded by woods full of oaks and maples whose leaves had turned vibrant shades of red and yellow. Meticulously kept grass showing signs of fall surrounded the house. She swung into the gravel driveway and parked next to a big green Cherokee, then got out of her car and approached the porch. A cozy wooden swing swayed in the breeze to the side of the door. O'Roarke's home was as overpowering as he was.

She rang the doorbell only once before he flung it open. He'd been waiting for her. Very flattering. Very dangerous. "Hi."

Behind him scampered fifty pounds of dog. Circumventing his master, the dalmatian pounced on her. Beth let the dog lick her until O'Roarke tugged him back. "Down, boy. Come on, Quint, she's mine tonight, not yours."

Wincing inwardly at his phrasing, Beth dropped to her knees and nuzzled the dog. He was warm and real and soothed her nerves. "He's beautiful."

"So are you."

She stood and tried to close down. She wished she could shut out the sight he made, barefoot, wearing those disreputable jeans and a thermal navy blue shirt that... *Get control, girl.* "Before I come in, let's not forget the ground rules."

"Ground rules?" His tone lost some of its warmth.

"This is just sex, O'Roarke."

He scowled and stepped back. "Just sex. Fine."

Wary, she entered the foyer as he led the dog to the rear of the house—the kitchen?—and closed a door. She got a glimpse of the interior off to the left—log walls, worn leather furniture, a fieldstone fireplace, a wooden floor with plush rug, large framed firefighter prints hanging everywhere.

He was on her the next instant, from behind, encircling her, smothering her with his heat.

It was like trying to fight a forest fire in the middle of a drought. Everywhere he touched, her skin burned. His fingers on her waist were like flames, flaying off layers of skin to reach her nerve endings. Like an out-of-control blaze, his body singed hers with no mercy. Just as before, she couldn't think with the sizzling intensity of his touch.

It's just sex, she reminded herself. He was cooperating in the deception—ripping at her jacket, tearing off the plain cotton blouse she'd put on with jeans. She hadn't fussed. Nothing was special tonight. It wouldn't have mattered what she wore. In seconds her clothes were gone, then his. He didn't say anything the whole time, just yanked her around and crushed her to him.

"Protection," he said in almost a growl as he pulled away to get it.

She stopped him with firm hands on his shoulders, then

leaned down, reached into her bag and ferreted out the condoms she'd filched from the storage room.

He gave them a cursory glance and tore one out of her hand, letting the rest fall. He rolled it on, backed her up against the wall, lifted her and plunged into her. "Lizzie, oh, God, Lizzie."

Dylan plundered her body—there was no other word for it—and it was over in minutes. He sagged against her, thinking he'd rammed into her with all the finesse of a bull, up against his foyer wall as soon as she walked through the door. It wasn't even that she'd made him angry by saying it was all sex. It was what happened when he got near her, got to touch her, got to be inside her. His civilized nature turned primitive; he became an animal. That it seemed to happen to her took the edge off his feelings of remorse, but not enough.

He drew back slightly, and she whimpered. Just like the last time, her body clung to his, inside and out. Still inside her, he brushed her damp hair off her sweaty face and kissed her nose. She was too dazed with passion to resist the tenderness, and he savored her pliancy. When he felt her sanity return, signaled by the slight stiffening of her body, he scrambled for a way to keep her close.

"I don't know about you," he whispered, "but ninety seconds is a record for me."

He felt the giggle more than heard it. Holding on tight to him, she responded in kind. "Well, I probably could still catch an eight o'clock showing of the new Mel Gibson movie."

"Not on your life, Winters. I haven't had nearly enough of you yet." He slipped his hand behind her knees, threw her over his shoulder rescue-style and carried her to the bedroom in the back of the house.

Two hours later he rolled over in the bed, waking from a sleep brought on by more lovemaking. He yawned, then frowned. Beth was already up. Lying back on the pillows, he watched her for a minute. "Where are you going?"

Fully dressed, she was at the foot of the bed, stuffing something into her duffel bag, which he'd retrieved for the indisputably erotic condoms. The moon slanted in from the four wide doors across the room, bathing her in an eerie glow. She glanced at him, then away. "Home."

That zinged his pride. He pushed himself up to lean against the headboard. "Why don't you stick around?"

She hefted the bag to her shoulder. Her hair was still mussed from their lovemaking, her face still flushed. "Why?"

"Have a beer. Maybe order a pizza."

"No, that's not a good idea."

A thought struck him, cramping his gut. His whole body tensed. "Do you have something else to do? *Someone* else?"

"Of course not." Well, at least she sounded as disgusted as he with the idea that she could see another man after this…cataclysm they'd experienced together.

"So, stick around."

She shook her head vehemently. "Listen, O'Roarke, we're not buddies here. This is just sex, plain and simple. You haven't forgotten that, have you?"

"Maybe just for a minute."

Did she have to look so horrified? he thought in dismay.

"Do us both a favor and don't forget it." Her voice was a tortured whisper.

Damn her! She was at the door by the time he bounded out of bed and grasped her arm. "Wait."

She turned away from him.

"I want to know when we're going to do this again."

Pivoting slowly, she looked at him with bruised eyes. "When?"

He couldn't fathom why this was so hard for her. Was he repugnant to her in every way but sexually? The thought notched up his temper. "Yeah, when. You're a good lay, Winters. And I like to have the best."

Her chin rose. "All right, Sunday. Same place, same time."

"Fine." He dropped his arm. "I'll *pencil* you in."

TWO WEEKS LATER, just past midterm, the academy was filled with excitement over the newly completed simulator room, over recruits who'd mostly scaled the academic hump—the second half of the curriculum was nitty-gritty hands-on stuff—and over instructors who'd found a way to coexist.

Dylan had managed the latter by tangling frequently with a punching bag he'd set up in the weight room. Slugging it out with an inanimate object, like now, took the edge off his misery and his anger.

Punch, punch. He ignored the pain in his gloved hands, the sweat soaking his navy gym shorts and tank top.

What the hell's the matter with you, O'Roarke? You're acting like you've lost a battle with a fire. He hadn't lost anything, except maybe a little pride.

You couldn't lose a person you'd never had.

Punch, punch, punch. The ache escalated to a dull throb.

Wiping the perspiration off his brow, he thought back on the past two weeks. They'd had sex. God, he was getting to hate that phrase. A lot. But it was accurate. They'd had sex. In more ways than Dylan had ever imagined, except in his randy teenage days. It was torrid, wild. A young man's fantasy. But not his. Who would have thought?

Punch, punch, punch, punch. When the pain shot up his arm, Dylan backed off and sparred with the bag.

There was never any foreplay. And when he tried to cuddle her afterward, she drew away, dousing his euphoria. She'd quench the physical hunger just fine, but she'd leave him parched for emotional fulfillment. The worst was when she got up immediately and took a shower, washing away his scent, obliterating all traces of him from her body. It was only in those split seconds right after she lost control, after he emptied himself into her, that he really *had* her. She'd immerse herself in him, sink into his body like water into dry ground and hold him as tightly as he held her. Although he suspected she would stop even *that* if she could, for those few precious moments, he put up with the rest. That and because his body craved her. He thought it would wear off, but it didn't, and he worried that there was no cure for the narcotic obsession he'd developed for her. He needed sexual rehab, he thought with grim humor.

As October drifted into November, and the cold weather set in, Dylan had never been more wretched.

Punch, punch, punch, punch, punch.

BETH WASN'T HAPPY. Maybe O'Roarke thought she was just fine, but she wasn't. Often she went outside running, like now, which she hated, just to clear her head, garner some resolve. She hadn't dressed warmly enough today—she was in shorts and a thin sweatshirt—and she was cold. It was getting harder and harder to stay impersonal, to remain distant. To keep it just sex. She'd managed to do it, but with excruciating difficulty. Sucking in air at the crest of a small hill by her condo, she tried to block out how subtly O'Roarke had lured her in. Every single time he hoarsely uttered, "Lizzie," and touched her with those wonderful hands, she wanted to give in, relent, open up to him. And each time he protested—nonverbally, but it was as loud and demanding as an ambulance's siren—she lost more of her reserve.

Running faster, she winced at her behavior over the past few weeks. She'd purposely kept herself detached in small ways. She allowed no intimacies, no talk, not even the naughty kind she suspected he was good at; she didn't invite him to her house and she left his body, then his home, as soon as she could tear herself away.

Working beside him at the academy was equally painful. He'd been trying hard with the recruits, making a valiant effort to instill caution and prudence in them, qualities foreign to his nature. And he did it for her.

Slowing to a fast walk—she'd exceeded her limits and was struggling for air—Beth thought about how she'd met him halfway at work. She designed lessons that recognized the iffy nature of some emergency calls and had the recruits brainstorm alternatives. When Reed mentioned a new set of videos, she previewed and ordered the films, which could have been made by O'Roarke's mental twin. The cocky paramedic narrator recognized the need for circumspection *and* the risky nature of the business in humorous presentations and role-playing episodes.

The recruits were well-adjusted and progressing fine.

She was the one who had regressed. She, who had to fight every single day to keep from caring about a man the way she'd once cared about Tim. She stopped herself from falling for O'Roarke by picturing Tim's smiling face, by consistently pushing to the foreground of her mind the fact that she had lost one man—and it had almost killed her. That was what kept her from letting O'Roarke into her heart.

Tim's face. And the face of her baby, who'd died with him.

CHAPTER NINE

FROM ACROSS THE ROOM at Logan's Party House, Dylan looked at the bar and glowered as Eric Scanlon tucked a strand of hair behind Beth's ear. Something about the quiet intimacy of the gesture got to Dylan more than if the captain had kissed her. That Beth stiffened and backed away was the only thing that kept Dylan from going for Scanlon's jugular.

That would be a nice show, O'Roarke, in front of a hundred members of the Rockford Fire Department. Maybe you could ruin Tom Jackson's retirement party.

"Dylan, honey, are you okay?" Marilyn Stevens scraped her long red fingernails down his suit-coat sleeve and moved closer.

"Sure. Why?"

"You're grippin' that beer so hard you're gonna break the glass." She leaned over and squeezed his biceps. "You've gotta watch out with these muscles."

As genuinely as he could, Dylan smiled at her. Beautiful Marilyn, with the hourglass body, mane of golden hair and heart-shaped face. She was dressed in a knockout little black thing guaranteed to spike any normal male's temperature. His type exactly. So why did she leave him colder than water trickling into his turnout coat? Maybe he wasn't trying. He swept his knuckles down her classically curved cheek. "Having fun?"

"Just being with you is fun, Dylan." She leaned into him, one full breast brushing against his arm. He felt his body stiffen—not from desire—and inched back. "Though later tonight will be even better."

Dylan sighed and slouched against the pillar. *Don't bet on it.* He hadn't been with a woman other than Beth since Francey's wedding. Unintentionally his gaze locked with the scorching stare of the only woman he wanted tonight. Beth had obviously witnessed the exchange with Marilyn and wasn't happy about it. She looked so sexy in the short silvery dress that shimmered around her every time she moved. Damn her, why couldn't she admit her feelings for him? That was probably the most maddening thing about this whole mess.

He'd thought the same thing two nights ago after they'd made love—correction, after they'd had sex—and he'd asked her about this evening.

"I don't suppose you want a ride to Tom's party Thursday?" he'd asked casually as she performed her usual ritual of dressing and leaving him alone in bed. "Since it's Veteran's Day Friday and the academy's closed, I thought we could...do something after the retirement dinner."

She'd hesitated, then eased down next to him on the mattress. Her silky auburn hair fell into eyes whose tenderness warmed him. Then she'd doused the feeling with her next comment. "I'm going to the party with Eric."

Struggling to keep his face blank, he'd said, "I see. And is he allowed at your condo?"

She'd had the grace to blush. "He's picking me up, yes."

"And taking you home."

She'd nodded. "Eric's in charge of Tom's party. I've been working on it with him since the beginning of October. I'd made plans to go with him a long time ago."

Furious, Dylan had gripped the brown striped sheets they'd just tangled together. "How convenient."

She'd watched him for a minute, then risen, picked up her duffel bag and silently left his house. Her standard exit.

"Dylan, sweetie, someone's wavin' to us." The speaker was Marilyn, his last-minute date, because he couldn't face Scanlon and Beth alone.

Rousing himself from the unpleasant memories, Dylan caught sight of Ben Cordaro motioning him over. "Must be time for dinner."

He kept his hand at the small of Marilyn's back—*try, O'Roarke, try*—all the way to the table. Four seats were empty, the others occupied by Ben and Diana, Francey and Alex, Jake, Reed, a pretty brunette, and Chuck Lorenzo and his wife.

"Come sit near me, buddy." Francey patted the chair next to her. "I never get to see you anymore." After he made introductions and took a seat, Francey leaned over so only he could hear. "Beth's sitting at this table, too. Is that okay? Dad said you're getting along better."

Life's full of little ironies, Grandma Katie used to say. *Get used to them.* Jeez, she was haunting him these days.

"It's fine," he said tightly. "So, tell me what's going on at the station."

Right before dinner was served, Scanlon escorted Beth to the table. They looked stunning together, both polished and sophisticated. Again, introductions were made.

"Everything okay?" Ben asked after they sat down.

"Of course." Scanlon's arm went around Beth's shoulders, and he squeezed her affectionately. "With a partner like this, who's organized to a fault, how could it not be?"

Ben examined her closely. "Something wrong, Beth?"

"No, no." She picked up her water glass and avoided Dylan's eyes.

Chitchat was made. Dylan wondered if anyone was as uncomfortable as he. Hot currents shot between him and Beth, but no one seemed to notice.

Francey didn't appear disturbed. "I haven't seen much of

you since you went to that conference in New York, Beth. Did you get to have any fun while you were there?''

Dylan knocked over his water glass, and as he cursed, then mopped it up with a napkin, Beth answered. ''Fun? Oh, sure, it was okay.''

''She met up with an old friend there and he took her out on the town.'' Dylan's voice was gravelly, like he'd just inhaled gray smoke.

''Who?'' Francey wanted to know.

''Josh Carrington.''

Ben asked her, ''The FDNY trainer?''

Beth nodded.

''Did you make arrangements for that exchange program we discussed?''

''Yes. Didn't I tell you about it?''

''No, you've been too busy since you got back.''

This time, it was Beth's wineglass that toppled over. Scanlon cleaned it up.

Dylan caught Reed Macauley's eye across the table. His arched brow indicated that he, at least, was aware of the tension.

Alex sneaked his arm around his wife and squeezed her neck gently. ''Those plans Dylan brought back for the simulator room have kept us all busy. What did you think of the safety project, Beth?''

''O'Roarke did a nice job with it.'' She turned to Eric, without a smile or nod to Dylan to accompany the compliment, and said something Dylan couldn't hear.

He wanted to reach over the table, grab her by the shoulders and shake her until she acknowledged him, but he didn't, of course. He knew when to back away from the beast before he got burned.

They were called to the buffet table, and the meal passed uneventfully, but Beth was a wreck. By the time dinner ended and the program was over, she thought her nerves might snap. She wasn't sure how she got through the tributes to Tom. All she could see were O'Roarke's eyes, alternating between anger and hurt. She could barely look at him, which seemed to make him angrier. But the sight of him in a charcoal-gray sports coat and lighter silk T-shirt under it made her hands itch to touch him and her heart ache from not being with him. After the program, while people were mingling at the bar, she excused herself and headed for the ladies' room. In the hallway, she ran smack into him.

"Oh, excuse me."

She moved to pull away, but his hands had come up reflexively to steady her, and he held on. "I don't think so."

She looked down. "Let go of me."

He didn't budge.

She was forced to meet his eyes. "You're going to create a scene, O'Roarke." Her voice was a harsh whisper.

After a moment's hesitation he released her, and she circled him and fled down the hall to the bathroom.

Hastily, she ducked inside. She had to have a minute to compose herself. Catch her breath. Steel herself against him and his effect on her.

Staring into the mirror, she almost didn't recognize the woman reflected back at her. In the plush lounge—mauve carpet, light rose walls, frilly cushions on wicker chairs—she shook her head. Not her style. Then she looked closely at her image. Who was this woman? Her eyes were full of flaming emotions. High color ran from her neck to her cheeks. Even the short, cap-sleeved, above-the-knee silver sheath didn't feel right sliding against her skin. She'd been wearing clothes lately that Chelsea and Francey had encouraged her to buy— the green blouse, the strapless dress, this dress that she'd purchased years ago for a fireman's ball. She closed her eyes to block out the sensuous woman in the mirror. That wasn't her.

She heard the door open, then the loud snick of the lock.

Raising her lids, she faced in the mirror the cause of her metamorphosis. Dylan O'Roarke.

His face like a thundercloud, he leaned against the wall and stared hard at her. She opened the purse she clutched in her hands, drew out a brush and ran it through her hair. With a calm she did not feel, she said, "What are you doing in here?"

"Where the hell do you get off?" he asked in a deadly sober voice.

As if addressing a recruit who questioned a decision, she raised a brow. "Get off?" Finishing with the brush, she found her lipstick.

"What makes you think you can treat me like you treat everybody else?"

Struggling for her legendary cool, she managed to outline her mouth in honey-raisin without making herself look like a clown. "I don't know what you mean."

He shoved away from the wall and came up so close behind her, she could feel his heat. The gray of his outfit deepened his eyes to a steely blue. He pinned her with his blistering gaze in the mirror. "It's bad enough you're here with Scanlon. I'll be damned if I'll let you treat me like one of the guys."

His voice was so raw, she felt it pull her down and under. Into deep, icy water that would surely drown her. She had to find a lifeline. Meeting his gaze, she said, "You *are* one of the guys, O'Roarke."

She thought that would do it. Send him out of the ladies' room and out of her life.

But she'd underestimated him. He clamped his hands on her shoulders. Into her ear, he said silkily, "Yeah? One of the guys? That's not what you thought two nights ago when you dug your nails into my back as you came—*three* times."

Closing her eyes, she prayed for strength. "That was just sex."

His fingers bit into her. When she looked at him in the mirror again and saw pain instead of fury, she was tempted to give in, give him everything he wanted. Frightened by her reaction, she summoned her anger and rounded on him. "Oh, don't look so hurt, O'Roarke. You brought Barbie tonight." Beth was beyond caring what she revealed. "But she's your type, isn't she? Big and blond and buxom."

"There are advantages to dating Barbie."

Beth rolled her eyes. "Spare me the details."

"No, I won't. You need to hear a few things. I like being with Barbie because *she* wants to talk before we jump into bed. *She* asks me about my day, how I'm feeling."

Pricked with guilt, Beth jerked her shoulders. He didn't let go. "Like I said, spare me the details."

He towered over her. Beth had to force herself not to shrink from the inferno of his anger. "And when she does want to be intimate, she *makes love,* something you wouldn't know about."

In spite of her resolve, Beth blurted, "What do you mean?"

"I mean—" he shook her, not gently "—that when Barbie looks at me, she really sees me. She touches my face for no reason. She rubs my back when it doesn't even hurt." A final shake. "She kisses my spine just for the hell of it."

Beth cringed at the image of another woman fondling him.

He was too angry to notice. "And Barbie calls me by my first name when I'm inside her."

Beth's throat closed up.

"And—" he stepped back and let go of her, as if he'd touched hot coals "—she doesn't pull away as soon as we're done. She doesn't wash every remnant of my touch and smell off her."

Beth could feel the color drain from her face. When he edged back, she raised a hand to her mouth and covered it.

O'Roarke stared at her for a moment, then uttered a crude expletive, turned and stalked out the door.

At TEN O'CLOCK the next morning Beth did something she hadn't done in almost twenty years. Still dressed in the long-sleeved flowered pajamas Chelsea had gotten her from Victoria's Secret, she sank onto the carpet in front of the cedar chest at the foot of her bed. Running her hand across the smooth surface, she smiled at the memory touching the wood evoked.

She'd just come to live with Mary and Bill Mack. A shy, introverted child of eight, she'd kept her distance when Bill had lugged the chest into her new bedroom—the whole top floor of a Cap Cod house on Camden Lake. *This is for you, Beth. I always wanted a little girl to build one for.*

Mary had stood in her plain cotton house dress, her hands clasped in front of her. *Inside is something I made myself, honey.*

Gingerly now, as if probing an open wound, Beth raised the lid of the chest. Even the smell was the same. *Sachet.*

Beth bit her lip then took a deep breath. She wouldn't cry. She wouldn't taint the wonderful memories that were housed in this chest with the horrific ones that had followed.

After a moment she was able to look at the dolls. She'd collected them since she was adopted by the Macks. Some were made by her new mother, others given to her by Tim and his parents, but they were all handmade. They were carefully set between layers of tissue paper. On top was the last one she'd gotten, from Tim, on their daughter Janey's second Christmas. It was an ice skater doll, dressed in a short white skirt, matching sweater, with a red Christmas scarf wrapped around her neck. It had been attached to the ice skates he'd bought Janey, ice skates that— No! No bad memories. She coughed to stop the emotion. She fingered the note. *The doll's for Mommy, kiddo. The skates are for you.*

Beth put the skating doll aside. Next was a newborn doll that bore a remarkable resemblance to Janey's dark-haired, dark-eyed looks. Beth fingered the delicate diaper and the lace-edged pink booties. Her heart thumped hard as she remembered Janey's soft little-girl's clothing and precious baby smell.

Beth set down the newborn and picked up the bride doll Tim had given her on their wedding day. He'd had that one made to look just like her—long auburn hair to her waist, freckles, the dress matching the white wedding gown Tim's mother, Leona, had sewn for her. He'd snuck in her room the morning of the wedding and placed it on her pillow. The note read, *Ready, Bethy baby?*

A little farther down in the chest was a high-school-graduate doll complete with teal blue cap and gown—Lakeville High's color. Then the Tim football player. Lovingly she traced the number thirty-four and tugged at the chin strap of the helmet. He'd given it to her just after Mary and Bill had died in the boating accident. This note read, *You'll always have me.* She had to close her eyes a moment. Swallow hard. Take a deep breath.

Rustling more tissue paper, she drew out a doll given to her to celebrate her confirmation, its pristine white veil falling down the back of the lacy dress; Beth reverently shined the white patent-leather shoes with her thumb. There were several holiday dolls. Christmas—its note said, *I love you best at Christmas*—Easter, Valentine's Day. Even a leprechaun doll for St. Patrick's Day; Leona Winters had been Irish. At the bottom, she found the very first doll Mary had made for her. It was a little girl who resembled Beth when she'd come to them: huge hazel eyes, a shy half-smile, in an outfit that matched one Mary had also sewn for her upon her arrival. Its card read, *Welcome to our home, dear little girl.*

Beth sank back on her heels. She'd set each doll, sitting

up, around her, so many of them, they almost completely encircled her.

Bravely, she faced her past—the *good* part of her past—for the first time in almost twenty years. With it came an enormous sadness, but also a strange calm. Those twelve years she'd lived with the Macks had been good years, despite Bill and Mary's tragic boating accident, Mike's heart attack and, later, Leona's stroke. She'd held on through it all, managed to survive, love and live life to the fullest.

She picked up the Tim doll in one hand and the baby doll in the other. Until the last tragedy. After that, she couldn't hold on any longer. If it hadn't been for the members of the Lakeville Fire Department who saved her life, then adopted her as their pet project, she wouldn't be here today.

Firefighters. How strange. They'd saved her once.

A face with cobalt blue eyes appeared before her mind's eye. Hugging the dolls close to her heart, she asked herself if God had sent her another firefighter to save her once again.

Several minutes passed before she took a deep breath, set the dolls down and reached over to the nightstand for the phone.

"YOU DUMB-ASS son of a bitch." Dylan shut off the engine but didn't get out of the car. He continued to curse himself until he ran out of swear words. Shaking his head, he pounded the steering wheel. When nothing worked to alleviate the pressure cooker inside him, he forced himself to look at her condo, a green-shingled two-story nestled between a pair of similar units. He should start the car and drive away. He didn't need crumbs. He was Dylan O'Roarke, the great ladies' man.

Who was so completely pussy-whipped he'd come as soon as she'd snapped her fingers. When she'd called this morning, he'd been sound asleep, having wrestled with the blankets till dawn.

"This better be good," he'd muttered groggily as he'd nudged the receiver to his ear and opened one eye to see that it was ten-thirty.

"I think it is. Were you asleep?"

"Yeah." Then, meanly, he'd added, "Who is this?" though he'd know that breathy voice anywhere.

"It's Beth."

He hadn't said anything.

"I, um, I was wondering if I could see you tonight."

Fully awake, he'd dragged himself up, stuffed pillows behind his head and tugged the sheet up. "In the mood for some hot sex, sweetheart?"

Momentarily she'd been quiet. Then she said, "I'd like to see you." Her voice was quivery and raw. If he hadn't known better, he'd have thought she was on the verge of tears. Despite his anger, it softened him.

"Fine with me."

"What time is good for you?"

He'd made a date with Marilyn for eight, even though he'd sent her into her apartment alone last night. "About six."

"All right." She'd cleared her throat. "Why don't you come here?"

The phone had slipped from his grip. He'd scowled as he brought it to his ear. "Why?"

"I just want you to."

Silence.

"Please."

Outside of sex, she'd never once said that word to him. "Makes no difference to me. What's the address?"

He'd refused to let himself wonder why she'd asked him to her house. He supposed she felt guilty and this was some kind of concession. "Well, sweetheart," he said as he exited the car, took the concrete sidewalk to her door and rang the bell, "it ain't gonna be enough. I can tell you that now."

She answered on the first ring, her face unnaturally pale

and her china-doll skin taut across her cheekbones. "You look like hell," he said unkindly.

Dylan could practically hear his grandmother's admonishment as she dragged him to Sunday school each week. *The greatest sin is intentionally hurting someone.* He winced in shame.

Beth rubbed her fingertips under her eyes. "Oh. I didn't sleep last night. I put some makeup on...."

Her vulnerability made him feel like a heel. And it surprised the hell out of him. She always went toe-to-toe with him. When she stepped aside, he entered her apartment and scanned the first floor. Stairs straight ahead, big living room to the right, furnished with earth-tone colors, overstuffed couches. He could see a dining room and kitchen to the back. It was plain, tidy and stark—just like her.

"This suits you," he said, then shrugged out of the jacket he'd thrown on over jeans and a denim shirt and placed it on the banister.

"Does it?" God, why was her voice so soft?

He faced her. "Where's the bedroom?"

She nodded upstairs. "First door on the right." Staring at him with an expression he couldn't read, she wrung her hands together. "But I thought you might want something to drink first."

He glanced at his watch. "Well, I've only got two hours."

"Two hours?"

"I have a date with Barbie at eight."

"You've got a date? After..." The words trailed off.

"Yeah, why not?" he said. She really brought out the best in him.

Without answering, she stepped into the sunken living room and crossed to the coffee table. He followed her. "I bought a bottle of red wine. I saw you drink some in New York. And I made some hors d'oeuvres."

"Lizzie Borden can cook?"

That got her hackles up and restored some color to her cheeks. "As a matter of fact, I'm a very good cook. Or at least I used to be. I haven't cooked in years."

"Too feminine an activity for you?"

Instead of responding to the insult—she'd been dodging all of them—she shook her head. "Sit down."

He sat on the couch and studied the living room. Nothing personal was displayed, not a picture or memento in sight. She really was a robot. An image of her kneeling between his legs loving him belied the thought so he pushed it away as fast as it had come.

"It's Merlot."

"What?"

"The wine." She held out a delicate crystal goblet.

Careful not to touch her when he accepted it, he lifted the glass and clinked it with hers. "To another great fu—" She clapped her hand over his mouth before he could finish the offensive comment. Then, gently, her two fingers outlined his lips. She'd almost never touched him outside of bed, and that awareness infuriated him, causing the slow burn inside him to escalate. When she dropped her hand, he arched a brow. "So, do we have anything to talk about?"

"It was a nice party for Tom, wasn't it?"

Wrong choice, sweetheart. "Did Scanlon spend the night here?" he asked nastily.

Tilting her chin a bit, she looked him straight in the eye. "I haven't slept with another man since you came to the academy."

He ignored the bumping in his chest that signified hope. He was done hoping—that she'd care for him, that she'd treat him like a lover. He put his glass on the table and stood. "Well, then, no wonder you're so hot for me." He reached over and grabbed her wrist, dragging her to her feet. The roughness of the gesture caused her to spill some wine on her pant leg. For the first time, he noticed she was wearing a peach outfit, the kind Francey chose when she got all dolled up. A one-piece thing, made of clingy material that dipped low in front. It was sexy as hell.

"What's going on, Beth?"

Her eyes were wide. And frightened. God, he hadn't meant to scare her.

"Nothing."

He stared hard at her, then said, "Fine. I'm restless. Let's go upstairs."

"You go ahead. I want to wash out this stain."

With one last look, he released her arm and headed for the steps.

Beth made her way to the first-floor bathroom. Mechanically she got a cloth and dabbed at the wine; her hands shook. *I can't do this. It's too scary. Too risky.*

But he had a date in two hours. *Want to think about that all night, Lizzie?*

"No, damn it," she said aloud. She didn't. She wouldn't.

She stared at the woman in the mirror. *Playing the doormat isn't going to fix this.*

She lifted her chin. *All right, then.*

Purposefully, she bit her lips to give them some color and patted her cheeks to redden them. Then she unbuttoned two buttons on her outfit and headed upstairs.

He was seated at the foot of the bed on the cedar chest, his shirt off, holding one boot, which he must have just removed, staring at the two large aquariums built into the wall.

"I know," she said from the doorway, indicating the fish she loved to watch as she fell asleep. "They're perfect pets for me. No touching, no nurturing involved."

He let the boot fall and angled toward her. "Actually, I was thinking they were beautiful." He yanked off his other boot and socks, then looked at her. He was clothed only in his jeans. Flooded by a rush of feeling for him, she didn't trust herself to speak. His gaze turned hot at her look.

She crossed the room, kicked off her flats and climbed on the bed so she was kneeling behind him. He stared ahead. His bare back presented several possibilities to her. Then she remembered his words. *Barbie likes to rub my back, even when it doesn't hurt.*

Yeah, well, Barbie, you've given your last massage for a while. Slowly she raised her hands and began at his neck. The muscles there were roped tighter than a safety knot. She kneaded his deltoids carefully. Lovingly. After a few moments his head fell forward and he groaned. Encouraged, she moved closer so that her spread thighs flanked his hips. *She kisses my spine for no reason.* Beth's lips met the middle of his spine with a feathery touch.

Abandoning his back, she knelt and ran her hands down his shoulders, then around to his chest and the dark springy hair that had beckoned her for weeks. Suddenly he grabbed her wrist and stopped her.

"What's going on, Beth?" His voice had resumed its earlier harshness.

"Nothing's going on." She cleared her throat. "Dylan."

If an entire body could stiffen all at once, his did. "What did you say?"

"Nothing's going on, Dylan."

It was like going forward without a seat belt in a car crash. In seconds she was on his lap. His eyes smoldered like red hot coals. "What are you pulling?"

She met his look unflinchingly. "I've been wrong."

"About what?"

"Not giving you what you need."

A look of disgust infused his face, and he tried to push her away. "Don't do me any favors, Winters."

She put her arms around his neck and held on tight. "I'm sorry, that came out wrong. I'm not very good at this."

"Just say what you mean."

She could almost hear the blood pumping through her

veins, feel the beat of her pulse at her neck. Ignoring the panic, she said, "I'm ready to give more." She swallowed hard. "To take more...from you."

He dragged her arms from around his neck and manacled each wrist with his fingers. "Why?"

"Because I want it." When he didn't say anything, she lifted her chin and tried to sound feisty. "So do you." His gaze remained hard; she asked achingly, "Don't you?"

An eternity passed until his eyes softened. Until the hard line of his mouth melted. Right onto hers.

It was like no other kiss she'd ever received or he'd ever given. It smothered her in tenderness; he tilted his head, slanted his mouth, giving, taking. Loving.

When he finally pulled away, he whispered against her cheek, "Why did you make me wait so long?"

The hurt in his voice cut her like a knife. It was harder to hear than his earlier cruelty. "I'm sorry."

"Don't be sorry. Tell me why."

"I can't. I never talk about it."

"Please, just tell me something."

Like a blind person groping her way, she searched inside herself for the words that once came naturally, for feelings that used to be so easily expressed. At last, surprisingly, she found a little of the old Beth. "I...I've lost..." Oh, God this was so difficult! "I've lost a lot of people I loved in the past." She buried her head in his shoulder. "A lot."

His hand locked on her neck. "I'm sorry."

"I can't tell you any more right now. Please, let that be enough. For now."

His lips in her hair, his hand stroking it, he whispered. "Someday...will you try?"

It took more courage than she ever thought she had to give a simple nod.

"All right."

Pulling away, he eased her around and lowered her to the

bed. Covering her body with his, he looked deeply into her eyes. "Say it again."

She didn't pretend to misunderstand. "Dylan."

"Again."

She threaded her hand through his unruly hair as she'd longed to do for weeks. "Dylan, Dylan, Dylan."

His eyes misted.

"Make love to me now," she whispered. "Please."

Purposefully he lowered his head. The drugging kiss went on forever but then she pushed at his shoulders.

When he drew back, his look was quizzical, his eyes wary. "What is it?" he asked with a slight edge to his voice.

"You've got a phone call to make."

He frowned.

"Your date. Call her from downstairs. I don't want to hear it. Tell her you can't make it tonight."

The jealous tone earned her another kiss. "Stay right where you are," he ordered. Then he rolled off her, springing lithely to his feet.

He was at the door when she called after him. "O'Roarke?"

He circled. "Yeah, Winters?"

"Tell her you won't be calling again. That you're out of circulation."

Arrogantly he hooked his thumbs in the belt loops of his jeans. "You gonna tell Scanlon the same?"

Her voice lost its teasing. "I already did."

AFTER HIS PHONE CALL, Dylan hesitated in the doorway of Beth's bedroom, struck by how different it felt from when he first saw it. His senses were on red alert, like they got when he entered a burning building. He was acutely aware of the ticking of a six-foot grandfather clock in the corner; there was the slight hum of the motors from the fish tanks. And permeating the air was the faint womanly scent of Beth.

She'd changed into something so sexy it made his mouth dry. She stood at the window, peeking out through half-closed blinds, her profile toward him. Her face was somber, but untroubled.

He crossed the wide expanse of rug, and as he neared her, his sensory awareness kicked into overdrive. Though she stood in the muted glow of a corner lamp, which gave the room a dreamy intimacy, he could see her clearly. Involuntary tremors coursed through him, and he stopped to garner control. As a rookie at one of his first fires, he'd gotten scared to face the red devil. He remembered halting then and garnering his strength to take that next, crucial step that would forever alter his life. He was on a precipice like that now. With joy in his heart, he closed the distance between them.

She glanced back and gave him a tender, private smile. He lifted his hands and rested them on the thin black straps that hugged her lovely sloped shoulders. He ran his fingers along the straps, over her shoulders and to where they met the material. Then he traced the silk to her waist and to where it fell over her gently rounded bottom. He squeezed her flesh and felt a jolt of awareness—desire, maybe—go through her. "This gown is lovely," he whispered so close to her ear he could almost taste the lilac flavor of her hair. He kissed her neck.

"Chelsea bought it as a gift."

"Remind me to thank her," he said.

Slowly, with aching gentleness, he turned her. Then his hands seared the same path they'd taken on her back, and Dylan followed them with his eyes. Beneath her breasts, the silk gave way to lace so sheer it momentarily stole his breath. She shivered as his knuckles grazed her soft, straining flesh. When he looked up, her eyes were on him. They were green, one of the myriad colors of fire.

Leaning down, he brushed her forehead with his lips, then

her just-closed eyelids. His voice was raw, unfamiliar, when he said, "I want to steep myself in you."

"I want that, too. Touch me everywhere."

In slow motion, he explored the full length of her arms with his fingertips. In their path, tiny goose bumps followed, but she didn't shiver. Heat simmered just beneath the surface of her skin.

She did moan as he knelt on one knee, buried his face in the flat stomach he'd kissed a hundred times, but everything was different now, precious, almost sacred.

His hands kept up their sensual exploration, but his mouth begged for equal time, so he rose, lifted her arms and drew Chelsea's gift over her head. Then he led her to the bed.

Beth followed his silent commands. She sank onto the mattress, stretched out flat and allowed him to raise her hands over her head. Her knuckles skimmed the slats of the oak headboard. And still his fingertips kept up the search with tantalizing possessiveness. He traced the inside of her arm, the curve of her breast. When he drew back, she opened her eyes and watched his tongue trace her kneecap, then down her calf to her ankle.

"Dylan..."

He stopped. His eyes widened, the low flame of desire smoldering in them. He lowered his body to hers.

She frowned at the denim that met her bare, overly sensitized skin. "Too many clothes," she murmured, unable to form a complete sentence. "Off."

A shock of black hair fell over his brow when he shook his head. "Not yet. I want this first time to last."

First time.

Beth was powerless to stop the web of sensual arousal he wove around her. All she could do was moan when his tongue traced her collarbone, dipped into her cleavage, encircled the hard buds of her nipples. She sighed when his lips brushed her belly, briefly closed over the sensitive area between her legs.

"Let me in, Beth. Everywhere."

"Yes."

Long moments passed. He turned her over and continued the gentle exploration. He began to talk, croon, really. "So soft, just like silk...mmm, a nice gentle curve...such womanly flesh." The erotic litany increased her arousal. She buried her face in the pillow, clutched at its corners and finally squirmed. "Soon, Dylan, please."

"No, no, not soon, love."

At the endearment, tears pricked behind her lids. But she battled them. This was too right for crying. Instead, she relaxed and not only allowed the hypnotizing seduction, she partook of it, encouraged it, willingly, joyously.

"Stay still now. Don't move."

Though she protested when he left her, she did as he instructed. Muffled noises from the bathroom made their way to her. Then he returned; she smelled her body lotion, felt its slippery warmth from his heated hands.

Incoherent sounds escaped from her several times as she succumbed to his soul-searching massage. At some point, she reached a mind-altered state, conscious only of his hands on her, the pressure of his fingers, the smell of her lotion, the carnal scrape of those jeans she loved as he straddled her.

And then he turned her over.

Dylan thought he'd never in his life seen anything lovelier.

Glazed eyes locked on his. Emotion gathered in the back of his throat, briefly clouded his vision, temporarily immobilized him. As if she sensed, maybe shared, the feeling that swamped him, she lifted her hand and traced his lips with her fingers.

His breathing quickened and, drawing back, he slid off the bed, then shucked his jeans, grabbed a condom from the dresser where she'd set them out and rolled it on. Then he stretched out beside her. She turned and gave him a surrendering smile.

He spread her legs. Never losing her gaze, never losing the intimacy he'd established, he pushed into her and said, "Lizzie."

She closed her eyes at the name, at the possession. "Dylan." She breathed it lovingly.

As he'd done with the foreplay, he drew out the consummation. Taking long, lazy strokes. Changing their position. Her moans stretched together into one long, sexual chorus. Sweat gathered on her brow. Her lips fell open. Her chest began to heave.

He gave into it, then, increased the pressure, quickened the pace. Still it took moments for them both to ignite. Release hit them like flashover, burning away all previous hurt they'd caused each other, hollowing out new corners in each of their hearts for the other.

Dylan gladly let the flames consume him.

CHAPTER TEN

IT WAS ON HER DESK Monday morning. Too small a thing to send her into such paroxysms of terror. Just one beautifully shaped peach rose in a cut-glass vase.

Pushing away the demons and ignoring the fact that she was late for exercise class, she dropped her bag and crossed to the flower. For just a moment, she savored its sweet scent, its exquisite shape, its soft petals.

With the rose fragrance wafting through the office, she tugged off her black sweats, then hurried to the arena, greeted the recruits and began the warm-up. Then she ran laps with the class. But exercise didn't interfere with her memories of the weekend just spent.

They'd sat on her bed facing the fish tanks. Naked. Sated. It was late Friday night, and the evening had been a sensuous feast, a healing banquet, one they both needed.

"Tell me about your fish," he said as he brushed her hair. "What kind are they?"

"That pretty blue one there is a betta. It's also called a Siamese fighting fish. You can only have one in the tank, 'cause they eat each other."

"Hmm, sounds like our office the last few weeks." He bit her shoulder lovingly.

"Since you mention it, the betta is most ferocious when attacking rival suitors."

He scowled. "You told Scanlon you were unavailable, right?"

"Uh-huh."

"Are there are others who need to be put on notice?"

"No." She bit the inside of her cheek to hide a smile. "But speaking of that, see those white fish with black and yellow stripes? Those are angelfish."

"Yeah?"

"Well, the single male angelfish has a harem of female fish."

"Very funny."

"And their names all start with M."

"I got a brush in my hand, Winters. Just right for paddling."

She giggled. It felt so good to have fun with him.

"What are those markings on their bodies?" he asked.

"Some people have commented the markings look like Arabic script. In Zanzibar, an angelfish was spotted that supposedly had, 'There is no God but Allah,' written on one side."

"What does this one say?" His mouth flirted with her ear; he spoke in a sexy whisper.

She turned her head, her lips almost grazing his. "It says, 'All those women were right about Dylan O'Roarke.'"

His kiss was passionate and consuming.

When he'd drunk his fill of her, he resumed brushing her hair and inquiring about the fish. "The orange ones outlined in black look like firefighters."

"They're clown fish."

"They tell jokes?"

She elbowed him. "Actually, they're an interesting species. In the ocean, they have a symbiotic relationship with sea anemones. The anemone sprays the clown fish with a mucuslike substance, which allows them to live within the anemone's tentacles for protection but kills all predators. In return, the clown fish goes to the surface and lures larger fish to the anemone as its food."

Abandoning the brush, Dylan moved closer, placing his

legs on either side of her, and enfolded her in his arms from behind. They touched from head to toe. Serious, he murmured, "I'll be your anemone, Beth. I'll protect you from everything." When she stilled, he waited. Then, as if to lighten the moment, he'd cupped her breasts. "I can think of a way you can feed me."

Afterward, as they lay together, only the glow of the tank illuminated their sweaty skin; the repetitive bubble of the water soothed their erratic breathing. Dylan said, "You know a lot about fish."

Sleepily, she indicated a row of books on the shelf above the tank. "I've read about them. I enjoy it. And I grew up on a—"

She stopped abruptly.

"You grew up where?"

Here it was. The first of many inquiries she knew would come from him. Though it scared her, she said, "On a lake."

"Oh. Did you have a fish tank, too?"

She stiffened.

His hand closed over her waist. "Just a little bit, honey. I know it's hard for you, but share a little bit with me. Please."

On a precipice of trust, she waited a very long time. Facing away from him, she finally whispered, "No fish tanks. But we had a dog. A big collie that looked like Lassie."

"What was his name?"

"Her. Edna."

"Edna?"

Beth smiled at the memory. "My father's old girlfriend's name was Edna. My mother, Mary, thought there were similarities."

"How old were you to know that kind of thing?"

"We got the dog when I was twelve."

He squeezed her shoulder in thanks for the confidence, so she found the courage to go on. "I came to live with them when I was eight."

Tension crept into him—she could feel it—but she didn't turn around. Hiding in the darkness, she spoke softly. "I was adopted by Bill and Mary Mack after spending a year in foster homes."

"What happened to your biological parents?"

"My mother was killed by a self-induced drug overdose. I never knew my father." Dylan sucked in his breath. "Don't feel bad. It was not...pleasant living with her. Finding the Macks was a godsend. They were wonderful to me."

"Did you...did you lose them, too?"

She nodded.

"Can you tell me how?"

Beth felt panic shoot through her veins. She hadn't talked to anyone about this since Tim. "I—I..."

Patiently Dylan waited, hugging her, watching the fish cruise and dart.

"It was a boating accident. They loved the water. They were out for a night ride. I was studying for a final exam and didn't go with them." She shuddered. "I wished I had."

His arms tightened around her, enfolded her in a blanket of warmth. "I'm glad you didn't." After a moment he asked, "What happened to you?"

"I went to live with our next-door neighbors, Mike and Leona. They were my parents' best friends."

"Did you adjust?"

"Uh-huh."

"Did they have any kids?"

"Yeah, one. We got to be—" she hesitated only briefly "—good friends."

Dylan said nothing for a long time, as if he was waiting for her to go on. But she hadn't been able to tell him more. She'd used up her capacity for confiding.

"Ms. Winters?" Connie Cleary was beside her, healthy sweat on her now fit body. Beth focused on the young woman. She'd stopped running; they all had. "Our, um, laps are done."

"Oh." Beth blushed. "Sorry. I was somewhere else."

"Are you okay?"

"Yes, of course. Let's do some flexibility exercises."

Beth tried to concentrate on the class. She noted that Barnette looked tired and missed several commands, and Wanikya appeared even more somber than usual. But then she zeroed in on Tully's smiling face, which reminded her of Dylan, and in the middle of leg extensions she was back on that bed with O'Roarke quicker than a flash fire.

"A promise?" he'd said warily in response to her request. It was Saturday afternoon and raining; the temperature had dropped to forty. They'd not left the house since he arrived the night before.

"Give me an hour," she whispered, sitting on the bed in a forest green teddy.

"With what?" He was in black boxers, lazing against the pillows.

"With your body."

"To do?"

"All those things you did to me last night." She paused. "Let me touch you like I've always wanted to." Beth was as shocked by her proposal as she was by the sultriness of her voice. For a second she'd been frightened that he could turn her into someone she didn't recognize.

But Dylan laughed, hugged her and asked how he could possibly lose on a promise like that.

Ten minutes later Dylan was flat on his stomach, moaning, long and loud into the pillow. "You touch my butt one more time, Winters, and I can't be held responsible for my actions."

"You're such a smooth talker, O'Roarke. You've really got a way with words." Just for good measure, she bit his cheek, then soothed it with the baby oil she'd fetched from her bathroom and heated in the kitchen.

Twenty minutes later he was on his back and swearing. "Damn it, Beth, you can't possibly expect me to take any more of this."

She kissed his chest. "You promised."

"My arms are tired."

"I've seen you haul hose longer than this." He groaned. She said, "Don't you dare let go of that headboard. It arouses me, seeing you defenseless like this."

Massaging her way down his body, she reached his flat stomach. "That night of the first basketball game, in the office, when you lifted your shirt to wipe your face, my mouth went dry when I saw this." Her tongue drew circles around his navel.

"Be-eth!"

Bypassing the part of him that stood at attention, she kissed his thigh. It became rock hard, and she lingered there. When she reached his calf, she poured more oil on her palms and kneaded it into his muscles. His hips ground into the sheets.

"Remember when you hurt your calf on the treadmill?"

He made an incoherent sound that she took for agreement. "I wanted to touch you all over." She switched to the other calf. "Intimately. Do you know how much you excite me?" Once again, her voice was a stranger's and her confession foreign. Beth had never in her life behaved this way.

Eagerly she went back to his thigh. With her mouth. "I want you to want me like I've wanted you, O'Roarke."

"I do, oh, I do."

"I'm not quite certain." She took his marble hard penis into her slippery palms. And rubbed. Slowly. Up and down. "Maybe, but I've got—" she squinted at the clock "—four more minutes to make sure."

"You're heartless, woman."

"Ah, Ms. Winters, we lost you again." Beth returned to the reality of the recruits, whom she'd obviously neglected a second time. "And your face is red." Cleary spoke, but the rest of them gazed at her with avid interest—and a bit of amusement.

"Sorry," she said brusquely. "Let's head to the weight room." There, at least, the recruits could work on their own. Beth couldn't seem to string two coherent thoughts together. As they mounted machines and spotted for each other, Beth walked around, gave some recommendations, then sat on the padded bench against the wall to oversee them. Once she was idle, the lure of her memories drew her to the final day of her marathon weekend with the recruits' favorite lieutenant.

"I have to go out today," he'd said, sliding off her and sinking into the mattress.

She'd struggled to sober up, but she couldn't shake the sexual buzz induced by thirty-six hours of Dylan O'Roarke. "Oh, sure, it's okay."

"No, really, I wouldn't go, but I promised."

"It's fine."

She sprang off the mattress, where they'd been playing with the condoms, this time the edible ones, which functioned as toys, not contraception, much like edible panties. She grabbed a white terry robe, donned it and faced him from the foot of the bed. "You've got a life, I understand."

He moved to the end of the bed, spread his knees and tugged on the sash of her robe. Unsteadily she came to stand between his rock hard thighs. With just his nose, he nuzzled open her robe. "Don't shut down on me, honey. I made a commitment to Mrs. Santori at Dutch Towers that I'd help her husband move some furniture today."

"Oh."

"Come with me."

Beth shook her head. It might be good to get away from him for a while, to collect herself.

"*Please.* I don't want to be without you."

She'd tried to resist, but in the end, she'd accompanied him. They'd even dressed alike, in jeans and flannel shirts.

The Santori apartment was located on the fifth floor of Dutch Towers, which was around the corner from Quint/Midi Twelve where Dylan had worked since he'd graduated from the academy. Housing seventy senior citizens, the complex boasted neat, inexpensive accommodations, social areas, a big yard and a convenient location. Beth knew from Francey that the older people were sweet on the fire department whom they called regularly to check gas leaks, put out stove fires and deal with small medical emergencies. Jake Scarlatta was their favorite. It appeared O'Roarke ran a close second.

"*Mathone,* Dylan, you came." A small woman, gray hair scraped back in a bun and an apron over a pink-checked housedress, opened the door to them; she reached up and kissed Dylan's cheek.

"Josephine, you wound me. I *said* I'd be here."

"A young boy like you has other things to do on a rainy Sunday afternoon."

Smiling, Dylan dragged Beth from behind him. "I brought the only other thing I wanted to do with me. Josephine Santori, this is Beth Winters."

"Welcome to our home, Beth."

The old woman said something in Italian as she ushered them into the living room. "I think so, too, Josephine," Dylan said.

"Mama, I told you not to bother the boy." From a door off a hallway, a big, burly man without a hair on his head chided his wife. He wore brown pants and a green sweater and reminded Beth of the old men who'd lived on the lake when she was a child.

"I'm glad to help, Moses." He winked at Josephine. "It impresses my woman."

Dylan introduced her to Moses Santori, who said, "He really comes for Mama's cookies."

They laughed, but Beth was made uncomfortable by the closeness among them. She felt herself getting pulled in, dragged under and swept away by the current of O'Roarke's life.

Josephine said, "Our Joey should be helping." Another firefighter, Joey Santori, was their grandchild and Francey Templeton's former fiancé.

Dylan didn't say anything.

"Our Joey's been a mess since Francey married that rich guy," Moses told Beth. "He don't help nobody anymore."

Throwing an arm around the older man, Dylan scowled. "I got better muscles than that punk, anyway. Come on, show me the furniture Josephine is badgering you to change around."

"Can I help?" Beth asked.

"No, it's man's work." Moses Santori was of another generation. Dylan's wink warmed her as he followed the older man down the hall.

Josephine faced Beth. "I'll get coffee and some cookies while we wait. Sit down, please."

Beth perched on the edge of the slipcovered couch. While Mrs. Santori was in the kitchen, Beth noticed that crocheted articles were everywhere—afghans, doilies, a rocker seat cover. Beth perused the walls, too, then the shelves on the far wall.

And froze.

Josephine came in and found her that way. Tracking her gaze, the older woman smiled wistfully. "You like my dolls?"

Beth nodded.

"I made them all myself."

"They're—" she coughed to clear her throat "—they're beautiful."

"Go look close."

Forcing herself to move, Beth rose and crossed the room, wondering fleetingly if it was coincidence or another example of fate intervening. Gingerly, she picked up the bride doll, much like her own. "For your wedding?"

The old woman nodded as she sat in a rocker and sipped from a fragile china teacup. "I made that doll and all the bridesmaids. Moses is there, too. I wanted to remember my wedding day."

Beth found the groom, resplendent in an old-fashioned tux. "He's handsome."

"Later, I did my sons and grandsons." Mrs. Santori waved her hand to indicate the menagerie; she'd captured images of all of the people she loved in cloth and buttons and beads.

Beth's heart pounded like a trip-hammer when she picked up the last doll. It looked like Dylan in his RFD uniform. "Is this Joey?" Her hand shook.

"No. It's Moses again. He was a fireman, too."

"Oh."

When Dylan and Moses returned, they joined the women for cookies and coffee. While Dylan sampled what Josephine labeled crispets, Italian spice balls and fruit bars, Beth nibbled on a sugary confection. But her gaze kept straying to the dolls.

"Your woman likes Mama's dolls," Moses observed bluntly.

Caught, Beth flushed.

Dylan cocked his head. "Really?"

Beth said, "They're lovely."

After packing up not only cookies, but some of Mrs. Santori's lasagna for dinner the next night, Beth and Dylan returned to her place. Once inside the door, he stole her breath with a kiss, robbed her sanity with an intimate dip into her shirt and irrevocably absconded with her heart as he swept her up in his arms and carried her to the bedroom.

Later that night, as they lay spoon fashion in bed, Dylan tugged up the sheet to cover them. "You liked the dolls, didn't you?" he said idly.

She stiffened.

"Beth, what is it?"

She knew what he was going to do—push for more. She wasn't sure she was capable of giving it.

"Beth?"

She shook her head, burying her face in the warmth of his arm.

Dylan didn't say anything for a long time. Then, in a tone she'd never heard before, he asked, "You know why I go to Dutch Towers so much?"

"Why?"

"I was close to my grandmother. I was an only child, and my mother died when I was five. Dad spent a lot of time at the station house, so I stayed with her and Grandpa." She could hear the smile in his voice.

"It was great being out of the city and getting so much attention from them. Grandpa was terrific and taught me a lot about being a man, but I loved Grandma Katie more than anyone in the world. And I miss her."

Beth squeezed him tightly.

The next words were wrenched from him. "She died in my arms, Beth. A myocardial infarction, when I was seventeen. I came over after school and found her on the floor." He drew in a deep breath. "I wanted to die, too—she'd been such a big part of my life." A long pause. "I went into EMS because I thought if I'd known more, I could have saved her."

She turned in his arms and brushed his knitted brow with her lips. "You couldn't have saved her. You must know that now."

"Now I do. But then—" He broke off.

She drew his face into her breasts. "I'm so sorry."

"Reed thinks it's why I have this driving need to save everybody. Because I couldn't save her."

"Oh, Dylan."

"I've never told that to another soul."

Her throat clogged. "Thanks for telling me."

He didn't respond for a long time; then he pulled away and stared at her bleakly.

She knew what he wanted...needed.

Turning around in his arms, she settled against him. "I had...have a doll collection."

"You do?"

"It was special."

This time, he squeezed her, for comfort and encouragement.

"They were all handmade, like Mrs. Santori's. Chronicling my life."

"Can I see it?"

"I'm not sure, Dylan." She kissed his hand. "I don't share stuff like this. Ever."

"I don't talk about Grandma Katie, either."

She got the message. "I'll think about it. That's the most I can give right now."

"It's enough," he whispered achingly. "For right now—"

Once again, Beth was brought back to the present by Cleary. "Ms. Winter, we're done in here. We're leaving, but don't mind us. You go ahead and, ah, do whatever you were doing."

The recruits chuckled all the way out of the weight room.

Beth sensed that her hard-nosed reputation was shattering. Right along with the protective shield that had kept her sane for years.

Both scared her to death.

DYLAN RUSHED through the academy doors for the second time that morning, and into the arena where the recruits were lined up for roll call. He scanned the area for Beth but didn't see her. The gym had been set up for EMS practicals today, simulations of activities they'd have to perform to pass the state exam. The recruits would be tested in three areas of practical skills—hemorrhage control, primary assessment and airway management and oxygen therapy. Then to become a Certified First Responder, they'd have to take a written exam. Dylan and Beth had made sure their tests and practicals were harder than the state ones, so the recruits wouldn't have a problem passing—except for maybe Tully.

Chuck Lorenzo wandered among the standing-at-attention group, as did three other instructors. Dylan joined them, wondering where Beth was. As he went up and down the two lines, he frowned. She'd awakened at five to get here for her exercise class; he'd tried to snuggle with her a bit before she got out of bed, but she was all business. He'd left her house while she dressed, detoured to an all-night superstore to get the rose, stopped in here with it and had gone home to shower and change.

"Lieutenant O'Roarke?"

Dylan looked at Tully. "Yes, Recruit Tully."

"You're, um, just standing there staring at me."

Dylan recovered quickly. "I was looking at that poor excuse for a knot in your tie."

Tully reddened. "I can't tie them good."

Dylan was about to joke when he saw the sadness in Tully's eyes. "Never had a dad to teach me," the recruit confessed.

Giving the kid a comforting smile, Dylan winked. Now that they were into the second half of the class, the officers were less formal with the recruits at roll. "That's okay, Tully. Women love to tie ties for men. They can't resist a man in need."

"Is that so?" The familiar voice came from behind him.

Dylan pivoted to face Beth. Bombarded by emotion at just the sight of her—jeez, now she even looked sexy in her uniform—he nevertheless summoned a devilish smile. "Yes, ma'am. They can't keep their hands off you when you need help with ties." His searing look said, *Remember New York City.*

Winters coughed and turned to Cleary. "Do you think that's a sexist statement, Recruit Cleary?"

Cleary hid a smile. "Yes, ma'am."

"Hmm." Beth tipped Cleary's hat a bit and said, "We'll have to think of a way to retaliate."

Dylan wanted to whoop. A few weeks ago, Beth would never have joked with the recruits.

As Chuck Lorenzo called the recruits to attention again, Dylan stood behind them and covertly watched Beth. She'd gone to stand with Lou Giancarlo. Dylan was keeping his distance because he couldn't trust himself near her. She'd made him promise, and he'd agreed, to keep it very cool at work; no touching, no personal talk, no sexual innuendo. He'd run his hand down her cheek and told her he wouldn't touch her and he'd try not to say anything out of line or indicative of the change in their relationship in front of anybody else. But to expect no personal remarks at all, especially if they were alone, was unrealistic.

Scowling, he remembered the second promise she'd exacted from him, one he *really* didn't like...

"No, Beth, I won't agree to that."

They were in her bathtub. It was a huge whirlpool in a surprisingly large bathroom. She nestled her back against his chest. "Hear me out, please."

Rubbing the washcloth down her arm, he grunted agreement.

"Let's keep the change in our relationship quiet. Just for a while. I can't answer any questions about us yet. I don't even know how *I* feel about this. Don't make me explain it to anyone.''

He didn't say anything, but he tensed.

She pushed her fanny against his groin, angled her head and reached her arm behind her to bring his face close. ''It's so new…so scary,'' she'd said against his lips. ''Let me get used to it between us before we go public.''

But Dylan wanted everybody to know about their relationship. Should he give in on this one? *Learn the wisdom of compromise, Dylan; it's better to bend than break.* Jeez, he thought, scowling, Grandma Katie's words came back to him at the damnedest times. Then he smirked and pulled Beth closer. His grandma would have loved Beth and the sensual closeness Dylan had with her. An earthy woman, Katie O'Roarke knew what was important—and what was *right*. So he agreed to what Beth wanted.

Once the practicals began, he crossed to Beth. She stood in the corner as Lorenzo divided the recruits into thirds, assigned them their first station and gave last-minute instructions. There were paramedics at each station to conduct the practicals. Dylan and Beth would rate the recruits. She handed him a clipboard as he reached her.

''Hi.''

''Hi.'' There was a reddish mark just under the right side of her collar, and he remembered how his mouth had made it last night. Gripping the clipboard, he struggled to keep his first promise.

She averted her gaze and stared at the group. ''Thank you for the flower. It's lovely.''

''Didn't send you into a panic, did it?''

Still not looking at him, she smiled slightly. ''I managed.''

''Good. Shall we split up or do the assessments together?''

She looked at him. Her eyes burned briefly with emotion. ''We'd better split up.''

He arched a brow.

KATHRYN SHAY   195

"I won't be able to concentrate with you near me, O'Roarke. I already made a fool of myself at exercise class this morning."

"I can't wait to hear about it," he said, pleased.

"In your dreams." As she pushed off the wall and walked away, she called over her shoulder, "Start with station two."

"Yes, ma'am." He gave her back a salute.

Dylan crossed to the hemorrhage station just as Tully volunteered to go first. "You're on," the supervisor, an off-duty paramedic firefighter, told him. Sandy Frank sat in the designated victim's chair. The recruits would take turns being patient and Certified First Responder on the scene. The CFR was required to talk through the process as he performed it.

"First," Tully said, "I'd use universal precautions." Though they didn't actually don gloves, goggles and mask for practicals, a student would fail automatically if he forgot to indicate the initial procedure. The supervisor nodded that Tully was protected. "Next, I'd locate the wound and staunch the blood." Tully stretched out Frank's left arm and took a sterile pad to cover her fictional gash.

"It's still bleeding," the instructor said.

"I'd elevate the arm." Tully raised the patient's arm to a right angle.

"It's still bleeding."

"Then I'll wrap it in gauze." With his big hands, he wrapped the gauze as surely as he handled a basketball. Dylan knew he was right about this kid being a good firefighter.

The instructor once again said, "It's still bleeding."

Tully scowled.

Come on, Dylan thought. *Locate the brachial artery under her arm. We went over this last week.*

The four recruits in his group were silent. They knew he'd fail if he missed this.

"Um... Oh, wait, I know—locate the artery under her arm and apply tourniquet-like pressure."

Dylan said, "Yes!" closing his fist and jerking down his arm.

The recruits laughed.

This was going to be a great day.

It was lunchtime before he was able to talk to Beth again. She was working at her desk when he got to the office, her cute glasses perched on her nose. Looking up, she said, "Oh, good, there you are. I need the assessment sheets so I can compile all this information."

He wished she'd smile, or do something to indicate what she was feeling, but he forced himself not to dwell on it. Crossing to her desk, he handed her his forms. He glanced at hers. "How'd they do?"

"Pretty good. Lots of fumbling," she said dryly. At practicals, the recruits always got nervous, and their hands shook as they wrapped bandages or examined patients. "I was a little surprised at Barnette, though. He messed up on the ABC's of patient assessment." They'd taught the students a mnemonic device to remember how to assess a patient: check Airways, Breathing, Circulation, see if there was a Disability, Expose the body for injury. "So far, Barnette's gotten perfect scores on the tests."

Dylan edged his hip onto the perimeter of her desk. "Sometimes it doesn't transfer. The best book learners don't always make the best firefighters and CFRs."

"I told him I'd work with him at six. He'll miss your basketball game."

"This is more important."

She cocked her head at his easy acquiescence.

"I *can* be reasonable," he said innocently.

She rolled her eyes.

"Let's see if you can be, too. Come to lunch with me."

Her face paled, and she glanced at the flower. "I don't think that's a good idea."

He didn't say anything.

"You said you understood about keeping this private for a while."

He crossed his arms. "No, I said I'd go along with it. I don't understand it at all."

There it was again. That scared, vulnerable look suffusing her face. It melted his insides like candle wax.

"Oh, all right," he said. "I'll go see if Jake would like my company." She was so relieved it angered him. "But I want to see you tonight."

"So soon? We just... I thought you'd at least wait until—"

That made him mad. He got up and closed the door and leaned against it. "I want to be with you tonight. I don't necessarily want sex. Maybe we'll just have dinner, watch a movie, sleep in each other's arms." He branded her with an impatient stare. "That's what people who care about each other do, Beth."

A rainbow of emotions filtered across her face. She bit her lip, the gesture almost making him retract his demand. Damn it, though, he wasn't asking for that much. And he sure as hell wasn't going to let her fears keep them apart.

Silently he watched her struggle; she took in a deep breath, fingered the rose, then looked at the ceiling. Finally her gaze landed on him. "Can I have some of Mrs. Santori's lasagna for dinner?" she asked, obviously trying for a light tone.

"You can have anything you want, Beth." He did not return her levity.

And the realization that he was dead serious frightened even him.

CHAPTER ELEVEN

THEY HADN'T MADE LOVE in four days, and Dylan couldn't have been happier about it. He felt as good as he had when he'd dragged his first victim out of a fire. Heading toward the EMS office Friday at noon, he wondered if he should press his luck and try to get Beth to go to lunch with him.

How the mighty have fallen. Yet another of Grandma Katie's favorite phrases. Who would have thought Dylan O'Roarke would be satisfied to simply sleep with the same woman four nights in a row, wake up with her and be as gratified as if they'd spent the hours at a Roman orgy?

But he was, because Dylan wanted her heart more than her body. Whistling Sonny and Cher's old song, "I Got You, Babe," he walked through the doorway—and stopped dead in his tracks.

Beth wasn't there, but Francey and Chelsea were. Francey was decorating the wall behind Beth's desk with black crepe paper. Chelsea was blowing up black and white balloons and had tacked a couple onto Beth's desk. They'd hung a four-by-four sign by the window that read, Over the Hill.

His pulse rate sped up; hoping this wasn't what it looked like, he stepped to the side of the door and casually leaned against the wall. "Hi, guys. What's going on?"

Francey glanced over her shoulder. "Hi, Dyl. We're taking Beth out for lunch but wanted to surprise her first."

"Surprise her?"

"Yeah, Dad's got her in his office so we could decorate.

But she'll be here any minute.'' Finished with the last of the paper, Francey jumped off the chair.

Just as Beth walked through the door.

Francey and Chelsea yelled, ''Surprise!''

Dylan watched Beth's eyes narrow on her friends, then scan the decorations, catching a glimpse of him in the process; then her gaze landed on a cake on the computer table. Her face reddened, and he could tell she was embarrassed.

''Happy Birthday, Beth,'' the women chorused.

Dylan's heart plummeted. He crossed his arms and tried to stop his disappointment from surfacing, but it floated to the top like pieces of wood from a shipwreck. To cover his reaction, he pushed away from the wall and moved to the table. On it was a rectangular cake, decorated with the vivid blue EMS star of life and the words read, Happy Fortieth Birthday, Beth.

Appropriate decal for her, he thought, with a mixture of hurt and resentment. Her whole life was work.

It certainly wasn't him.

He turned to find Beth watching him. He didn't say anything. She started to say something to him, then clamped her mouth shut. But heated mercury wasn't as volatile as the look that passed between them.

''...that you don't like celebrations,'' Chelsea was saying. ''But we couldn't just do lunch and presents for the big four-oh.''

God damn it, not only had he not known it was her birthday, he hadn't even known how old she was.

Francey turned to Dylan. ''Could we, Dylan?''

''Pardon me?''

''We couldn't let Beth's fortieth birthday go with only lunch.''

I would have been happy just to know about it.

''No, of course not. Birthdays should be shared.'' He gave Francey a weak smile. ''You know how I feel about them.''

Rolling her eyes, Francey said, "Yeah, the ultimate birth-day boy."

Beth paled. Good. He wanted her to know he was hurt. Some part of him that he didn't like wanted to hurt her back. Tossing her a piercing look, he said, "Happy fortieth, Winters," and walked out of the office before he did anything he'd regret.

And, by all means, he didn't want to reveal a hint of their relationship to her friends. As he walked down the hall, he thought miserably, *What relationship?*

Beth was quiet on the ride to Minx's in Chelsea's sporty red Camaro. She only half listened to Chelsea's latest con-flicts with Billy Milligan, who was demanding more com-mitment in their relationship.

"I guess I just know he's not the one," Chelsea told them.

"Then you'd better stop it now," Francey advised. "I wish I'd never let it go as far as I did with Joey."

Was the same true for Beth? Should she cut it off now before she hurt Dylan more? she wondered as they walked into the restaurant, got their table and perused the menus. She couldn't forget that look of unhappiness and disappoint-ment in those blue eyes that had come to mean so much to her.

Sighing, she peered up from the menu to find Chelsea and Francey exchanging worried glances. Finally Francey said, "You're angry at us for decorating the office, aren't you?"

Beth smiled. "No, of course not. It's fine."

"Honestly?" Chelsea asked.

She reached out and squeezed both their arms. "Yes, hon-estly." Her heart broke a little at their concern. Beth hadn't realized how much she'd cut people out, limited their in-volvement in her life. She'd been doing it to Francey and Chelsea for years. Had they suffered, too, like Dylan?

"Oh, good. We thought maybe we'd made a mistake."

No. I made a mistake. A big one. "I appreciate the gesture.'' To lighten the moment, she said, ''Except now everybody knows I'm forty.''

Francey laughed. ''Dylan will rag on you for this one.''

You don't know the half of it.

''What was the matter with him, anyway?'' Francey frowned. ''Something's got his jocks in a twist.''

''Maybe Barbie's giving him a rough time,'' Chelsea quipped.

Barbie would have told him it was her birthday.

''Nah, Dylan doesn't let—''

''Did I hear my favorite firefighter mentioned?'' Beth looked up at one of Dylan's M-girls. Skeins of blond hair framed a youthful face with a full, sensuous mouth. Which one was this?

''Hi, Missy.'' Francey's greeting was polite.

''Hi. You didn't bring that handsome hunk with you, did you?''

Beth stared at the waitress.

''No, we left him at the academy, sulking.''

A line creased Missy's smooth forehead. ''I haven't seen much of him. He said he wasn't dating for a while.''

For a while, Beth thought.

''But I'm gonna surprise him this weekend.'' Missy giggled girlishly, the action calling attention to her voluptuous breasts and tiny waist. ''Make him dinner, bring it over...''

Beth dropped her gaze to the menu. This was unbearable.

''Just a word of advice,'' Francey told her. ''Dylan doesn't like surprises. I'd call first.''

Missy shrugged, took their order, then left.

''Damn.'' Francey scowled. ''I hope she doesn't surprise him. Dylan will have a fit.''

Chelsea nodded. ''Maybe you should tell him what Missy said when you get back to the office, Beth.''

Oh, God.

At what must have been Beth's bleak expression, Francey

braced her arms on the table. "Beth, something *is* wrong, isn't it?"

I don't want anyone to know...you said you understood.

No, I said I'd do it. I don't understand at all.

Nodding, Beth hesitated a long time before she found the courage to answer. "It's not Barbie that's got Dylan's jocks in a twist. It's me."

Misunderstanding, Francey raised her brows. "Oh, I'm sorry. I thought you were getting along better."

Beth sighed. "We are getting along better."

Chelsea frowned. "I don't understand."

Beth took a deep breath and made a momentous leap of faith. "Dylan and I...we're...we've become...close."

Chelsea and Francey still looked quizzical.

Beth coughed. "We're, um, sexually involved."

Both women gaped at her in stunned silence.

"No, it's more than that. We're friends, too."

"You're kidding." Francey's mouth was still open.

Beth shook her head. "I wish I was." But did she really? *Would I go back to the way things were?*

She thought of the past twenty years. How she systematically excluded everybody from her life for fear of losing them. Except these two women. And how they had, unacknowledged by Beth, been the source of so much joy.

Please, Beth, let me in, Dylan had asked her many times.

Tim's and Janey's faces flashed in front of her eyes. Did she dare let Dylan in and risk that kind of loss again?

She looked at Francey and Chelsea. She'd let them in. And they were both firefighters.

Back to cosmic unity.

Suddenly Beth realized she was tired of being alone.

"No, that's not true. I'm glad it happened."

"Then tell us about it," Francey said simply, and covered Beth's hand with hers.

DYLAN HAD LIED. As he stared out his bedroom window, sipping his second Manhattan, he thought about why. Though he rarely fudged the truth—he preferred dealing with reality—he'd lied today because reality was too hard to face. He'd gone to Ben and said he was ill and wanted the rest of the day off. Since Dylan had rarely asked for any special consideration and was often the last to leave the academy or the fire station, Ben told him to go. His old friend had looked worried.

Dylan had driven home, gotten on his motorcycle—though it was really too cold to be riding in mid-November—and sped out of Rockford like a man on fire.

In a way, he was. He'd been burned, badly.

Now, at six at night, blisters were beginning to form around his heart. Which was very close to breaking.

Dylan remembered his grandpa's funeral when he was twelve. Though she'd been distraught about the death of the man she'd married at seventeen in Ireland, Grandma Katie had held Dylan close and quoted one of the Greek philosophers she'd read. *If you want life to be pain free, you'd have to be a god or a corpse.*

Well, he knew he was neither, because this hurt. Too much, he guessed. In some corner of his mind, he knew he was overreacting. But Beth had always provoked irrational responses in him.

Maybe he would have been more sane about it if he hadn't gotten his hopes up. He glanced at the bed. They'd made so much progress. She'd come here the past four nights and willingly and happily cuddled with him under the covers. They'd stared through the four sliding glass doors at the trees losing their leaves and talked about winter. Did she like it? Did she ski? True, she hadn't confided all her secrets yet, but she was sharing her present and talking about her future, and he'd had hope.

He took a slug of the drink. Strong stuff that he'd planned would numb him. It was doing its job.

The doorbell rang.

Quint barked.

Despite his pique, Dylan smiled. Quint was probably hoping it was her. He adored her. Every time she came here, he'd lick her all over, and last night the dog had crept into bed with them. Dylan found Quint snuggled under her arm this morning.

He ignored the bell as long as he could. Finally he headed to the foyer, barefoot, in only jeans and an open flannel shirt. "Come on, buddy, it's not her. She doesn't want to spend her birthday with us. It's been all smoke and mirrors."

Well, no more. Whoever was at the door, he'd invite them in, start right now overhauling his life, putting out the blaze that burned inside him for a woman who didn't want his fire.

No, correction, she wanted his passion. She just didn't want the rest.

Quit feeling sorry for yourself, Grandma Katie would say.

Shut up, Grandma, he thought as he pulled open the door.

Beth stood on his porch. Wrapped in a long gray raincoat, she was shivering.

"Well, if it isn't the birthday girl."

"Hi."

"What do you want?" He ignored the bleakness in her eyes, the desolation on her face. He'd paid attention to both too many times, and look where it got him.

"Are you really sick?"

He stared at her.

"Ben said you'd gone home ill."

"I'm not sick. I needed to think about some things."

She wrapped her arms around her waist. "It's cold out here. Can I come in?"

"No."

Beth stared over his shoulder; he tracked her gaze. From

here, the open door to his bedroom was visible; muted lights cast the back of the house in a romantic glow. How ironic.

When he looked at her, she was biting her lip. "Is…is someone here?"

He shook his head. "No one's here, Beth. But you're not coming in. Go home. I don't want to see you tonight." He moved to close the door.

She put her foot in it. The slim lines of her ankle were accented by the strappy black shoes she wore. For the hundredth time he wondered how she could appear so delicate on the outside and be steely on the inside. And cursed himself for caring. Still, he softened his tone. "Look, I'm not going to slam the door in your face. But I don't want you here. Close it on your way out." He turned and left her on the porch.

In his bedroom, he sank onto the bed, closed his eyes and threw a hand over his face. He wasn't going to do this anymore. He was done with it. It wasn't too late get out. It would be hard, but—

He felt the bed sag. Opening his eyes, he found her seated on the edge of the mattress. She'd removed her coat, and the clingy black-and-white flowered dress she wore distracted him for a minute. It had ruffles down the front, was a silky material that hugged her curves and… Shit, he wasn't going to go there!

"I won't be seduced out of this, Beth."

"Not even after I apologize?"

He sprung up, like a charged hose out of control. Grabbing her arm, he tried to stem the force of his grip. "Do you even know what you're apologizing for?"

Slowly she lifted her chin; he'd come to recognize the gesture was one of bravado when she was frightened. "Yes."

He stared at her.

"I should have told you it was my birthday."

"Why, Beth? Why should you have told me?"

"Because we're close enough for you to know about it. For us to have celebrated it together."

His grip eased. "But are you comfortable with that yet?"

"No."

"Are you ever going to be?"

"Dylan, I'm trying."

To be fair, she was. He knew it was hard for her. But, damn it, he still didn't see why. Everybody lost people they loved. And it didn't affect them like it affected her. "Tell me. Why is it so hard?"

Her eyes clouded with pain. Intense pain. "I told you I lost people I loved."

He smoothed his knuckles down her cheek. "I know. But sweetheart, everyone has."

She shook her head. "I lost…more than most."

"Who? Your mother. I know. And your adoptive parents."

Bleakly she stared over his shoulder and continued the list. "The couple who took me in. Leona and Mike Winters. Four years after the Macks. Mike had a heart attack. Six months later Leona had a stroke."

"Oh, baby, I'm so sor—" He stilled. "Did you say Winters?"

She nodded.

"You took their last name?"

"No." Her expression was grim. Slowly, her hand crept over to his. She linked their fingers. "I married their son, Tim, when I was seventeen."

Tim. Dylan remembered the night in the storeroom when she'd called that name.

He felt sick. "At seventeen?" Then it hit him with the force of a battering ram. "Oh, God, he died, too, didn't he?"

She looked at their entwined hands. When she raised her eyes, his heart, which he'd foolishly thought hurt before, groaned with the pain he saw there. "Yes. Tim died, too."

"No!" BETH BOLTED upright in bed; breathing hard, sweat bathing her naked body, she shivered. It was only seconds before she felt Dylan's arms come around her, cocooning her with his warmth. "It's all right, sweetheart, I'm here."

Trying to shake off the dream, she snuggled into him. After holding her for a moment, he eased them onto the pillows, tugged up the comforter and rubbed her arms soothingly.

"Bad dream?"

As she nodded into his chest, she breathed in his scent. That, more than anything, calmed her.

"About Tim?"

Again, the silent acknowledgment.

"I'm sorry."

"I hadn't dreamed about him in years. Lately...since you...the dreams have come back." He waited. "I never talked about this, but you've gotten me to. It's not buried anymore."

"Some still is. Maybe that's what's trying to come out in the dreams."

Shaking her head, she burrowed into him. "I know you want to know more. But I can only talk about it a little at a time."

He brushed back her hair and continued to rub her arm. "Honey, maybe it would help to get it all out."

Oh, God, she didn't want the pain. Like a patient denying an illness, it was easier to ignore reality.

"If you can't tell me about it, you could go talk to Reed."

She drew back. "No. I've found a way to cope."

"By keeping it in. Cutting yourself off."

She settled into him. "It worked until I met you."

He kissed her hair.

"Please let it rest awhile. No more revelations now." Beth knew it wasn't enough. He'd wanted to know how Tim had died, but she couldn't tell him.

Finally he said, "All right, but I don't think this is the best decision." And the tension in his body let her know he wasn't happy. What if she could never tell him?

She drew away to look at him. "Dylan, what if I can *never* share everything with you?"

Moonlight bathed him in a golden halo, but his face was shadowed with hurt. "You will."

"But what if I can't?"

"Beth, we'll work it out. Trust me."

With memories of Tim's death haunting the fringes of her consciousness, she willed herself to trust him. "All right."

He hugged her, slid down into the blankets and, both their heads on one pillow, they fell asleep.

HE CASHED IN on that trust Monday afternoon. She should have known he wouldn't wait long. She was at her desk when he poked his head in the door. "Aren't you coming?"

"Where?"

"To the meeting about the Immaculate Conception Christmas party."

Her heart began to hammer in her chest. "Dylan, I told you I don't take part in that."

"Yes, but I thought this year, you'd...well, I guess I just assumed some things would change now."

She stared at him bleakly.

He stepped inside, closed the door, leaned against it and fixed her with a stare that told her he would not be put off. "You don't celebrate holidays."

She shook her head.

"Why?"

She could feel the color drain from her face. Her hands trembled.

"Listen, I know I said we'd take it slow. But this isn't something we can wait on. Thanksgiving's a week from Thursday."

As an excuse to look away, she glanced at her calendar. "I know."

"We'll be spending the day together, won't we?"

"No. I work at the ambulance company on holidays."

"Not on this one, Beth."

There it was again, his demands. His unshakable belief that he could change everything. She raised her chin. "Yes, Dylan, I *am* working on this one. I've already signed up. No one else wants to work holidays." At his implacable glare, she added, "I don't have anywhere to go, anyway."

"You do now. My father and I are invited to the Cordaros'. Come with us."

She shook her head.

"Look, I'm trying not to push you, but I can't bear the thought of you working through Thanksgiving and Christmas."

Agitated, she stood. He was steamrolling right over her objections. He was expecting too much. "I'm working, Dylan. And I'm not doing the Immaculate Conception party. You'll have to accept that."

He stepped toward her and broke his promise not to touch her at work. With his trademark tenderness, he brushed his knuckles down her cheek. "Let me replace the old memories with new ones, baby."

"I'm trying. But you ask too much."

"I'd never ask more than you could give."

She drew back from his mesmerizing presence. "You are now. I can't do it."

DYLAN POUNDED the computer, taking out his frustrations on the poor machine in Reed's office. The EMS computer was down, so he'd sought out another and ended up at Reed's. For the past week, since Beth had refused his invitation to spend Thanksgiving with him, it was hard to work at his own desk, anyway.

He typed, *When was the first female career firefighter hired in the U.S.?* and followed it with the answer—1976. Each week, he made out a separate copy with the answers in case…in case something happened to him. Somehow, now, the idea disturbed him, whereas before it had always been a fact of life.

Of the 260,000 firefighters nationwide, how many are female? Three percent.

Who were Roxanne Bercik, Fleur Lombard and Kristine Meyer? They were the first female fire chief, the first female firefighter to die in Britain and the CEO of the International Society of Fire Service Instructors.

And last, *What qualities can make women better firefighters and EMS personnel than men?* He typed the answer. Women are usually smaller and can get in tight places, and they're more flexible; they are also the most stubborn, unyielding, hardheaded, frustrating…. Whoops, he'd gotten carried away.

Deleting the personal remarks, he reread this week's trivia and printed a copy with the answers and one without. He stood as Reed entered his office. "Done yet?"

"Yeah, I just finished."

"Can I get a sneak preview?"

Dylan handed Reed the list without the answers. After a moment, Reed chuckled. "All women questions?"

Distracted, Dylan nodded.

"Speaking of women…"

Shit, he was so obvious. "I've got to post the questions." Dylan strode past his friend and headed out of the office. "Thanks for letting me use your computer."

He stopped when he heard Reed say, "I might be able to help out with Beth, O'Roarke."

Dylan turned and leaned against the closed door. "It's that obvious?"

"It was at Tom's retirement party." Reed smiled his fatherly, I'm-gonna-help-you grin. "You two were shooting sparks off each other so bad I'm surprised the tablecloth didn't catch on fire. These past two weeks, it's been more like simmering embers."

Resigned, Dylan sauntered over to a chair and fell into it. "She doesn't want anybody to know about us, though she did tell Francey and Chelsea."

"What's there to know?"

"Want the prurient details, counselor?"

Reed arched a brow.

"I'm sorry. Hell, I don't even know how to describe what's going on between us. And there's a lot I can't say because she told me in confidence."

"How do you feel about her?"

"The sixty-four-thousand-dollar question."

Reed scowled, as if something just occurred to him. "Look, Dylan, Beth may appear tough, but she's not. I've worried about her for years. If this is just another fling for you, maybe you should think twice about it."

"It's not like that."

"How is it, then?"

"I...care about her. She's the one who's holding back."

"Really?"

"Funny, isn't it? The tables are finally turned on Dylan O'Roarke."

"No, I don't find it funny. What are you going to do about it?"

"What *should* I do?"

"Is she worth waiting for?"

That he could answer. "No doubt in my mind."

"Then don't push her. Let her take her time. My guess is she's scared to death."

Dylan pointed a cocked-gun finger at Reed. "Give that man a cigar."

"WHAT ABOUT CLEARY?" Ben Cordaro rubbed his eyes as he sat behind his desk the night before Thanksgiving to confer about a recruit profile.

Reed said, "Testing indicated all systems go. She's got a good grip on the role of a firefighter at the station and on the fire ground."

They'd gathered for psychological and physical evaluation of the recruits. Dylan asked, "How's her fitness?"

Beth answered. "Just about there. By graduation, she'll be top notch."

Dylan's warm look of approval made Beth's insides contract. "You did a good job, Winters."

"Thanks, O'Roarke."

After they filled out the forms on Cleary, Ben glanced at his watch. "Diana's picking me up in half an hour. We're due at Ma and Pa's. Let's finish up."

"Preparing for Thanksgiving dinner?" Reed asked.

Ben nodded. "Yeah. We've got a houseful coming tomorrow."

Dylan stilled. Beth caught the slight tensing of his body, invisible to anyone who didn't know that body the way she did.

"Sure you won't change your mind and join us, Reed?"

Beth watched Reed struggle to maintain his bland expression. "No, thanks, I have other plans."

A kindred spirit, she thought. Isolated in his own way.

"You, too, Beth." Ben smiled. "You won't take Francey up on her offer?"

Dylan's head snapped up. "Offer?"

"Francey asked both Beth and Chelsea to come for Thanksgiving at Pa's. Chelsea's going to her sister's, and Beth…" He turned to her. "Ambulance work, right?"

Avoiding Dylan's eyes, she nodded.

"I guess you and your father, and of course Jake, are the

only two outside of the family, Dylan.'' Ben glanced at the folder. "Barnette's last.''

Reed scowled at the forms as he spoke. "Some funny reactions on his testing.''

"Like?''

Reed explained Hoyt Barnette's unusual responses to the goal-oriented questions. "He appeared gung ho, initially.''

"Maybe a little too gung ho.'' Dylan lazed in his chair. "I wonder sometimes about that type of firefighter.''

As they discussed Barnette, Beth's mind wandered. She and Dylan had slept together every night since Veteran's Day. Sometimes they'd made love, sometimes they hadn't. Would she stay with him tonight even though she had to be at the ambulance at six in the morning? After she had refused to spend Thanksgiving with him, would he even want her to? She knew she'd disappointed him.

Coward, an inner voice accused. *He didn't ask for that much.*

Oh, but he did.

You're still a coward.

"Dinner's at five, but come early. Francey's making hors d'oeuvres.''

"Francey's cooking something?'' Dylan sounded shocked. "I don't believe it.''

As they all rose and crossed to the door, Ben chuckled. "Marriage has really domesticated her.'' He clapped Dylan on the shoulder. "Time you thought about settling down yourself, boy.''

As they exited the office, Dylan walked ahead of her with Ben, and Beth fell behind next to Reed. Casually, Reed said, "So you're working tomorrow?''

Beth sighed in spite of herself.

"Come on in here a minute,'' he suggested when they reached his office.

Looking into his kind brown eyes, Beth felt a little more

ice around her heart melt. Like frostbite warming up, it was painful—and she knew, if she allowed it to continue, the pain would get worse. Still, she said, "All right."

She stepped inside, and Reed closed the door. Once again Beth was engulfed in the comfort of his office. She wandered to the window and looked out on the parking lot. Huge snowflakes swirled to the ground. For a moment she pressed her forehead to the glass. It was cold. At only six o'clock, it was already dark. Rockford winter was on its way.

"I'd like to help." Reed's voice matched the concern in his expression.

She pivoted to face him. "Help?"

"I don't like holidays much, either, Beth."

"I told you once I don't talk about this."

"I know, and I'd respect that if it wasn't for Dylan."

Her eyes narrowed. "O'Roarke came to you about me?"

"No, I approached him about you."

"Why?"

"Because things between you two have changed. Because I see a different kind of fire now in both your eyes when you look at each other." He paused, then added, "Because I care."

"You and Dylan have become friends."

"I'd like to be your friend, too, Beth."

"We've known each other since you came here years ago, Reed."

"Have we?"

"You mean because I don't reveal much about myself."

"Nor do I."

"No, you don't." She cocked her head. "Why is that?"

"I've got my own private demons to fight."

For the first time since she'd known him, Beth saw an old and painful weariness etched into Reed Macauley's face. "Sometimes too private," he added.

"What do you mean?"

"Storing unshared grief is like wearing lead shoes. After you walk around in them awhile, you don't even realize how heavy they are, how they weigh you down, hold you back."

She stared at him blankly.

"Let him in, Beth. It could mean true joy for you."

More ice was chipped away, threatening the numbness that fit her like an old slipper. "I'm not sure I can risk it again, Reed."

He nodded. "I know the feeling. But ultimately, Dylan won't settle for less."

"No, he won't." Beth crossed to the door. When she reached it, Reed called after her.

Briefly she hesitated, then turned to face him.

"Tomorrow, on Thanksgiving, you've got O'Roarke to be thankful for."

"*Now.*" The word and what it meant were wrenched from her.

Reed told her bleakly, "All any of us have is *now.*"

CHAPTER TWELVE

"COME ON, FRANCEY, baby. You can do better than that."
Nicky Cordaro egged his sister on—in the guise of encouraging her—as she faced Jake Scarlatta across the table on Thanksgiving day. Francey and Jake were perched on opposite dining-room chairs, arms raised at right angles, palms interlocked, elbows digging into Grace Cordaro's heirloom, which had been cleared for their traditional arm wrestling contest. They looked incongruous in their holiday finery—a gorgeous violet calf-length dress for Francey and a sharp gray cotton sweater and matching pants for Jake. Dylan, too, had dressed up, in a blue silk shirt Beth had said made his eyes look like sapphires.

"She's doing her best," Jake said dryly. "What can you expect from a girl?" To belie his words, sweat had beaded on his brow as he struggled to force her arm down.

A vein throbbed in Francey's neck. "Shut up, Scarlatta. Distracting me won't help."

Gus Cordaro smiled at them. "Ah, just like the good old days."

Dylan noticed the fleeting shadows of sadness on Diana Cordaro's face. Watching their children from the doorway, she leaned into her husband and he kissed her hair. She'd missed her kids growing up. It must be hard to be faced with that—especially on a holiday.

I don't celebrate holidays. Dylan pushed thoughts of Beth away. As a firefighter, he'd gotten damn good at keeping images out of his head.

With a renewed burst of adrenaline, Francey edged Jake's arm back an inch. Their clasped hands vibrated.

"Come on, kiddo, do it." Francey's brother Tony, who was walking his cranky eleven-month-old son, Ian, back and forth, put in his encouragement.

Francey's forearm muscles bulged.

Ben said, "Hold on twenty more seconds, honey, and you beat your record."

Despite his funk, Dylan smiled at them. Jake and Francey's arm wrestling was an ongoing contest that Francey was determined to win someday.

Jake put on the last push.

Ben counted aloud. "Fifteen…ten…five…okay, that's it."

Slowly, Jake's arm took hers down.

"Ten seconds longer, France," her father said.

Alex, who'd been lounging near the sidebar, crossed to his wife. "You're getting better, sweetheart." He kissed her nose.

The look she gave him—part sexy, part unadulterated love—made Dylan's breath catch. He wanted that kind of devotion.

From Beth.

"Well, at least I lasted ten seconds more on you." She scowled, marring her perfect brow. "Only five on Chelsea, though. I bet she could beat you."

"Not a chance."

The family laughed.

Restless, Dylan rose from the table and headed to the kitchen for a beer. Standing by the window, he watched the snow fall in heavy flakes around the bare trees. He checked the clock. Three. He didn't know how late she was working. Or even where she was. He wondered—worried—if the roads were slippery.

She hadn't come to him last night. She'd stayed at the academy to talk to Reed, and Dylan assumed she'd follow him home when she was done. She hadn't. He'd almost called her several times, but ultimately he'd gone to bed alone, wondering what was going to happen to them. He knew he was pushing her, but he simply couldn't settle for what she was offering.

Sick of covering the same ground, Dylan wandered to the back of the house, where Ben and Gus had winterized a huge enclosed porch. With a glowing wood stove in the corner, warm cedar paneling and windows highlighting the falling snow, the scene was Courier and Ives perfect.

Winter used to be my favorite time of year. It was so beautiful on the lake.

Damn.

He set his beer on the table and noticed a photo album there. *Wedding.* Francey had given one to all the attendants and her grandparents. Against his better judgment, he sat down and opened the book full of memories. The photos were blown up—

Francey and Alex, arms linked, smiling as if nothing could ever hurt them again.

Ben and Diana, their expressions revealing a deep and unshakable love that had lasted through years of separation.

Gus and Grace. They'd just celebrated their fifty-fifth anniversary.

Tony and Erin.

Everybody's a couple, Dylan thought. Except him. Something that had been just fine before now.

He turned the page…and there she was.

Beth wasn't fond of getting her picture taken. But the photographer had gotten a couple good shots of her. One photo caught her on the beach, splashing in the water. Pretty whimsical for Lizzie Borden. Another showed her standing next to Francey on the pier. God, that sarong made his mouth water. How had he ever thought her looks were ordinary? The last picture captured her face in a closeup. Smiling, he traced his thumb over the delicate arch of her brow, that full bottom lip. He smoothed his fingertip over a few freckles which had disappeared since then.

A shadow fell over the book, and he glanced up.

Jake stared at the open page. "Want to talk about it?"

Dylan sighed. "Not much to say."

"Something's going on between you two."

Since Beth had confided in Chelsea and Francey, Dylan felt comfortable telling Jake. "Yeah."

Taking a seat across from him, Jake stretched out his legs on a worn hassock. "She looks at you like Diana looks at Ben."

Dylan's head snapped up. "Does she?"

"And you look at her the way Ben looks at Diana. You got it bad, buddy."

Running a restless hand through his hair, Dylan said, "Afraid so." He stared hard at Jake. Since his best friend Danny's fall from grace, Jake had been more introverted than ever. He'd always reminded Dylan of John Wayne in *The Quiet Man.* "Can I ask you something?"

"Sure."

"If you had to do it all over, would you marry Nancy again? Even though the relationship didn't work?"

"It didn't work because I cut her out after Danny left town."

"Why did you?"

Jake shook his head. "Danny and I had done everything together—high school football, the academy, in each other's weddings, same crew in the RFD. Hell, our kids, Jessica and Derek were born only two months apart eighteen years ago. When Danny came unglued, I didn't know how to handle it."

"You talk to anybody about it?"

"Nah. We didn't have a Reed Macauley in the fire department then. I kept it all inside.'' He stared at Dylan. ''It's still there, I guess.''

''It's hard for me to understand keeping to yourself so much.''

''Like Beth.''

Dylan nodded.

''At least I had Jessie. She forced me to communicate more than I would have.'' Jake watched him intently.

The doorbell sounded. Dylan asked, ''Who else is coming?''

Jake rose. ''It's probably Jessica. She was going to try to get away from Nancy's for dinner here.'' Looking at the album, Jake playfully punched Dylan's arm. ''Come on out with me. We'll get Jess and the family and play some poker before we eat.''

Stop being maudlin, Grandma Katie would say. *There's no point in wishing things were different. See where you are and what you can do with that.* He also remembered Grandma Katie's resolution to live life to the fullest after his grandpa died. She'd played bridge, continued to read and even joined a widows' square dancing group. Her example was good for him. Dylan closed the album and stood, thinking, *Okay Grandma, you win.* Following Jake down the hallway, he thought about where he was and made a list of what he had to be thankful for. He reached the living room just as he tallied up health, good friends and a job he loved as a very good place to be.

Ben, Diana, Alex, Grace and Gus all surrounded Francey, who stepped back from a big hug with their just-arrived guest. Dylan knew Francey and Jessica were close.

But when Francey moved aside, he saw it wasn't Jake's daughter.

It was Beth.

THE LOOK on Dylan's face when he spotted her in the entryway was almost enough to make Beth turn tail and run like a rookie panicking at his first fire.

But she didn't. Because the emotion revealed there only matched what she felt for him. For better or for worse, she was ready to pursue it—totally.

In a flurry her coat was taken and she was ushered into the living room; someone stuck a glass of Chardonnay in her hand. Then Jake's daughter arrived. All the while, Dylan tracked her with his gaze. All he'd said was, "Hello, Winters," but he'd watched her every move.

When they conned him into playing cards, she took the opportunity to devour the sight of him. He looked tired. He probably hadn't slept well. In her usual cowardly manner, she'd avoided him—and any pressure he might put on her—by going home last night. She'd lain in her bed and watched her fish and thought about Reed's words. In the middle of the night, when she awoke from the nightmares, she'd gotten out her dolls and placed them on the mattress. They weren't Dylan's arms, but they helped.

"Any action today, Beth, on the ambulance?" Ben asked as he shuffled the cards.

"We had a save."

Dylan looked up sharply at the slang for rescuing someone that everybody thought was a goner. "Really?"

"An old woman took a bad tumble down the stairs. We managed to get her to Emergency in time, but we had to do some fancy footwork."

Jessica looked up from her cards. "Your job must be so rewarding."

"It is," Beth said. But not rewarding enough to stay for another shift today. When hers had ended at two and they'd asked her to sign on for a second round, she'd opened her mouth to say yes. But then she remembered the woman who almost died, and she thought about dying herself—which hadn't scared her since before Tim and Janey's deaths. Today, the thought frightened her. So she'd gone home, changed into the green blouse Dylan had seemed to like and a short black skirt, and shown up at the Cordaros without phoning.

"Dinner's in half an hour," Diana called from the kitchen.

"Game's over, anyway," Gus said. "I got a royal flush."

Amidst the groans, the table was cleared and set for the meal. Since Beth had been told there was nothing she could do, she watched the activity from the sidelines. After a few moments she saw Dylan head for the stairs, probably to the bathroom.

Hmm.

When she was sure no one was watching, she followed him.

The john was at the end of the long second-floor hall. She could hear him inside. Leaning against the wall, arms closed over her chest, she waited until he opened the door.

He acted startled to see her.

For about two seconds. Then he dragged her inside, slammed the door and locked it. "I'm goin' crazy not being able to touch you."

He backed her against the wood panels, framed her face with his hands and devoured her mouth. Her response was gratifying.

Then he raised his head and, with shaky fingers, unbuttoned the green blouse. Pulling down her bra, he suckled her voraciously.

She groaned—and then started to giggle.

"What's so funny?" he asked, sliding his hand up and down her stockinged thigh.

"You are. For weeks you've been ragging on me for more than sex. Now you're like an animal."

He looked at her, and what she saw in his eyes leveled her. "This is what commitment does to me," he said simply.

Swallowing hard, she drew his head down and whispered against his lips, "To me, too."

Minutes later, Francey knocked on the door. "Ah, Dylan...or whoever, dinner's ready."

Dylan called out, "Enjoy it, France."

Beth giggled again.

They were barely under control when they came downstairs, Dylan first, then Beth a few moments after. No one commented that they were absent together or seemed to notice the telltale flush on both their faces. But someone had seated them next to each other.

After everyone took a place at the table, Beth felt a second of panic when she realized where she was—at Thanksgiving dinner—and what she was doing. She hadn't sat down to a holiday meal since she was twenty years old. Half a lifetime. Dylan's hand crept to her knee. Under the table, she entwined her fingers with his as Ben raised his glass and grasped Diana's hand.

"I want to make the toast. Happy Thanksgiving to everyone, and today, I'd like us all to be thankful for new beginnings."

He clinked his glass with Diana's.

Francey clinked hers with Alex's.

Dylan turned and clinked his glass with Beth's, then echoed Ben's sentiments. "To new beginnings."

ON THE FOLLOWING Saturday morning, Dylan lazed in Beth's bed, clothed only in navy sweatpants, one of the fish books spread open on his lap. Taking her concession about Thanksgiving to mean real commitment, he'd never been happier. He just hoped he could keep it light enough to let her get used to the idea and not spook her.

"Listen to this," he said with a marked note of mischief in his voice.

Beth was ironing her uniforms. Dressed only in a flannel

shirt he'd left at her house along with some other clothes, she looked adorable. "I can't wait," she said dryly.

"The mating habits of your fish are interesting. Take the betta. The male courts the female with a graceful dance. If she's interested, the female folds her fins. He nibbles at her scales and may even bite her."

"Typical." She shook her head as she passed him to hang up a shirt.

When she got close enough, he grabbed her arm and nipped the flesh. "Wanna let me bite your fins, baby?"

She swatted his hand away, but chuckled all the same.

Dylan continued to read, and she began to press her trousers. "When he knows he's got her, the male betta builds a nest for the eggs, leads her under there, entwines himself around her and turns her on her back."

"Sounds familiar."

"Hush. The angelfish is more fascinating. In order to entice the female, certain species of the male change colors. Then he makes excited swimming movements. The courtship takes ten to twenty minutes."

"Not enough foreplay," Beth said. Good, he thought. She was getting into this.

"The fairy basset's the best. At dusk the male displays to a nearby female." Dylan lifted each arm and took turns flexing a muscle. "Think that's displaying?"

Giving him a sideways glance, she said, "I think you've lost your mind."

Dylan read on. "His dorsal fin and spines stand upright... hey, sort of like an erection—"

"You're making that up, O'Roarke."

"Honest to God, it's right here. Anyway, this fish gets his spines and fins up and swims backward and forward to show off his body. Then he rubs against the chosen female's belly and—"

"Stop, this is nuts."

"Okay, I'll go on to their spawning habits." He searched the page. "Here it is. The female betta releases her eggs, then the male fertilizes them. When they're done, he kicks out the female because she may eat them. He guards the nest until the eggs hatch."

When she didn't comment, he continued, "The male clown fish also guard the eggs and often care for the young until they reach sexual maturity, when they leave to find their own anemone."

Still, she didn't say anything.

"Beth? Is something wrong?"

"No, go ahead, I'm listening."

His brow furrowed. "Here it is again. When the female angelfish lays the eggs, the male tirelessly guards them—fans water across them, defends them against big fish." Dylan put the book down. "This whole fish kingdom is really into male nurturing. It kind of appeals to me."

He noticed then that she'd gone perfectly still.

"What's the matter, honey?"

She switched off the iron, crossed to the bed and sat down facing him. Her eyes were huge and unhappy. "Dylan, do you want kids?"

"Yeah, of course. Don't you?"

"No. I'm never going to have children."

He opened his mouth to speak, but shut it when a thought hit him. Finally he said, "*Can* you have them?"

"Well, I'm forty, so it's late to conceive. But I'm physically capable." Briefly her eyes darted away, then returned to his. "But I never will, because emotionally I couldn't risk the loss. So if taking this any further—" she made a gesture that included the bed, her room, him and her "—is dependent on having kids…maybe you should reconsider seeing me."

"Beth, this isn't something that has to be decided now."

"It's already been decided."

"You really mean this, don't you?"

"More than I've ever meant anything. And don't think I'll give in on it like I did on Thanksgiving. This is nonnegotiable."

His back stiffened. "Thanks for informing me."

"I just don't want you to have any false expectations or get your hopes up."

That made him mad. "You're something else, you know that?"

"What do you mean?"

"What do *you* think *this*—" he made the same sweeping motion with his hand as she had "—is all about?"

She stared at him blankly. A vein pulsed in her neck.

"I already have expectations and high hopes." When she remained silent, he said, "I love you, damn it."

Still, no response.

"You don't feel the same way about me, do you?" he asked tightly.

She pinned him with an angry glare and said between clenched teeth, "Yes, as a matter of fact I do."

His heart rate went into arrhythmia. He thought it might explode with joy. He hadn't known how much he needed to hear that. When he collected himself, his mouth quirked. "Don't be so mushy about it, Winters."

Though her smile was sad, she did bestow it on him. Inching over on the mattress, she looped her arms around his neck. "I love you, Dylan. More than I thought I could love anyone again."

Holding on to her waist, he swallowed hard.

Against his lips she whispered, "Your declaration wasn't exactly all hearts and flowers, either."

He whispered back, "I've never said those words to a woman before. I love you, Lizzie. So much it makes me crazy."

She touched her forehead to his. "We *are* crazy. There's too much against us."

"We can compromise. If you really won't have kids because you can't handle the risk of losing them—like you've lost all the others in your family—I'll accept that. *If* you promise to give me everything else."

She waited a very long time. Which was all right with him because he wanted her to be sure. "I can do that, eventually. Just don't rush me, okay?"

"Okay." He held her a moment longer, then eased her back to the bed. "Now, fold up your fins and let me rub my spines against your belly."

HOYT BARNETTE smiled as two of his favorite instructors, O'Roarke and Scarlatta, told the recruits about night evolutions.

From his perch on a desk off to the side, Lieutenant O'Roarke joked. "You're gonna get your first taste of night fires, kiddies. Get ready for it."

Scarlatta continued, "It's a whole new ball game, ladies and gentlemen. The rules change in the dark."

Hoyt couldn't wait to get into that burning building at night and show his stuff. He'd perform better than he had in those damn practicals if it killed him. He couldn't believe he'd messed up a week ago when the recruits were finally asked to demonstrate what they knew. Faced with a phony patient to assess, he'd choked.

His recriminations were interrupted by Instructor Winters skidding into the doorway, her face red, breathing fast. "There's been an accident out front. Ben was pulling in when a vehicle veered off Scottsdale Road and hit the academy sign. Quint/Midi Twelve's on its way, but Ben wants all certified medical personnel out there." She threw Lieutenant O'Roarke his jacket and shoved her arms into hers, momentarily setting down the ever-present ALS bag. "Let's go."

O'Roarke was out the door in a flash. Lieutenant Scarlatta

stared at the recruits. "All right, grab your coats. But don't interfere. You might as well see this firsthand."

Blustery late-November wind hit Hoyt in the face as they exited the front door; they crossed the grass to about ten feet back from the car. Hoyt huddled next to the other recruits and watched the scene. Man, this was great. This was what it was all about.

The late-model station wagon had crashed head-on into the school sign. The rear of the vehicle was intact, indicating the gas tank was safe, but the front was crunched metal and shredded tires; the roof was partly concave. The car rested precariously at an angle on the passenger side. The elderly seat-belted driver was pinned by the activated air bag.

Battalion Chief Cordaro stood on the left side of the vehicle; Winters hovered behind him, as did O'Roarke and Scarlatta. "The door's jammed," Cordaro said, "and the car's at a bad angle. Gas tank is safe, but the position isn't. It could tip over at any time. Stay back, everybody." He circled the car to assess the situation.

"I hear moans." O'Roarke stepped closer to the car. "Driver's conscious." In gloves, but no mask or goggles—Winters would get him for that, Hoyt thought—he reached through the broken glass of the window. "Slow pulse. She's having trouble breathing. She needs immediate intervention."

Sirens sounded, still far away. Stabilizing and extrication equipment would arrive, but would it be in time? Hoyt realized this must be what it felt like to make life-and-death decisions.

TREVOR TULLY watched with excitement as Winters crossed to the end of the grass and craned her neck to peer down the road. "The trucks are coming." She'd cupped her hands around her mouth to yell. "They'll be here in seconds."

Trevor's excitement turned to horror as O'Roarke yelled,

"We don't have seconds," reached for the back left door and pulled it open. The car shimmied with his action.

Cordaro called from the other side, "O'Roarke, what the hell are you doing? The car's gonna—"

Trevor couldn't believe his eyes. O'Roarke climbed in the back seat.

"Dylan, don't!" The shout came from Winters as she raced from the road.

Trevor shivered and rubbed his hands together. "Damn, why'd he do that? They told us a thousand times never to touch a vehicle unless it's been stabilized."

Ace Durwin huddled next to him. "He felt the pulse and knew the victim was ready to buy it. He'll stabilize her head with his hands and do a jaw-thrust maneuver to keep her airway open."

"A calculated risk," Wanikya put in.

"That could very well get him killed." Durwin again.

"Killed?" Trevor blanched.

"The car's in bad shape. The roof looks like it could cave. If it does, O'Roarke could be hurt bad. Or he could be trapped. And if the gas tank's affected when the car shifts…"

Cordaro shouted to everyone to stay back; Scarlatta made sure no one was close to the car. Instructor Winters stood by, cool and calm, her face devoid of emotion.

Trevor felt sick inside. O'Roarke was a great guy. Jeez, no one had ever been as nice to him as the lieutenant. If something happened to him… Trevor felt like bawling and puking at the same time.

Sirens sounded, closer now.

Please, God, let help get here. Let him be all right.

CONNIE CLEARY watched Quint/Midi Twelve arrive and assess the scene. As the captain in charge spoke quickly to Battalion Chief Cordaro, Connie moved around the car. Ms.

Winters stepped back as the accident team set up their equipment.

Hesitantly Connie crept up behind her instructor. Everyone thought Ms. Winters was a cold fish, standing there unaffected by the danger Lieutenant O'Roarke was in. The guys were making comments about the Ice Lady. But Connie suspected something different.

As Quint/Midi Twelve took the few necessary minutes to stabilize the vehicle, the earsplitting roar of the generator rent the air. Ms. Winters flinched. Her face was white, her hands shaking. The woman didn't like any show of affection, Connie knew that. Still, she raised her hand and clasped Ms. Winters's shoulder. The instructor turned, surprised by the contact. When Connie witnessed the stark terror in her mentor's eyes, she squeezed her shoulder. Beth Winters was hurting. She looked at Connie with undiluted fear; then she turned back to the scene.

Connie didn't say anything; she left her hand where it was and watched the firefighters set up the well-known extrication tool, the Jaws of Life. In seconds, the men inserted the tool in the jamb in the driver's side and pried open the door. With another tool—a ram—they jimmied the roof. The ambulance crew behind the two firefighters handed the rescuers a neck brace and readied the backboard. Connie only half watched as they secured the patient, eased her out and settled her onto a stretcher. O'Roarke was still in the back seat. Ms. Winters trembled all over.

Connie smiled as a cheer went up from the recruits. The victim was alive. Thank God.

Everyone stilled when the car shifted. The roof caved in right above the lieutenant.

Instructor Winters moaned and clapped a hand to her mouth in horror. Connie blinked back tears. Lieutenant O'Roarke was trapped inside.

"GET HIM out of there!" Ace Durwin said under his breath. The other recruits, except Cleary, remained rooted to the ground. The cold November wind whipped around them as they battled their emotions.

Once the elderly patient had been wheeled away, they all held their breath. The expert firefighters stabilized the station wagon with more chocks, then one guy ducked his upper body into the back seat.

"I need the smallest ram," he called out.

A burly firefighter handed it to him.

Ace held his breath as precious seconds ticked by. Finally, the firefighter eased his head and torso out of the car and backed up; his hands were under O'Roarke's armpits as he dragged the lieutenant out and onto the ground. At first Ace wondered why the team hadn't braced him like the victim. *Please, don't let him be dead.*

Praying like he'd never prayed before, Ace watched as the firefighters formed a wall around their brother, making it impossible to see what was happening.

Then Ben Cordaro shouted, "He's okay."

Instructor Winters was frozen. The firefighters shifted, and Ace could finally see.

O'Roarke was sitting up on a blanket. His sleeve was ragged; a bruise darkened and swelled the side of his face. Several small cuts bled minimally.

Cordaro knelt, said something to O'Roarke, then stood and turned away. His hands were fisted and his jaw was tense. In a booming battalion chief voice, Cordaro called over his shoulder, "Beth, get him inside and fix him up. Then let me at him. I'll have his ass for this."

Ace looked at the instructor.

Or to where she'd been standing. He scanned the area.

Beth Winters was gone.

CHAPTER THIRTEEN

"OF ALL THE RECKLESS, unprofessional things you've done, this takes the cake." Ben Cordaro paced his office, his voice growing louder with each word, his face redder; he was like an erupting volcano. Dylan had never seen him explode before. "Not only did you endanger your safety, but you set an unforgivably bad example for the recruits." Ben fumed silently for a moment, then threw a book on his desk and kicked the wastebasket.

Sitting on a chair, Dylan stared at the floor and didn't answer. He tried to ignore the pounding in his head and the throb in his shoulder—along with the ache in his heart.

Which made him glance at the clock.

"Am I keeping you from something?" Ben asked tightly. "A hot date who'll coddle you and tell you what a hero you are?"

Dylan shook his head. He was worried about Beth, who, he'd been told by Jake, had left the accident scene, and the academy, as soon as she learned he was all right. He was sure he couldn't begin to fathom the terror she must have felt those few minutes he was trapped in the vehicle.

I lost people I loved.... Yes, Tim died....

Ben rounded on Dylan. "I asked you a question, Lieutenant O'Roarke."

Woozy, Dylan leaned back in the chair and tried to stem the wave of dizziness. "No, I don't have a date. I'm just worried—"

A knock on the door interrupted him.

"Come in!" Ben barked.

Reed Macauley entered the battalion chief's office, looking somber and intent. He reminded Dylan of a doctor with bad news. "You need to lower your voice, Ben. I could hear you down the hall."

"Good. I want everybody in the place to know he's getting his ass kicked."

Reed scowled and leaned back on his heels.

"And don't you dare take his side."

Raising an eyebrow, Reed said quietly, "I wasn't about to. I'm just as angry at him as you are."

Ben faced Dylan again. "Beth Winters was right about you."

Bull's-eye. She was right. He was wrong. He knew it now. He just wanted to get to her to tell her. "Yes, she was."

Cordaro's brow furrowed, and he gave Dylan a sideways glance. "You won't get off that easily. I'll have your card for this."

"Rightfully so."

"May I make a suggestion?" Reed's voice was calm.

Ben took a deep breath, stuck his hands in his pockets and nodded.

"Report his actions to the brass. But before you do anything irrevocable, require O'Roarke to meet with me for an undetermined duration to work on the *problem* he has with his hero complex."

"They won't go for it this time."

"Cite his honors. The chief isn't going to do anything too drastic to him after all that publicity in New York a couple of months ago. Unless you force the issue."

Ben shook his head. "I don't know."

"At least wait for a report from me before you make any decisions."

Ben raked a hand through his hair. "I don't know, Reed," he said again.

Reed crossed to Ben and studied him. "Maybe you're too involved to be objective. My guess is you're reacting out of the fear you felt for his safety. You obviously care about him like a son, Ben."

Exasperated, Ben said, "You're probably right. Much to my dismay." He scowled at Dylan. "God help the woman who loves him."

Well, that did it. Drove the stake all the way into Dylan's heart. She *had* been right. He was a powder keg, emotionally unstable, a jerk, a real asshole—

"Dylan, come on. You're about to keel over."

He looked up. Reed stood by the chair, staring down at him. Apparently he'd closed his eyes. "Come on?"

"I'm driving you home."

"But I have to—"

"Damn it, O'Roarke, do as you're told and *shut up!*" Reed had never once lost it with anybody, as far as Dylan knew. Man, he was really in deep shit.

They left Ben without another word, retrieved Reed's leather coat and headed for the parking lot. The temperature had dropped considerably, and Dylan shivered despite his heavy jacket. Feeling the way he had when the ChemLabs explosion knocked him across the yard last summer, he swayed on his feet as Reed unlocked the Bronco's doors.

"You okay?" Reed asked.

"What do you think?"

Once inside, he lay back against the seat and closed his eyes again. All he could see was the fleeting glance he'd gotten of Beth's face when the firefighters around him had briefly parted. God, what had he done?

"I need directions to your house." Reed started the car.

"I want to go to Beth's."

Shifting sideways in the front seat, Reed shook his head. "Dylan, you can't do this to her repeatedly. You know how she feels about loss."

"I know. I've got to tell her, though, make her understand what I've finally learned."

For a long moment Reed studied him; then, obviously convinced, he put the car in gear and drove to Beth's. They didn't talk. Dylan's bruised and battered body needed to garner its strength. He guessed he was in for a real battle.

"We're here."

Dylan must have dozed off. He opened his eyes to see they'd arrived at Beth's condo. It was dark, but he could see her car was parked in its space. He glanced at the house. A light shone from the front bedroom window.

"She's probably looking at her fish."

"Her fish?"

"She has two big aquariums. She watches them when she's upset. I think they calm her. Make her feel secure."

"It's going to take more than fish to soothe her tonight."

Dylan faced Reed. "I know. I'll do whatever I have to now."

"You love her, don't you."

"Yes."

Reed surveyed the house. "Want me to come in? It might be rough."

"No. I need to be alone with her."

Reed reached into his pocket, ferreted out his wallet and extracted a card from it. He wrote on the back. "That's my business card, but I put my home phone number on it. I'm heading there now. Call me if you need me. I'll be in all night."

Dylan nodded and reached for the door handle.

"Good luck."

"Thanks." Again the bracing air smacked him in the face, making his head thrum. He felt shaky and nauseated, as if he'd swallowed smoke, but he wasn't sure it was the result of his injuries.

Approaching the door, he hesitated. Instead of ringing the

bell—he was afraid she'd ignore it—he decided to use the key she'd given him. Just before he stepped inside, he turned to see Reed wave from the car and pull away.

The condo was eerily silent. The last few times he'd been here, they'd played oldies CDs and he'd even gotten her to dance with him. She'd come so far, and he'd ruined it by... He clenched his fist, then winced at the pain. God, he'd really blown it.

In the hallway he removed his wet boots, then noticed the mud on his uniform and the torn sleeve of his jacket. He discarded the jacket, wishing he'd cleaned up before coming over. Jake had patched his cuts and checked him out, but Dylan knew he must look like hell.

Slowly he ascended the stairs. His heart hammered in his chest. For the first time in his life, Dylan feared he wouldn't be able to get what he wanted. What he needed to live the rest of his life.

He could practically see Grandma Katie in front of him, her hair pulled into a bun. She was sixty-five and it was completely white then. He'd wanted to go to college, be the first O'Roarke to do so, but he'd doubted his chances of success. Wrapped in a gray sweater she'd knitted herself, sitting amidst her books, she'd said, *If you think you can, you can; if you think you can't, you're right.* It had been the week before she died, and he'd never seen her alive again.

He raised his eyes heavenward. *If you're up there, Grandma Katie, please say a prayer I can do this.*

Dylan's progress up the stairs was slow. Finally he reached the top, and then the bedroom doorway.

His throat closed up when he saw her. She sat unmoving on the floor in front of her open cedar chest, her beige coat lying crumpled on the rug beside her. He had to step around her boots, which had muddied the carpet; her purse spilled out next to them. Even her uniform was wrinkled.

She didn't look at him until he knelt. He cupped her cheek

with his palm. She closed her eyes and leaned into it. He glanced down. "These are your dolls."

She nodded.

"Show me."

Again she nodded.

He sank onto the carpet without taking his eyes off her. Her skin was chalky, and he could see the blue veins at her temples and under her eyes. Her mouth looked a bit swollen, and he guessed she'd bitten her lips as she watched him at the accident. Her eyes were bloodshot.

When she reached down, he really looked at the dolls for the first time. About a dozen were set out in a half circle. She picked up one. It was a bride doll, similar to one of Mrs. Santori's. "Tim gave me this on our wedding day. It looks just like I did."

Dylan fingered the long auburn hair. "Yours used to be long?"

Once again she nodded.

Putting it down, she pointed to several dolls positioned together. "He gave me a doll on every holiday." She peered at Dylan, her smile painful to see. "He loved holidays. Just like you do. He made such a fuss."

The lump in Dylan's throat grew.

She picked up another doll and held it out. He took it, still watching her face; then his eyes shifted down.

For a moment he didn't understand.

He held a baby doll. With deep brown eyes and a shock of brown hair. A baby doll. A baby…

Oh, no, please, God, don't let this be what I think it is. Please, please, please.

"Her name was Janey. I got pregnant before Tim and I were married. I had her just before my eighteenth birthday."

Dylan's fingers clenched on the doll.

"Tim was ecstatic to have *two girls* in his life. And I

wanted a family, since I'd never grown up with one. We were really happy about her, despite the circumstances.''

Dylan swallowed hard, blinked several times. He knew what was coming.

She picked up another doll. It was a tiny ice skater, with a festive Christmas scarf looped around its neck. She handed it to him. ''Read the note.''

He took the skater in his other hand. The letters blurred, but he managed to read the bold scribble. *The skates are for you, kiddo. The doll's for Mommy.*

''Tell me,'' he uttered hoarsely.

Her face was a mask of agony. ''Tim and I had skated on the lake for years. He bought Janey skates for Christmas when she was two and a half. But it had been a warm winter, and I was worried about the ice.'' She stared over his shoulder, as if reliving the incident. ''He said I was being silly. We all bundled up Christmas morning. Tim brought his and Janey's skates down to the dock.''

''Not yours?''

She shook her head. ''I'd slipped the night before trying to replace a light on the Christmas tree, and my ankle was swollen.'' She stared at him. ''Strong ankles are important in ice skating, you know.''

''I know, honey.''

''So I sat on the dock and watched them.'' Beth bit her lip.

''Tell me. All of it.''

''She did pretty good. Tim held her hands, and I remember how her little knees wobbled. Her giggles rang out over the lake. No one else was out Christmas morning. It was a perfect setting.''

That turned obscene. Dylan was numb.

''Then…then…I heard this huge crack. The sound was so loud…I wasn't sure what it was.'' She looked at Dylan with wide, tormented eyes. "All of a sudden they were in the water. They fell so fast, in seconds."

He set down the dolls and reached out to her grasp her hands. They were arctic cold.

"Tim surfaced, holding on to Janey. He said…he said…"

"What did he say, sweetheart?"

"I started out onto the ice, and he screamed at me to get back. To go get help."

"That was the right thing to do."

She shook her head. "I ran to a neighbor who called nine-one-one."

"What happened?"

"By the time I got back to the dock, they were gone."

Dylan's eyes filled. "Oh, sweetheart."

She lifted her chin. Her eyes were bleak but dry. "I jumped in after them."

"Oh, no, Beth, you didn't." Her face was obscured by the moisture in his eyes.

"It didn't matter. I didn't want to live without them, anyway. So it didn't matter."

Dylan couldn't speak. Even at Grandma Katie's funeral, he hadn't felt this deep, wrenching sense of loss. Beth freed one hand from his and reached out to wipe a tear from his face. He just looked at her.

How had she ever survived?

Finally he asked, "What happened? Who saved you?"

Shrugging, she looked at the ceiling. "The Lakeville Fire Department arrived in minutes. Four guys. I knew a couple of them. They had a rope—one guy risked his life by easing out flat on the ice to pull me in." She smiled weakly. "He was just like you, heedless of his own safety."

"Beth, I—"

Abruptly she stopped his words with her fingertips. After a moment she continued talking. "They got me out. I was in intensive care for days. I didn't want to live." Her voice cracked. But still, no tears. Dylan imagined she'd cried them out over the past twenty years. "They wouldn't let me go— the firemen. They came every day to see me. Sent their wives, their friends, their ministers. They all pulled me back from death."

"That's why you work at the academy training firefighters, isn't it?"

"Yes. I love the fire department."

He smiled sadly. "So you left Lakeville?"

"I couldn't bear the reminders. The firefighter who rescued me—Johnny Waletsky—got me an ambulance position in Rockford. I wanted to help people, like the rescue workers helped me. I had lots of money to live—" again her voice cracked "—because I sold all that lake property I'd inherited from the Winters and Macks. I couldn't be near the lake anymore." She looked at him again. "I still have a lot of money, Dylan," she said irrelevantly.

He moved closer to Beth, and she let him tug her onto his lap. He nestled her face into his neck, and his other arm encircled her. "I'm so, so sorry."

She nodded, snuggling into him.

"I can understand why you don't want any more children. And why you hate Christmas."

"It's why I've kept my distance from everybody. Connie…she's the same age as Janey would have been."

Mention of the recruit brought back the events of the afternoon. "Beth, about today…"

Her body went totally limp, as if the weight of his foolishness was too much to handle.

"You've been right all along. I'm careless with my safety." His grip on her tightened, and he cringed as the significance of his outlook registered. Damn, he'd been so cavalier. So unknowing.

"You were right," he repeated. "I didn't recognize the preciousness of life."

She still said nothing.

"I'll change. It all fell into place this afternoon, anyway. But now, hearing this, I promise I'll be different."

After a moment she drew back and faced him.

His hand went to her hair, brushed it from her cheek. Feeling his eyes fill again, he whispered, "Please, give me another chance. I'll be meeting with Reed. I'll work all this out. I won't take any more chances." He glanced over at the dolls. "Especially after knowing this."

Her eyes were deep green and mysterious.

"Please, Beth, I'll stay safe, just for you."

SHE STUDIED DYLAN as she brushed the hair from his forehead. A huge angry welt scored his left temple. Several scrapes marred that classic jaw. Exhaustion made half-moon smudges under his eyes. His uniform was torn and dirty.

It was too late, she thought with a touch of panic. Today, when she watched him climb into that station wagon, she realized it was too late. It had been déjà vu, the loss of Tim and Janey all over again. But she'd known, as the vehicle teetered, that if Dylan survived, she wouldn't be able to leave him. It was too late. Her heart had signed on for life, even though her mind hadn't caught up with it yet.

She loved Dylan O'Roarke as much as she'd loved Tim Winters.

He gazed at her with agonized blue eyes.

She cleared her throat. "Yes."

His jaw dropped. "Yes? After what I did?"

"Yes."

Closing his eyes, he crushed her to him. "Oh, honey, I promise—"

She shook her head. "I know. You already said. Don't talk anymore. Please."

That didn't mean they wouldn't have this out, she thought as she crawled off his lap, stood and took his hand. He'd *have* to change his ways. Older, wiser now than she was with Tim, she'd insist on it. But with everybody's help—hers, Reed's, the fire department's—Dylan would become less reckless, more careful.

He rose—wobbly—to his feet. Though the catharsis of telling him about Tim and Janey made her weak, she drew him to the bed, made him sit and slowly undressed him. She kissed each bruise on his chest, arms and legs. When he was naked, she shed her clothes, then pulled down the covers, pressed him into the mattress and settled in front of him, spoon fashion. He was exhausted from his physical ordeal, and she was drained from her emotional confession. She nestled against him and said only, "I love you, Dylan. Sleep."

"I love you, too, Lizzie." They were the last words she heard before she drifted off.

Hours later she awakened sexually aroused. She thought she'd been dreaming, that he'd been touching and kissing her only in her unconscious, but it had been real. As soon as she opened her eyes, he mounted her and thrust inside her. "Lizzie, Lizzie."

She didn't speak, just allowed the sensations to overcome her.

After a shattering climax together, he let his full weight sink into her and said again, "I love you."

THE NEXT MORNING, the academy instructors gathered for a staff meeting after roll call while the recruits were taken on routine inspections by station house personnel. Ben wanted to wind up the last few weeks of the class sure that all the pieces were in place. Graduation was three weeks away.

On an overhead he outlined what was left of their training. "Evolutions will begin the last week." At the end of training, recruits went through evolutions—several days and nights of training where they simulated the actual firehouse routine at the academy. "First we'll conduct a day of EMS calls, car fires and actual fires in the training building. Then we'll run them at night. Line firefighters will be here to help out, but it'll mean extra hours for us all. The recruits will be gone soon, and you can all have comp time then.'' When everyone agreed, Ben turned to Beth. ''When are the state practicals?''

Dylan stole a glance at her. She was staring down at her clipboard and didn't look up.

''Beth?''

Reaching over, Dylan squeezed her arm. ''Hey, Winters, you with us?''

Startled, she glanced at him, then surveyed the room. She blushed to see her colleagues staring at her. ''Sorry. Did you want to know something, Ben?''

''When are the state practicals?''

She consulted her notes. Dylan noticed her hands trembled. ''Next week. Thursday.''

''We gonna have a one hundred percent passing rate?'' Chuck Lorenzo, the captain in charge of training, asked.

Her smile was weak. ''I hope so.''

Dylan frowned. She'd had a rough few days, and the strain was showing in her concentration. Though they'd made breathless love last night, this morning she seemed subdued. She told him she was worried about his future in the RFD.

''The social activities?'' Ben asked Lorenzo.

''The recruits have the after-graduation party in place. And of course, there's karaoke Friday night.''

Ben groaned. ''I'm not singing.''

''Well, I hope *some* instructors participate,'' Lorenzo said.

''Dylan,'' Ben asked, ''how about the Christmas activities?''

''I called a meeting today to discuss recruit participation. With luck they'll be probies by the time the Immaculate Conception party takes place. I'm going to suggest they go ring the Salvation Army bells next week with us, and I put us in for a stint at the VOA.''

He could feel Beth's eyes on him.

"The Volunteers of America? What have you gotten us into this time, O'Roarke?" Eric Scanlon asked good-naturedly. Dylan wondered if the captain would be this congenial when he found out about him and Beth.

"I've signed us up for a Christmas food and toy distribution downtown at the VOA. Churches, places of business, all kinds of organizations send ten to fifteen volunteers to give out baskets to the needy."

"Sounds like it'll instill a real sense of community in the recruits," Ben commented. "All right, I guess that wraps things up. Let's hang on a few more weeks and then we can take a breather. You've all done a great job, and I'd like to see it end without any further escapades." He pinned Dylan with a glare.

Dylan cringed.

Beth frowned.

As the group filed out, Dylan waited for Beth to rise, but she remained seated. When everyone else was gone, she said, "I'd like to talk to you Ben, if you have time."

"I thought you might." He cocked his head at Dylan. "You want O'Roarke to stay?"

Beth nodded. Ben crossed the room and closed the door, then seated himself behind his desk. He glanced from Dylan to Beth as if expecting animosity to flare like visible sparks between them. "Go ahead."

"What are you going to do about yesterday?" Her voice was soft and neutral.

"I haven't decided yet. You'll want me to pull his card."

Beth shook her head. "On the contrary. O'Roarke's the best paramedic in the department. I'd hate to see his career go up in flames because of a mistake in judgment."

Ben knocked the side of his head with the heel of his hand. "I must have heard you wrong."

She gave another weak smile, then rose and moved behind

Dylan's chair. He held his breath as she placed her hand on his shoulder. Never in his life had he felt more supported. He reached up and laid a hand over hers, touching her openly for the first time at the academy.

"*I* was wrong about Dylan," Beth continued. "Not you. Your instincts and Reed's were on target."

The battalion chief stared at her hand on Dylan's shoulder. "I'm confused."

"I'm retracting my objections to his influence on the recruits. What's more, I'm asking you to consider implementing Reed's suggestions and to give him another chance."

"Why?"

Dylan kept his mouth shut. The ball was in her court. He was dying to see how she'd play it.

"He's learned a lesson about the importance of safety." She raised her chin. "We've been a good influence on each other. I think he sees why he does this kind of thing and that he needs help in figuring out how to control his behavior. I believe with all my heart he's going to change."

"Well, that's a testimonial I can't ignore." Ben's eyes narrowed on their hands. "Anything else I should know about?"

Beth swallowed hard. "Yes. Dylan and I..." She hesitated. "We're..." She squeezed his shoulder. "I'm in love with him."

Dylan looked at her in amazement, and Ben's brows arched in shock. He said, "You two? I can't believe it."

They both nodded.

"It's true," Beth said.

Ben watched them for long moments. "I see. And does this change in Dylan's attitude have anything to do with your feelings for him?"

"Absolutely."

"Fine. I'll consider your recommendation. Though I have to say that you're obviously no longer objective about this."

"No," she said sweetly. "But I'm right."

Dylan stood and drew her to his side. After a moment Ben rose, too. "Don't you have anything to say for yourself, O'Roarke?"

"Nah. She said it all." He grinned cockily, then grabbed Beth by the hand and walked out of the office.

STANDING JUST OUTSIDE the door to the classroom, Beth took in a deep breath. She'd made one big revelation today, and now she was about to make another. The thought of O'Roarke's stunned expression in the battalion chief's office made her smile and gave her the courage to go into the room where the recruits were signing up for the Christmas activities. Unobserved, she stood in the back and watched the show.

O'Roarke lounged on the front desk, casual as always. She winced at the sight of the bruise on his temple, but the rest of him looked remarkably better today. His uniform shirt pulled tightly across his chest, and a rebellious lock of hair fell over his forehead.

"So, here's a schedule for our end-of-year activities," Dylan was saying. "First we'll be ringing the Salvation Army bells the week before Christmas—you have a choice for which date to participate there. But the Volunteers of America food and toy distribution is the Saturday before graduation. I know it's a busy time of year—you have families. You can bring them along, if you want. But I think doing both these activities together is important."

"Kind of a bonding thing," Tully said. He was feeling pretty cocky, now that he'd passed everything but practicals and evolutions. He was going to make a good firefighter.

"Right."

"Bonding's happening Friday night at our karaoke party, too," Sandy Frank said. "Don't forget that, Lieutenant O'Roarke."

Dylan's blue eyes flamed with the challenge. "I tell you what, Frank. You get everybody here to commit to the VOA, and I'll sing at karaoke."

"Can't it be the other way around?" Austyn Myers asked, grinning. "We've heard you sing, Lieutenant."

Sandy picked up the gauntlet. "No, he has to perform if we get everybody to do the other stuff."

"Even Ms. Winters," Cleary said. She, too, had gotten spunky once she'd reached her peak fitness level. "She has to ring the bells and go to the VOA, too."

Wanikya spoke. "Hey, I'll even sing if Ms. Winters agrees to the Christmas stuff."

Good time to make her presence known, Beth thought, and strode down the aisle. Heads turned towards her, and the room fell silent. Out of the corner of her eye, she saw Cleary wink at Frank. Hmm.

When she reached the front, she gave Dylan her sternest look. The mischief in his eyes made the corners of her mouth turn up. She scanned the room, saw the poster sign-up tacked on the wall, took the marker out of Dylan's hand and crossed the room. With thespian flourish, she signed up for the VOA and the bells. Since she'd planned to do this, anyway, she might as well get her money's worth.

Turning to the class, she said, "Polish those vocal cords, Wanikya," and headed toward the door.

A burst of laughter followed her out of room. Just as she crossed the threshold, she heard Dylan say, "Well, now that's out of the way, I'd like to discuss something serious with you. Let's talk turkey about how recklessly you all saw me act yesterday. And why I was wrong."

At the exit Beth stopped. *Oh, God,* she thought, *this might just work.*

"ARE YOU READY for night evolutions?" Chuck Lorenzo asked Ace Durwin, who stood rigidly at attention.

"Yes, sir."

"Which truck position are you on?"

"I'm the officer, sir."

"Good." Lorenzo leaned closer. "At least you can keep the others from panicking." He turned to the rest of the recruits. "All right, ladies and gentlemen, this is your last drill. But if I see anyone treating it like a drill, you're out on your ass—even if there is only one week left." His eyes scanned the arena. "This is a firehouse. You are on the night shift. Your individual radios are the public address system. You will train, you will cook dinner, you will watch TV and relax. When a call comes in for your group, you will go. With a mouth full of spaghetti, if you're taking a leak—you will go. Got it?"

"Yes, sir," the recruits said in unison.

"Good luck." Lorenzo saluted them.

Swiftly the recruits disbanded. They removed their ties and hats and headed to their equipment. They checked that their goods were in working order, as a new shift at the firehouse would do. When they finished with the rigs, the alarm sounded.

Ace had fought fires as a volunteer, but still, the adrenaline pumped through his veins like water pulsing through a hose.

"Car fire at 1190 Scottsdale Road. Engine Four, go in service."

Ace Durwin was on Four.

He dragged his gear from his locker, jumped into his bunker pants and boots, hauled on his turnout coat, grabbed his helmet and was the first on the rig.

Directed to take the truck on a few turns around the parking lot to simulate the approximate length of a run—the accident was in the back parking lot—Brady Abbott drove a little fast; in two minutes they were at the scene.

Eric Scanlon and Herb Hanley were the observers. Both tough, but both fair. They stood back as the recruits dismounted the truck. Sandy Frank made the hydrant and got the water going, but fumbled with it. Austyn Myers donned his air mask and dragged the hose off the bed, with Abbott behind him. "Come on guys, faster. The car's burning," Durwin shouted as he put his headgear in place.

It always amazed Durwin how fast fire succumbed to its natural enemy, water. The engine blaze was out in minutes. Abbott continued to drench the vehicle.

Good, good, Durwin thought. *We'll get points for that. Even though we were slow with the water and hose.*

After the fire was out, Scanlon, pretending to be a police officer on the scene, questioned Abbott and Myers as they dumped the last of the water on the "red devil".

Durwin lifted his air mask. One down. He hoped the other evolutions went as well.

"TRAFFIC ACCIDENT at 1190 Scottsdale Road. Ladder Six go in service."

Connie Cleary bounded out of the kitchen, where she'd been setting the table. She flew to the lockers with her three housemates, and donned her goods in record time. Out of the corner of her eye, she saw Battalion Chief Cordaro with a stopwatch, and said a silent thank-you to Ms. Winters for helping her get in shape. They were in the truck, circling the parking lot and at the scene—which was the front area of the academy—in minutes.

The truck skidded to a halt. Harriet, the dummy, lay half under Ms. Winters's car. The instructor took the role of the driver of the other vehicle. Cleary approached her.

"I don't know how it happened," Ms. Winters began, throwing up her hands. "He's hurt. I think he's hurt. Help him."

"Please step back, ma'am," Cleary said. "We need the space."

John Wanikya pulled the Basic Life Support bag from the

rig, while Hoyt Barnette and Trevor Tully got the stretcher and set up the oxygen. Wanikya knelt in front of the patient. He began the assessment calmly, though Cleary had come to realize he wasn't the iron man everyone had thought.

"He's hurt," Ms. Winters repeated, crossing to the victim and getting in the way. Barnette intercepted her and dragged her aside.

Wanikya said, "We need the oxygen now, Tully."

The perfectly set-up mask was handed off, and Tully popped the tank.

O'Roarke came up to Cleary. "Are you the driver of the fire truck, ma'am?"

Surprised, she turned. "Um, yeah."

"That's my car there, behind it. I need to get out. I have a very important meeting. Could you move the truck?"

Cleary hesitated, then saw Battalion Chief A. J. Rooney snickering. At that moment she remembered him warning the recruits, in one of their frequent informal sessions, about the incredible gall of lay people at accident scenes. Her eyes narrowed on O'Roarke. "In your dreams, pal," she said under her breath.

"Excuse me?"

"I mean, no, sir. This is an accident and you're interfering. Please vacate the area." She stared over O'Roarke's shoulder. "The police are arriving now, so I suggest you cooperate."

O'Roarke's eyes twinkled. *Good girl.*

She turned to see Barnette and Tully strap in the victim, after Wanikya had stabilized her head and neck. Equipment was being cleaned up. She glanced at her watch. Only ten minutes had passed. It felt like ten hours.

IN THE ACADEMY kitchen, preparing the night meal as they would do at a firehouse, Trevor Tully noticed right away that Lieutenant O'Roarke and Firefighter Templeton, one of the line smoke eaters sent to help with evolutions, were missing. Knowing that meant they were out starting a fire that the recruits would have to put out, he sighed resignedly as the kitchen crew called the rest of the group for chow. Even before the radio blared, he knew he wasn't going to get the hot meal they'd spent hours preparing. The instructors had intentionally staged a call when they were about to sit down to supper. Oh, well, it was bound to happen at the firehouse. Might as well get used to it in training.

"Three-story blaze on Scottsdale Road. Engine Four, groups one and two, and Ladder Six, groups one and two, go into service."

"This is it, people," Battalion Chief Cordaro said. "Your big chance."

Trevor's heart raced. Though they'd been to area smoke-houses and fought smaller blazes, a night fire in the tower was the culmination of their training. Performance on these evolutions was crucial. Failure meant expulsion from the program. Thrilled to be on the tip of the hose, he donned his goods, raced to the truck and inhaled the cold night air.

"Ready for this, Tully?" Wanikya shouted as they roared to the scene.

Unable to resist, Trevor reached up and blasted the siren, then the loud horn. "Yeah, I am."

As they reached the fire ground and Hoyt Barnette took in the scene from his rig, his mouth went dry. Generators illuminated Battalion Chief Cordaro, who directed incident command. Winters and Lorenzo were with him, bathed in the flashing lights of the trucks. Must mean O'Roarke, Rooney, Scanlon and Giancarlo, who would have started the fires, were inside.

Barnette knew he was about to go inside a burning building. He'd done it on day maneuvers at the Hamilton smoke-house where they routinely trained, but this felt different. O'Roarke and the others would be watching him in particular because of his failure in earlier drills. And because he sensed they knew he was afraid. *Please, God, let me do this right, or I'll never be a firefighter.*

Would that be so bad? the little voice inside him asked for the hundredth time.

Quelling it, he donned his Nomex hood, secured the face mask in place, put on his helmet and started his air flow. Tully squeezed his arm as they entered the pitch blackness together. They humped the hose up the steps to the top floor.

There it was, the seat of the fire. Barnette began to sweat, and his vision was blurred. His arms felt too weak to hold the charged line.

Tully turned when he dropped it, but Barnette didn't stick around long enough to see the condemnation in his eyes.

BECAUSE HE'D ventilated by opening a window, as Tully doused the seat of the fire, Dylan witnessed Barnette leaving his partner.

"Shit," he said, and handed the clipboard he held to Scanlon. He raced toward the stairs and flew to the ground level, where Giancarlo sought a place to start another fire.

"Where'd he go?" O'Roarke asked.

"Who?"

"Barnette. He choked and came down."

"Never made it here. I been here the whole time."

Dylan felt a stab of anxiety. He must have gotten disoriented and gone to the second floor. "I'm going up."

He turned and ran smack into Tully.

Tully said, "I'm going with you."

Dylan nodded. They were halfway there when smoke billowed above them. He realized that Rooney was starting another fire in a second-floor bathroom. Barnette was wandering around up there. Tully's air pack beeped. Low oxygen. If Tully's was low, so was Barnette's. The recruits were almost out of air. "Go back," he said to Tully, as his face mask vibrated, then beeped, too.

Tully shook his head. "I gotta help."

Dylan knew the feeling.

A brother was in trouble. The firefighters had low air. Six months ago Dylan would have raced headlong to the second floor, heedless of his safety. But the boy before him would remember it the rest of his life. And perhaps risk his safety because of it. Then Dylan saw Beth's face, as she told him about her husband and child. He had made a promise. Tim Winters's death, and his baby daughter's, would not go unheeded.

Praying Barnette would be all right, Dylan said simply, "We're going for new bottles."

He took Tully's arm, turned and nudged the kid down the steps. To safety, which was, he'd learned, very important.

When they got to the bottom of the stairs, Giancarlo was just dragging a dazed Barnette out the front door. Thank God.

CHAPTER FOURTEEN

WITH STUDIED NONCHALANCE, Beth sat back in her chair on karaoke night at the academy. She'd walked into the gym with Dylan, dressed to kill in a slim green wool dress, cinched at the waist with a hammered-gold belt. Without warning, she had an attack of anxiety. So many changes were happening in her life that sometimes she doubted she could cope with them. Telling Tim and Janey's story for the first time and going public about her relationship with O'Roarke had stretched her nerves tightly.

To quell her fears, Beth concentrated on how the recruits had transformed the arena for the annual singing fest. A large area in front of the stage was sectioned off with room dividers. They were covered with black paper, and life-size white silhouettes of firefighters in action had been pasted on the background.

"Who did the silhouettes?" Francey asked from beside Beth. "They're terrific." Francey looked stunning in one of her mother's designs, a long-sleeved black pantsuit. This was a family night, and Ben had invited the whole Cordaro clan. Jake, though he'd gone back to the line last week, was also at their table. Sean O'Roarke, Dylan's father, was out of town.

"I don't know who drew them," Beth answered distractedly, thinking of what Dylan had said when she'd told him she had no family to invite. *You do now, babe.*

Ben leaned over. "Al Battisti did them," he said. "Odd, isn't it, what you don't know about people."

Bingo, Beth thought. She continued to scan the area. The tables were arranged cozily, with red and white checked tablecloths and karaoke song sheets spread randomly over them; candles graced the center of each, their flames casting flickering shadows on the walls. The stage was backed with black, too; ribbons of red and white crepe paper decorated it, along with white stars in the same material as the silhouettes.

"The recruits did a great job with decorating." Diana smiled and sipped a cappuccino. She looked as young as Francey in a simple indigo sheath.

"The transformation's unbelievable," Beth said.

"Francey says this is a tradition," Alex observed. "Haven't you seen it before, Beth?"

She shook her head. *I never allowed myself to attend.* "Um, no." She began to breathe a little fast.

Automatically she looked for Dylan. Dressed in black pants and a fiery red shirt with the sleeves rolled up, he stood by Tully's table talking to the recruit's mother. Just finding him across the room calmed her. *It's all right to be scared,* he'd told her. *I'll be there for you. Change is tough at first. But, Lizzie, think about the great life we're going to have.*

Determined to believe him, Beth conjured up images of the things in the past week that had gotten her through the upheaval in her life. Lovemaking that had transcended any physical contact they'd ever had, now that its foundation was commitment; helping Dylan and Jake decorate the common area for Christmas at Dutch Towers; dinner at Francey and Alex's, where Alex had told Beth about the firefighters' spouse class he attended at the academy. She smiled at the thought of the gorgeous hunk who loved her friend. He'd confessed to ongoing stress over Francesca's safety. But he was handling it. Just as Beth could handle the changes Dylan had wrought in her life.

The screech of the microphone distracted her. Brady Abbott, Ryan Quinn and Austyn Myers took the stage. The boys had been in charge of the whole night; they'd gotten the karaoke DJ, enlisted people to decorate and arranged for the food. She also guessed they were in for a few surprises.

"Welcome staff, recruits, family and friends," Brady Abbott said in a confident voice. "We've got a fun time planned. Although some of us have already chosen our songs this week, feel free to jump in at any time." He made a few razzing comments to Ryan Quinn.

"Enough, Abbott," Quinn said, jerking the mike away from him and handing it to the DJ.

The man smiled at their antics and announced, "As some of you know, we have about ten prepared songs tonight. Here's the first."

Beth watched as the curtain parted. Out came Connie Cleary and Sandy Frank. They were both dressed in high heels and mini-skirts that showed off their long, shapely legs. Sequined tops hugged them nicely, and their hair had obviously been styled. Immediately, catcalls erupted from all the male recruits. The women carried their bunker boots with them and set them down at the front of the stage. Each picked up a mike.

"This song is dedicated to our fellow recruits," Frank said. "Being female in this class has been…interesting. We want to thank you guys for all your help—" the audience laughed as the women rolled their eyes comically "—and let you know how we really feel about you."

Beth knew there had been pranks—stuffing their lockers with tampons, tying pink bows around their helmets and removing the toilet seats from their johns for a day—all in fun.

As Nancy Sinatra's "These Boots Are Made for Walking" came on, Beth chuckled. Cleary and Frank belted out their tune, all the while dancing around the bunker boots. The guys gave them a standing ovation.

But they didn't leave the stage. Cleary announced that they

intended to do another song right away. More cheers and catcalls. "Um, Lieutenant O'Roarke, would you come up here for a minute?"

Clearly Dylan knew nothing about this, though Beth suspected he'd been planning something all week with Tully and the guys; there'd been secret meetings and closed doors around the academy.

Grinning broadly, Dylan stood and made his way to the stage. The curtains parted, and Tully wheeled out a motorcycle. Then they held up a black leather jacket, which Dylan donned theatrically; the kids motioned for him to sit on the bike. Again he complied. Tully stepped forward. "Since we all know that Lieutenant O'Roarke doesn't always play by the rules, we thought we'd dedicate this song to him."

Again Cleary and Frank took the mikes. With Tully and Abbott and Quinn as backup singers, they launched into "He's a Rebel" by the Crystals. The audience roared. Beth snatched a quick glance at Ben, who still hadn't given his decision about yanking Dylan's card. Beth suspected he was deliberately making Dylan squirm. That Ben was laughing was a good sign.

When Dylan didn't return to the table after the song, Beth wondered what he was up to. She soon found out when he came out on stage for the next song, again with Myers, Abbott, Quinn and Tully. The guys wore colored shirts, but Dylan drew the crowd's attention, dressed in a white suit, like the one John Travolta wore in *Saturday Night Fever*. So, of course, no one was surprised when he burst into a rendition of "Night Fever" by the Bee Gees, complete with dance steps and hand motions. The guys bumbled along behind him. By the time he finished, the audience was howling.

After a few more songs, Quinn took the mike and said into it, "Okay, Wanikya, payback time."

Francey asked, "What does he mean?"

Dylan, in his seat and his own clothes, shook his head.

"Wanikya said he'd sing if Beth signed up to do all the Christmas activities with us."

Francey's eye's widened. "Christmas activities?" Then they narrowed on Dylan. "O'Roarke, if you pressured her..."

Beth touched Francey's arm. "He didn't. I wanted to do this. I loved ringing the bells yesterday."

Dylan gave Beth a sideways glance. *He'd* loved the dickens out of her afterward, telling her with his body how proud he was of her courage to face her ghosts.

Smiling at the thought, Beth watched as Wanikya, a little off-key, sang "I Am A Rock," by Simon and Garfunkel. After that the DJ took a break.

Ben turned to Dylan and Beth. "You've made a lot of unusual strides with the recruits this year."

Dylan and Beth exchanged hopeful looks.

"No, nothing's been decided yet," Ben told them. "The deputy is waiting for some information from Reed—and a recommendation from me." He paused. "But it looks good, O'Roarke."

Breathing a sigh of relief, Dylan leaned back in his chair. Things were so good he was almost fearful of the fates getting jealous. His eyes rested on Beth when she got into a conversation with Francey. His heart still ached for what she'd gone through. Reaching out, he placed his hand on her neck. She didn't flinch, didn't react to the public display. Maybe, just maybe... He put his thoughts on hold.

Jake, who was in on the conversation between Francey and Beth said to them, "Yeah. I heard a rumor about that."

"Billy lost it, according to Chelsea. He went wild when she told him she wouldn't see him anymore." Francey grimaced; she'd experienced some of the same problems with Joey Santori.

"I heard it happened at the fire station." Jake's tone was disapproving. "Why'd she tell him there?"

"She tried not to. But apparently Billy wouldn't let it rest when they got off duty and she refused to go home with him. She got so exasperated she told him."

"Personal matters should be kept out of the station houses."

No one commented. Dylan knew where Jake's concern came from. Since the debacle with his friend Danny, Jake had been a stickler about behavior in the firehouse.

"I don't think she precipitated this, Jakey," Francey told him.

Beth said, "Let's have dinner with her next week."

"Chels and I are both off Thursday. How's that?"

Automatically Beth turned to Dylan. "Is that okay?"

Dylan gaped. He couldn't believe she'd check with him. "Of course," he said hoarsely. She was delightfully oblivious to what she'd done, and to the fact that everybody else was as shocked as he was by her behavior.

The DJ was back from his break.

Ace Durwin, Jeff Griffith and Al Battisti went up to the mike. "We found these songs in the book and had the DJ put them together for us. It's music to pump up by before goin' to face the red devil."

"Isn't that cute," Beth said as they launched into a medley of songs that had fire in the title or in the theme, such as "Ring of Fire," "Great Balls of Fire," and "Smoke Gets in Your Eyes."

The audience gave the guys a big hand, and Ben told Dylan to get the tape for use at the academy.

Next, Giancarlo, Lorenzo and Herb Hanley approached the stage.

"We aren't gonna sing," Lorenzo said. "But as our contribution to the night, we've found the titles of some songs that we think fit certain phases of the recruits' experience here." He handed out scripts to Giancarlo and Hanley. "All right," he read from his notes. "How did the instructors feel when the 1999 fall recruit class arrived at the academy?"

Deadpan, Hanley spoke into his mike. "It's Gonna Take a Miracle."

The crowd laughed loudly.

"How do the recruits feel about coming to the academy every day?"

This time Giancarlo came forward. "Another Day in Paradise."

The recruits moaned.

Lorenzo's grin was broad. "How did the recruits do on confidence walks?"

"I Fall to Pieces," Giancarlo said. "And by week twelve, they were singing, 'Do That to Me One More Time.'"

Good-natured boos from the audience.

"Our impressions of the first time they fought a fire?"

"Send in the Clowns," Hanley replied.

Lorenzo winked at the audience. "How about why Cleary and Frank decided to become firefighters?"

"Girls Just Want to Have Fun," Giancarlo read.

And on they went till the audience was rolling in the aisles. Then Cleary and Frank came on stage again, still dressed to the nines. Something about them made Dylan wary.

"We'd like to do a final song," Cleary said. "As we said, being a woman in this place has been a unique experience. We couldn't have gotten through it without one person."

Dylan felt Beth tense.

"Beth Winters has been an inspiration to both Recruit Frank and me, by example, by her vast knowledge, by her unending selflessness in helping us—me—through this training." Cleary ran a hand down her sleek hip. "I couldn't have gotten into this skirt without you, Ms. Winters."

Everyone laughed, Beth included.

Sandy took the mike. "Seriously, Ms. Winters, you're a role model for all women in the fire department. We only hope we can do for other females what you've done for us. We'd like to dedicate this song to you."

Helen Reddy's "I Am Woman" began to play.

Dylan grasped Beth's hand, and she clutched it throughout the upbeat song. At the end of it, amidst thunderous applause Frank and Cleary made their way to Beth. Without censoring her actions, she stood and gave both of them a warm hug.

Dylan decided he'd go for broke, too. He'd been toying with the idea ever since he saw the song in the book. Without giving himself time to chicken out, he made his way to the stage and indicated his choice to the DJ. Then he took the mike from the stand.

"This," he said, "is dedicated to the special lady in my life." He paused dramatically. "The one I hope to marry soon." Without further explanation, he launched into Elvis Presley's "Can't Help Falling in Love with You."

Dimly he was aware of the utter quiet in the room. Of the fact that the clerical staff had come out of the kitchen and gathered around. He could see Beth's face as he sang the heartfelt words to her. He never took his eyes from hers, nor she from him.

When he finished, he kept staring at her. Then, amidst the clapping, she stood and, in front of God and the entire fire academy staff, wended her way through the tables, climbed the stage steps and hugged him.

"I love you, O'Roarke," she whispered in his ear.

"I love you, too." His eyes twinkled mischievously, "So, what about it? Wanna marry? On New Year's Day, maybe."

Beth smiled. She wasn't at all frightened by the proposal. It was, she knew in her heart, exactly what she wanted.

"Yes," she said simply. "New Year's Day sounds great."

AT DINNER on Thursday, Beth's stomach lurched when her fettuccine Alfredo was delivered. Sitting back, she sipped her

Chardonnay. It, too, went down sour. Surreptitiously she rubbed her palm over stomach and pulled on her striped top.

"You okay?" Chelsea asked. "You look a little green."

"My stomach's off tonight. No big deal." She glanced at the table and smiled. "We're so predictable. I always get the Alfredo, Francey gets the chicken and you get the angel hair pasta."

"I like that predictability," Chelsea said, her brown eyes melancholy. "It's stabilizing."

Beth tried her meal again, winding the dripping, creamy strands into a spoon with her fork. "I know you'd like to settle down. I'm sorry it hasn't worked out with Billy."

Before dinner arrived, Chelsea had related the unpleasant details of her split with Milligan and the even more unpleasant events since last week, when her entire station house had been thrown into havoc over their personal problems.

"Yeah, well," Chelsea said, "someday I'm gonna find me a man who's mature, thoughtful and terrific in bed." Her eyes narrowed on Beth, then Francey. "Like you two did."

Francey raised her brows. "I never talked about Alex's, um, performance."

"You didn't have to. Sexual gratification is written all over your face." She turned to Beth. "And yours."

Beth blushed, then lifted her glass. "He's stellar, just like all his M-girls said."

Again they laughed. Beth's napkin fell to the floor. When she reached to get it, the world tilted. Spots swam in front of her eyes. "I must be coming down with something. I feel dizzy."

"Getting enough sleep?" Francey's tone carried over the earlier teasing.

"Yeah, a lot lately. Dylan says now that I'm not fighting him anymore, I'm more relaxed. I even took a couple of naps this weekend."

They continued to eat. Beth picked at the noodles, nibbled on some bread and avoided the wine.

"I couldn't believe it when France told me he actually sang Elvis's song to you at karaoke," Chelsea commented. "And then he proposed."

"He's a—" Beth started to speak just as her stomach pitched. She stood abruptly. "I'll be right back."

Before Chelsea and Francey could react, Beth had bolted to the bathroom. She made it into a stall just in time to lose the contents of her stomach. Limp and bedraggled, she rose from her knees and went to a sink to rinse her mouth. Her friends arrived and led her to the alcove that served as a vanity.

"Sit," Francey said, indicating a padded chair.

Chelsea wet paper towels and blotted them on her face. Francey knelt in front of her. "You're flushed but not feverish." Taking her pulse, she said, "Everything seems okay."

"My stomach feels better now."

"It always does after you get sick."

Sighing heavily, Beth relaxed against the chair back. She saw Francey shoot Chelsea a speculative look.

"What?" she asked them.

"When was your last period?"

Beth thought back. "Right after we returned from your wedding."

Francey's eyes widened. "Beth, I've been married for almost three months."

"I know." Then it dawned on her. "Oh, that's okay. I'm irregular. I always have been."

"What's the longest you go in between?"

"It always comes by five or six weeks." She felt blood drain from her face. "I'll get it this time."

"Honey, you missed a time. At least one." Chelsea's expression was somber.

"But Dylan and I used birth control, every time."

"Have you been with anyone else?" Francey asked bluntly.

"No, of course not. I only saw Eric a couple of times after Dylan came to the academy and I didn't sleep with him."

"So if you are pregnant, it's Dylan's."

Beth felt a chill go through her. "I can't be pregnant. I'm forty years old. I'm responsible about sex. I—"

Chelsea stood. "Let's find out for sure." She checked her watch. "We'll stop at a drugstore on the way home. Get an early pregnancy test. You can find out in minutes."

Beth didn't move. Pregnant?

I'll never have children because emotionally I couldn't risk the loss.

She shook her head. It couldn't be.

Then she remembered when she discovered she was pregnant with Janey. She never even guessed, her periods were so irregular and she'd had no symptoms. It was Tim who commented that she hadn't menstruated in a while.

Oh, my God.

Beth buried her face in her hands.

No, please, God, don't do this to me. I'm not strong enough. I was just beginning to have faith that I could be—

Francey grasped her shoulders. "Beth?"

Chelsea said, "Honey, it's not the end of the world if you are. You're going to get married, anyway, so it's not a problem." Chelsea's voice was matter-of-fact.

Whipping her hands away from her face, Beth said, "Oh, yes, it is a problem. It's the end of everything."

"Why?" her friends asked simultaneously.

"Because I'm afraid to have another baby."

Again, they spoke together, "*Another* baby?"

The ladies' room door opened. At the interruption, Chelsea took over. She pulled Beth up and took her arm. "Let's get out of here. France, pay the bill, and I'll get the car."

They were at Beth's half an hour later, armed with the latest pregnancy test. Beth hadn't spoken all the way home. They'd gotten their coats off, and Francey and Chelsea sat in the living room across from Beth. Beth took the kit from Chelsea. Staring blindly at it, she said, "I was married and had a baby before I was eighteen years old."

Both women gasped. Francey said, "Oh, Beth."

"No one knew. I wasn't cutting you out. I never told anybody until Dylan." Beth smiled sadly. "But he wouldn't let it rest, he wouldn't let my secrets stay buried. Once I started talking, it all came out."

"Do you want to tell us about it?" Francey asked.

She did. Gazing sightlessly at the pregnancy test kit, Beth managed to relate most of the details. She didn't look up once, just stared at the test kit the whole time.

When she was done, she felt marginally better. She wasn't sure she'd done the right thing for her friends, though. Tears were streaming down their cheeks.

Francey grasped her hand. "Oh, Beth, I'm so sorry."

"Me, too." Chelsea locked her fingers around Beth's other hand.

"Now you understand why I could never risk having another child."

Neither woman answered.

"I can't risk it. I'd die if something happened to it." She squeezed the hands holding hers. "You can't know what it was like. I'd never live through the pregnancy, let alone the vulnerability of a child being a baby, a toddler."

She stopped, and Chelsea and Francey exchanged anxious looks. Then Chelsea stood. "First, let's see if there's something to worry about." She took the kit and scanned the directions like an officer reading a fire call report. "Just like the commercials say. Urine sample in this—" she gave Beth a small container "—then pour a few drops with the little bulb on the stick. Blue for yes, white for no." When Beth's hands trembled as she took the clear plastic container, Chelsea said, "Just get the sample, honey. I'll do the rest."

Zombielike, Beth headed into the bathroom. Numbly she got the sample, opened the door, let Chelsea and Francey in.

The women held hands as they watched the small tab.

Very quickly, it turned blue.

SOMETHING WAS troubling Beth. Dylan's sixth sense, the one that told him when there was fire in the walls, when a patient wasn't going to make it, told him so.

He stared at her across the room of the Volunteers of America distribution center. The warehouselike space was packed with gifts, food and toys. The smell of fresh baked cookies, hot chocolate and coffee, along with three ten-foot Christmas trees decorated with lights and streams of tinsel, scented the air. Combined with the carols playing over a loudspeaker, the atmosphere was festive. Despite that, Dylan felt a sense of foreboding.

"Hey, Lieutenant, you took the cushy job, I see."

Dylan turned to find Reed, bundled in jacket, hat and gloves, sipping a cup of coffee.

"Macauley, what are you doing here?"

"I thought I'd help out."

"Yeah, well, if you know what's good for you, you'll take a cushy job, too. Carrying those bags for the recipients in five-degree weather is worse than fighting a fire in that temperature."

"Couldn't be," Reed said easily. "No water to freeze on your eyelashes and wrists." He nodded across the room to Beth. "She came, too?"

Dylan smiled at her; at just that moment she caught his eye. The return smile she gave him was full of feeling—among them, fear. Why?

"Yeah, she did."

"She looks pale."

"Christmas is hard for her."

Reed nodded thoughtfully. "It's not an easy holiday." Shaking off the mood, he said, "Well, I'm gonna go haul turkeys. Catch you later."

Dylan checked his watch. Ten minutes until the crowd was let in. When he arrived with the recruits, a line of people already snaked down the sidewalk like a giant fire hose. They'd been there since seven this morning. The recruits were near the door, in their firefighter uniforms, as was Dylan—good publicity, Ben had said—waiting to carry out the goodies. Beth sat along a half wall; he'd gotten her assigned to checking off names of the recipients because he didn't want her walking around. She'd admitted she didn't feel well, but he knew, anyway. She'd been zonked out when he got to her house Thursday after she had dinner with the girls, and she'd left work right before lunch yesterday. Last night she'd fallen asleep in his arms as they watched their favorite sitcom. He crossed to her.

"Hi, babe."

This time, her smile was more genuine. "Babe is a sexist term, Lieutenant."

"But fitting. You look great in those red leggings and white shirt. A real babe."

"Stop."

He braced his hands on the table in front of her; he leaned over and whispered, "I'm never gonna stop, sweetheart. Loving you. Telling you how great you look. When we're eighty and living in Dutch Towers, I'll still be chasing you around the apartment."

He felt her stiffen. When he drew back, he was shocked to see tears in her eyes. Never once, not even when she told him about Tim and Janey, had he seen her cry. Multiple alarms went off in his head. "Beth, what is it?"

Just then, there was a ring, signaling the entrance of the clients. From working here in years past, Dylan knew there would be chaos in about thirty seconds. He looked to the door, then at Beth.

"I'm fine. Christmas stuff is hard for me, that's all." She shoved his arm. "Go away, O'Roarke. I'm okay."

Throughout the morning, Dylan was only able to catch glimpses of her as she talked to customers and handed over the toy bags that runners brought to her. Periodically the recruits came in to warm up; Cleary and Tully stopped to chat with her, then teased him about being a wimp because of the job he'd chosen.

Pizza for the volunteers was delivered. Worried, he managed to arrange his break with Beth. When she would only nibble on a cookie and drink some soda, his concern escalated.

"You really don't feel well, do you?" he asked, brushing back her bangs.

She shook her head.

Glancing at the clock, he said, "We'll leave in ten minutes."

Ten minutes later, Dylan was escorting a woman with four children to one of the checkers. The girl, about three, broke away from her mom and headed for the Christmas tree.

"I'll get the rascal." Dylan took after the child. He reached her just as she yanked some tinsel off the tree. "Okay, tiger, a little tinsel won't hurt," he said, swinging her up. He held her close for a minute, breathing in baby powder and milk—the scents of childhood—then pointed to the angel on the top. "Those dark eyes and dark hair are just like yours. I'll bet you're not quite as angelic, though."

He hugged her, then threw her in the air. She squealed with delight, drawing the attention of several people in the almost empty room. He'd just turned and headed toward the mother when he saw a commotion at Beth's table.

Panicking, he handed the girl to her mother and burrowed his way through the people who surrounded Beth.

When he got to her, he saw Reed kneeling in front of her. Beth was in the chair, bent over, her head between her legs.

"Breathe deeply, Beth. That's it." Reed's hand soothed her shoulder.

"What happened?" Dylan asked, his heart pounding.

Reed continued to rub her back. "We were just talking about you when the kid separated from her mother. I turned and saw you catch her, and when I looked back to Beth, she'd broken out in a sweat and was breathing fast. I think she's hyperventilating."

"I'm okay now." She sat up shakily.

Dylan knelt in front of her. When she looked at him her eyes were huge and haunted. Wetting her lips she whispered, "The baby looked so much like Janey...the tree...the tinsel...Tim used to toss her up...."

"Oh, God," Dylan said.

Reed had moved everyone back and retrieved their coats. "Want me to drive you home?"

"No, I've got my car. But you can stay with the recruits." Dylan stood, bundled a silent Beth into her coat and shrugged into his. He hustled her out of the huge room, wincing at the tune coming over the loudspeaker—"Have Yourself a Merry Little Christmas."

In the car, Dylan held her hand and apologized. "I'm so sorry. It was stupid of me to bring you here."

He drove for a few minutes before she answered. "It's not that."

"What do you mean?"

"It's something else." Her breathing started to quicken again. He thought about pulling over.

"Wait, sweetheart, until we get home."

He headed to her house because it was closer. She was eerily silent the entire way, but her hands trembled despite the fiery heat blasting inside the car.

In her condo, he removed their outer garments. Finally they sat on her couch.

"Hold me just for a minute," she said achingly.

He tugged her to him and soothed her arm. "It's okay, baby. It's a setback, but you'll get through it. I should have known not to push so hard."

"It's more than a setback." She took a deep breath. "I'm pregnant."

His breathing stopped. This was the *last* thing he'd expected. He couldn't speak.

"It's yours, of course." She touched his cheek. "Once you came into my life, there was never anybody else."

Reality began to dawn—and with it a joy he'd never known before. He reached down to touch her stomach. "Pregnant?"

She jerked back as if she'd been scorched, inching away from him. "No, don't do that."

Okay, he thought, *this isn't going to be simple.* Running a hand through his hair, he stared at her. "All the symptoms are there. I should have guessed." He narrowed his eyes. "And since we've been making love, you haven't had your period. It never occurred to me."

She bit her already raw lips. "Me, neither."

"Well, to say this is a surprise is an understatement."

"It's a tragedy."

He moved closer to her and grabbed her hands. "No, it's not. Look, I know you didn't want this. I was willing to go along with no children because it was what you thought you needed. But don't you see, fate's intervened. It was meant to happen."

"No, Dylan, it wasn't."

"I don't understand."

"I can't have another baby."

"Of course you can. We'll do it together."

"No."

An insidious fear snaked into his heart. "No? But you're already pregnant."

"I won't be as soon as I can make an appointment with my gynecologist."

He went cold all over. "Oh, honey, you don't mean that."

"Yes, I do."

"No, no, it's wrong." This time he did touch her stomach. "This is our baby you're talking about."

She wrenched away from him, stood, closed her arms protectively around her waist and paced. "No, it's not a baby. It's a few cells. That's all."

"It's our baby."

"No." She shouted the word.

He stood, too. "Beth…"

"No, I won't be talked out of this. Or seduced out of it. Or manipulated out of it like everything else."

That stung. But there were bigger issues to deal with.

"You can't mean you'd get rid of this child."

"It isn't a child."

He grasped her shoulders, not in anger but with utter gentleness. Just as gently he asked, "Is that how you felt when you found out you were pregnant with Janey?"

Her face paled alarmingly. Tears gathered in her eyes and fell mercilessly down her cheeks. "How can you say that? I told you about Janey, and now you use it against me?"

"I'm trying to save you from making the worst mistake of your life."

She stepped back, sobbing. "It's not a mistake."

"In your heart you know it is. Otherwise, you wouldn't be crying."

Swiping at the tears as if she could banish them, she struggled for air. Desperation, acute and jagged, was etched in her face. "I won't do this again. I won't put myself in that position again." Instead of moving away, she took a step toward him. She grabbed the front of his uniform shirt. "Don't you see, I'd die this time, Dylan. I couldn't survive it again. I can't risk it. I'd rather die myself than risk it.''

Chilling words came to him. *The female betta releases her eggs, then the male fertilizes them. When they're done, he kicks out the female because she may eat them. He guards the nest until the eggs hatch.*

Feeling like his heart had been ripped out of his chest, Dylan faced her squarely. Again, as gently as he could, given the avalanche of grief that threatened to suffocate him, he said, ''Please, honey, this is irrevocable. Don't do it.''

''I have to. You don't understand…you just don't understand how awful it was.''

Somewhere inside Dylan, a small part of him did understand. She'd been through hell, and no sane person would want to risk that again. But this was his child's life he was fighting for, so he had to be strong. ''You'll lose me, too. Along with our baby. The other—not having any kids—I could have handled that. I can never accept this…atrocity.''

Her shoulders shook. ''I have no choice, Dylan.''

He swallowed hard. ''There's always a choice, Lizzie.''

Stepping away, feeling like his world had gone up in flames, Dylan grabbed his coat and left Beth's house.

CHAPTER FIFTEEN

"I DON'T THINK SO Marilyn." Dylan, seated at his desk with his back to the door, spoke into the phone. He tugged impatiently at the collar of his blue shirt and shook his head.

From the doorway, Beth glanced at the clock. Almost nine. *He didn't waste much time.*

Not fair. She'd given up all rights late Saturday afternoon when she told him she was going to— She short-circuited the thought, as she'd done all weekend. It was the only way she could live with her decision.

Making as much noise as possible, she entered the office. He swiveled in his chair immediately. When his eyes locked on hers, Beth tried to steel herself against the wrenching sadness she saw there.

That she had caused.

"No, I don't think so," he repeated into the phone. "I need to go. I'll call you."

Beth tried not wince. He'd call Melanie or Missy or Marilyn now. He'd smother them with tenderness and make breathless love to them. Her head began to pound with images of Dylan with another woman. Her stomach roiled. Dropping her bag to the floor, she bolted to the bathroom and fell to her knees at the toilet. She was violently ill, shaking all over. When she was done, she sat back on her haunches and buried her face in her hands.

A rustling sound made her look up. Dylan stared at her for a minute, then knelt beside her and drew her onto his lap.

It was too much. She began to cry, deep, racking sobs that

filled the small room. He smoothed her hair. She felt a kiss she didn't deserve on the top of her head. Finally she quieted.

"I didn't make a date with her." His voice was gravelly.

"You will, though. Someday."

"Don't think about it now. We'll both be stronger by then."

Beth drew back and stared at him. "Why are you being nice to me? I thought you'd—" Tears welled again.

He wiped them away with rough fingertips. "I love you, Beth. I'm afraid I will for a long time."

"I love you, too."

His eyes misted and his hand crept to her stomach. She didn't—couldn't—push it away this time. He pressed gently. "I love both of you."

She started to speak.

"No, don't say anything. I promised myself I wouldn't keep on you about this. It's your decision." He eased her away and stood, then reached down, grasped her hand and tugged her up. She swayed on her feet. "You shouldn't be here," he said, steadying her.

She stepped back to stand on her own. "It's the recruits' last week. I have responsibilities."

He nodded. "Are you all right now?"

"Yeah. I'll splash some water on my face and brush my teeth."

"I'm going to go talk with Ben." His eyes said, *I need to get away from you.*

When she came back out to the office, she headed to her desk. On the way, she noticed Dylan's truck collection. *His toys.* She detoured to them. Slowly she fingered the shiny chrome and bright red paint. Someday he'd share this collection with his child. Eventually he'd have one with someone else. Would it be a boy or a girl? Would he want his daughter to be a firefighter?

No, stop, don't do this. It won't help.

Only one thing would.

She crossed to her desk, found her address book and dialed with shaky hands before she changed her mind.

"Westside Women's Center," said the female voice on the other end.

"Yes, I'd like to make an appointment to see Dr. Halladay."

"Dr. Halladay is out of town until next Monday. If it's an emergency, I can set you up with Dr. Johnson."

"No, no, I need to see Karen."

The woman hesitated. "We have a cancellation for Tuesday, December twenty-first."

"Fine. I'll take it."

The woman asked the pertinent questions as Beth blanked her mind. "Ms. Winters. What's the nature of the visit?"

Beth cleared her throat. "A pregnancy...termination."

"Oh. Well the doctor will need to talk to you before then."

"Fine I'll call her on Monday." Swallowing hard, Beth put down the phone. She closed her eyes and dug her knuckles into the lids. When she opened them, she saw Dylan in the doorway. His mouth was a hard slash of agony in his face. The skin was taut across his cheekbones. He watched her for a moment, then turned away and went down the hall.

Beth stared after him. She wished she could just sleep all day like she'd done yesterday; though she'd had horrid dreams, reality was worse. Images came to her from the nightmares—Janey's face on Christmas morning, then Janey falling into the frigid lake. Tim, when they'd first made love, then Tim's big, masculine hands clawing at the ice. Somewhere during those long hours, Tim's face had metamorphosed into Dylan's face. He was holding Janey, tossing her up in front of the Christmas tree.

Beth stood abruptly. Nine-thirty, the clock said. She had a meeting at ten. Hurrying, she climbed the stairs and made her way to Reed's office. The door was open, but he was on the phone. "Maybe, Tina. I'm not sure." He smiled, and despite her preoccupation, Beth watched him curiously. She knew nothing about his personal life.

"I don't usually do anything on Christmas Eve.... All right...I'll think about it." Again he smiled. "Fine, I'll let you know."

When he put the phone down, he stared at it. Beth sucked in her breath. She recognized the look, the struggle on his face. She knocked gently. "Reed?"

The expression was gone when he glanced up. Beth knew that tactic, too. "Beth, what can I do..." He stopped speaking when he really saw her. "Something's wrong."

"Do you have a minute?"

"Of course. Come in and close the door."

Shutting out the rest of the academy, Beth made her way to Reed's couch. Even the welcoming atmosphere of his office didn't soothe her today. "I have a favor to ask," she said.

"Shoot."

"Dylan..." She stopped. Cleared her throat. "Dylan's going to need some help...." She threw up her hands, then let them fall listlessly to her lap. "I don't know how to tell you this, but I've got to...for him."

"Just say it straight out. I can help you both."

"No one can help me, Reed. I thought Dylan could, but I was wrong." The psychologist waited. "We aren't getting married."

"I'm sorry to hear that."

"I'm pregnant."

Uncharacteristically, he showed surprise. Then he frowned. "Usually marriage is a good idea, then."

"I can't have it."

Again, the surprise, and some sadness. "I see."

"I...I had a child once. You didn't know that. She died. I can't risk it again. I won't."

"Oh, Beth, I'm sorry." He paused. "Would you like to talk about that? We might be able to find some alternatives. See things differently."

She shook her head. "I don't want to see things differently. I want to get past this. And I want you to help Dylan deal with it."

"Have you told him? About the baby?"

She winced at the word. "Yes. And my plans. He's devastated, of course. But I have no choice."

"There's always a choice."

"I can't survive it again, Reed."

He glanced at the phone. His face was full of empathy when he looked at her. "We can survive a lot more than we think."

Nervous, she stood. Stuck her hands into her pockets and paced. "No, not this. I only came here to ask you to help Dylan through it. He's having a rough time today. It will get worse. He won't tell you any of this to protect my privacy, but he'll need you."

"I'll be there for him."

"Thanks." She headed to the door.

"And for you, too," he called after her. She stopped. "I can help, Beth."

Without turning back, she shook her head. "No one can help now, Reed."

DYLAN WAS in the bay at eleven-thirty ostensibly checking hoses, but he needed the fresh air to clear his head. He hurt so much inside he wanted to die.

He still couldn't believe what had happened in the past few days. Pounding his fist on the rig, he leaned his face against the cool chrome. How could she do this? How?

"Dylan?" He glanced up to find Francey a few feet away.

He struggled for composure. "Hi. What are you doing here?"

"I came to see you." She stepped closer. "You look awful."

"Wild weekend."

Francey cleared her throat. "Dyl, I know."

His eyes widened. "How can you possibly know?"

"Beth told me and Chelsea. Actually we did the pregnancy test Thursday with her."

Slowly he nodded. "Did she tell you everything?"

The grim look on his best friend's face doused any flicker of hope he might have been secretly harboring. Francey knew Beth better than anyone. She'd know if Beth was really going to do this awful thing. "Yes. I know it all."

Francey stepped even closer and opened her arms. His defenses crumbled, and he went into her embrace. When his shoulders started to shake, she awkwardly led him behind the rig to relative privacy. He accepted the comfort for only a few minutes, then pulled back and swiped at his cheeks. "Sorry."

"It's worth crying over."

Dylan sighed, leaned against the truck. "I'm going to leave the academy right after graduation. I already talked to your dad this morning. I'll go back to any station house that has an opening, but I've got to get out of here."

"I understand."

"France?"

"Yeah?"

"When she does this, when she has the—" He couldn't say the word.

Francey nodded, indicating she understood. Her eyes teared up, which made his moist again.

"Don't let her do it alone. She thinks she can handle it, but it'll kill her. You and Chelsea go with her."

Francey swallowed hard. "Of course we will." She stared at him. "You're quite a guy, Dylan O'Roarke."

"Apparently not enough for her to risk this."

"I'm so sorry."

"Me, too."

ON FRIDAY, December 17, Beth sat on the stage next to Lou Giancarlo and Eric Scanlon dressed in her RFD issue navy blue dress uniform, hat and white gloves.

"I'd like to welcome all of you to the graduation of the Rockford Fire Department Fall Recruit Class of 1999." Chief Talbot smiled at the audience.

"And now I'd like to introduce the class of 1999."

Beth stood as the graduates marched military-style down the aisle of the auditorium dressed as she was, except with their brand-new RFD patches. Keeping her eyes straight ahead, she avoided looking at Dylan, who looked so handsome in his dress uniform she wanted to cry. Which was about all she'd done for the past week.

After the RFD color guard posted the colors and the Pledge of Allegiance was recited, the deputy chief gave his surprisingly humorous opening remarks. Beth forced herself to relax. They'd done a good job with this class. All the graduates were well-trained and would make excellent firefighters. That Hoyt Barnette had dropped out was a disappointment, but he'd told Reed in his exit interview that he believed in his heart he wasn't meant to be a firefighter. He was considering becoming a teacher, mostly because of O'Roarke, he'd said.

Don't think about him. Don't think about the situation.

The words had become a mantra she repeated several times a day. It was a tactic for survival, one she knew very well from when Tim and Janey died. She'd never planned to use it again.

"We'd like to show you some shots of what the class went through these thirteen weeks," the chief told the audience. "A picture says it better than any of us can."

Lights dimmed, and Beth sat back. She loved this part of the ceremony, so she was unprepared for the wave of nostalgia when the shots came on, backed by the music from *Jurassic Park*. Beth watched the images of the last three months—roll call, the first time the recruits donned their SCBAs, the tunnel-like maze with a trapped Harriet, driving the truck, the smokehouse. All the while a narrator told the audience what was happening. ''The recruits have learned many new skills and a new vocabulary—rig driving, pump operation, making a hydrant, using a K 12 saw, laying line, rope rescue and rappelling.''

A picture of Abbott rappelling off the Genesee Street Bridge came on, then one of Battisti cutting through a roof on an empty house, another of Frank crawling into the smokehouse and the words written on the wall—''If you can read this, then it's not smoky enough in here.'' Cleary appeared, too, in top shape as she shimmied up a rope at the end.

The instructors' turn came. Giancarlo with his famous poses, hands on hips, scowling at Abbott. Eric Scanlon, with his devastating smile, on the bottom of the aerial ladder where he would demonstrate proper climbing techniques. Chuck Lorenzo was next, holding up numbers to indicate scores on RTR's.

And there was O'Roarke wrestling with hose, wrapping a broken arm, ducking around Tully on the basketball court. When a photo came on of Beth facing Dylan across a desk, both with arms braced on the top, staring each other down, she sucked in her breath. The recruits cheered, but they didn't know that this story no longer had a happy ending.

Slowly, her hand crept to her stomach. *Why, God, why?* she thought bitterly. *We could have been happy.*

Dylan wanted to choke on his tie when the clips of Beth began—leading the morning exercise class at six, demonstrating the use of the oxygen canister, a rare photo of her smiling. Just looking at her hurt. Would he ever get over her? Damn, damn, damn.

After the pictures, Talbot introduced Ben Cordaro. "The RFD is rich with history and with pride," Ben began. "And it is with that pride that I will swear in the fall recruit class of 1999. Will the recruits please stand and repeat the oath after me."

The recruits donned their hats again, stood and repeated Ben's words in unison. "I, firefighter—say your name—do hereby pledge and declare that I will support the constitution of the United States and the constitution of the state of New York and that I will faithfully discharge the duties of the position of firefighter of the Rockford Fire Department according to the best of my ability."

With a rush of nostalgia Dylan remembered giving his oath, the pride he felt at finally achieving his goal. He never thought anything could make him happier than firefighting. He'd been wrong.

Despite his will not to, he sneaked a glance at Beth. She was pale, and makeup couldn't conceal the smudges beneath her eyes. He was shocked to see her hand resting on her stomach. Protecting his baby?

No, of course not. In four short days, that baby wouldn't exist.

He turned to see Wanikya, class valedictorian, approach the podium. The young man thanked Chief Cordaro for making minorities' and women's entry in the RFD smooth. He told a few stories about how the other recruits pulled him in despite his reserve. He credited the fairness and integrity of the instructors.

The last event was a recruit video scrapbook. The camera showed still photos of each recruit with their words of thanks superimposed over the pictures.

Ace Durwin smiled into the camera. "I'd like to thank my wife for supporting me at forty-eight in this new career. It's gonna be good, honey."

Brady Abbott credited his buddies Ryan Quinn and Austyn

Myers for getting him through, and mentioned how important teamwork was.

Trevor Tully grinned boyishly at the camera. He said, "I'd especially like to thank Lieutenant Dylan O'Roarke for teaching me not only what it takes to be a good, *safe* firefighter, but also what it means to be a man. He's been like a father to me."

Father. Dylan's stomach knotted.

It cramped mercilessly when Connie Cleary's pictures flashed on. There were several shots of her and Beth. Over them she said, "I haven't had a mother in ten years. I'd like to thank Beth Winters for filling that void in my life and for helping make me the woman I am today."

Dylan groaned inwardly, wondering if he could get through this ceremony, never mind life without Beth.

You can do what you have to do, Dylan, sometimes better than you think you can.

Will I be able to do this one? he asked Grandma Katie silently.

This time, there was no answer.

Dimly, he was aware of the rest of the program. At the end, he went through the motions of congratulating all the new firefighters and posing for endless pictures. He managed to stay on the other side of the room from Beth until Frank took his hand and dragged him to the large Maltese cross backdrop on stage. "I'd like a picture of you and Ms. Winters, Lieutenant."

Cleary had brought Beth.

Weakly Beth smiled at him. He tried to smile back.

"Get in close," Frank said innocently. "Come on, Lieutenant, slip your hand around that special woman in your life."

He felt Beth stiffen.

"Easy," he whispered, sliding his arm around the waist

he'd never expected to touch again. "Let's not spoil it for them."

"Of course." Her voice was full of tears.

"Now, guys, smile pretty for the camera."

His heart breaking because he couldn't have the woman who fit beside him like Eve did Adam, Dylan smiled.

THE MONDAY after graduation, the academy was empty of the recruits and much of the staff was on vacation. Though she felt physically drained, Beth had come to work because she couldn't stay home any longer. Over the weekend she'd questioned if she was losing her mind. She'd been unable to sleep, assailed as she was by doubts and inundated with images of the graduation.

He's been like a father to me.... I never had a mother.... Father...mother...father...

Beth thought she would scream if she didn't get away from herself. Intending to catch up on the mounds of paperwork, she entered the office. And caught her breath.

The room had been swept clean of Dylan's things. His area was like the shell of a house hollowed out by fire. His desk was cleared off. The boom box was gone—and already she missed the blare of his music. Everything had been emptied from the shelves except his fire trucks. As she crossed to his side of the room, her foot nudged an empty box on the floor.

"I didn't think you'd come in today."

She whirled. He was at the doorway, windblown and beautiful in jeans and fire department sweatshirt. His square jaw was tight, and his eyes were bloodshot.

"I have paperwork."

"I'll be out of here in a minute. I've just got one more box."

"No hurry." Her voice was scratchy.

She went to her desk as he crossed to the trucks. Opening her bottom drawer to stow her purse, she felt her eyes mist.

She glanced at Dylan. His head down, he carefully wrapped a truck in newspaper.

Before she could talk herself out of it, she drew the two presents out of her drawer and strode to his desk, as morose as a pallbearer. "I, um, got you these for Christmas."

He looked up from where he sat but didn't reach for the gifts.

"You don't have to take them if you don't want to."

"They're the first Christmas presents you've bought in twenty years, aren't they?"

Silently she nodded.

He took the brightly wrapped packages and opened the larger one. Despite the misery in his eyes, he smiled. "Where did you get it? It's unavailable."

She looked at the Washington DC 1/64th Seagrave Tractor. "Yes, I know. I had a friend in New York track one down after I saw it advertised in a flyer on your desk."

"It's beautiful." He stared at her. "Thanks."

"I ordered it a while ago. Since I'd teased you so much about your toys, I thought it was a way to show you I accepted that side of you." Her voice cracked on the last phrase.

He didn't answer, just coughed to clear his throat. He picked up the little square box. "Two?"

"Yeah. This one's more personal."

His hands shook as he tore open the small gift. Tenderly he drew out the medal. And smiled with recognition. "Saint Luke. The patron saint of EMS."

He turned it over. His badge number was engraved on the back. He didn't look at her right away, just lovingly traced the numbers. Finally, he raised his eyes and handed her the medal.

As if performing a sacred rite, she took it and looped it around his neck, letting the gold pendant nestle near his heart. She bent and kissed the top of his head. "Be safe, Dylan."

When he said nothing, she turned and went to her desk, carefully avoiding watching him pack the rest of the trucks. He finished in ten minutes. Out of the corner of her eye, she saw him carry the box to the doorway; he set it in the hall. Then, he got his coat from the closet while she pretended to look in the file drawers.

Please God, don't let me cry while he's here. Let him leave first.

"Beth." When she turned, he was in his leather jacket and holding a large, square package in his hand. "I debated whether to give you this."

She stared at him for a moment, then reached for it. In slow, precise movements, like she did everything else, she untied the ribbon, undid the tape, opened the box.

And gasped. Inside were two dolls, so lifelike she thought they might speak. One was a replica of Dylan—dressed as he'd been the night he got the *Firehouse* award. Even the shock of black hair on the doll's forehead fell the way his did. The boy doll was holding hands with the girl doll—who, of course, looked like her. She was decked out in the green strapless gown, right down to the shawl she'd worn that night.

Beth's eyes blurred, but she fought the blaze of emotion. She said only, "This was the first night we made love."

He smiled sadly at her phrasing. It hadn't been just sex after all.

"Where did you get them?" Beth asked.

"Mrs. Santori made them. I took your dress and my tux to her, along with some pictures." When Beth didn't respond, he continued, "I thought we could start your collection again…start new…I…" Choked up, he couldn't continue.

There was a long silence. She placed the dolls in the box and covered them. "Thank you." A pang shot through her when she thought of putting these dolls in the chest with the others, never to be seen, never to be enjoyed. To ease the clutch in her heart, she said, "You have your Immaculate Conception party tomorrow."

He nodded.

She stared at him. His eyes dropped to her stomach.

"I overheard you on the phone. Your appointment's in the morning."

She nodded.

"Take it easy for a while. After."

His kindness hit her like an emotional sledgehammer. She looked away.

He stood where he was for a moment, then came around the desk and placed a soft kiss on her forehead. "Take care, Winters."

She stared at the floor. "You, too, O'Roarke."

Thank God he shut the door on the way out.

Placing her head on the desk, she gave in to the sobs.

She didn't know how much time had passed when she heard a knock on the door. Reed pushed it open. "Beth?"

Sitting up, she wiped at her eyes. "I, um…"

He closed the door behind him and crossed to the front of her desk. "Can I do something?"

She shook her head.

"Dylan told me to come down."

A fresh bout of tears accompanied that news. Reed circled the desk, knelt next to her and ran a soothing hand down her shoulder.

When she finally pulled herself together, she said, "I can't stand this."

"Then maybe it's the wrong thing to do."

"Is it? How would I know?"

For a minute his face got bleak. Then he said, "Let's talk about it. I can help, Beth. I know it."

THE FRIGID DECEMBER wind blew Beth's scarf around her face as she approached the small cemetery plot. The graves looked different covered with snow. She adjusted the burlap she'd placed on the rosebushes earlier this year. Then she dusted off Janey's grave and lovingly traced the letters of her daughter's name. She did the same for her four parents. Finally she reached Tim's grave.

Kneeling on the hard, unyielding ground, she cleared his headstone.

Hi, Bethy baby.

Hi.

You don't look so hot.

She shivered. *It's only eight degrees, you idiot.* She stared at the grave.

You're sad.

I can't do this, Tim.

Of course you can't, sweetheart. You could never get rid of that baby.

But how can I take the chance again?

Life's one big crapshoot, Bethy.

Beth swallowed hard. *I talked to Reed Macauley. He said I have choices. I can get stronger.*

Good advice.

My job isn't enough anymore.

Of course it isn't. You need Dylan. And another family.

Beth waited before she said, *He probably hates me.*

He loves you more than life itself, just like I did.

Oh, Tim.

No, now stop. You've been given a second chance. To love and to have another child. My girl would never blow that.

Do you think I can do it?

I know you can. And he'll help you.

Beth placed her hand on her stomach. Lovingly she caressed it. After a moment she stood to go to the car where Reed waited for her.

Hey, Bethy, baby?

Yeah?

Bring him along next time. I wanna meet this guy.

She smiled at the grave. *You're on, Tim.*

THE HUGE AUDITORIUM had been decorated by the students of the Immaculate Conception School. Festive greenery drooped in places, big uneven snowflakes dangled in the air, and a Christmas tree sported lopsided ornaments. There were red and green signs everywhere in a childish scrawl. They announced, "We love our firefighters," "Keep our firefighters safe," and "Firefighters are the best."

As the students wound up a last off-key verse of "Frosty the Snowman," Dylan smiled at them from the podium. Imperfect children in an imperfect world. All of them were afflicted with Down's syndrome. The school, founded thirty years ago, took them at any age and all levels of retardation. And loved them. Just as Dylan would have loved—

No. Don't think about it.

Ruthlessly suppressing his emotions, he picked up the mike to play his annual part as emcee. "Those songs were terrific," he said, "only Rudolph, here, is really bothering me." The students laughed as a costumed Rudolph nudged Dylan once again. "No, Rudolph, I don't kiss in public. Now get away."

Rudolph pretended to cry.

"Kiss, kiss..." The kids cried out and clapped their hands at the ongoing disagreement between Dylan and Rudolph.

"All right, only if I can tell my jokes."

The audience moaned at the mention of the corny Christmas puns Dylan would recite. Dylan gave Rudolph a big smacker on his bright red nose, and the kids cheered.

With theatrical flourish, Dylan spoke into the mike. "What did the Italian angel say to the shepherds?" After a moment, he answered, "Pizza on Earth."

Again, laughter.

"What does a reindeer get on the beach?" A dramatic pause. "Sandy Claws."

More laughter.

"What did Santa say to Mrs. Claus when asked about the weather?" Quiet. "It looks like rain, dear."

Dylan felt better after the jokes. *Seek joy in what you give, not in what you get,* Grandma Katie used to say. And she was right, once again.

"I'd like to call Sister Sara up here to say a few words."

As tradition had it, the director of the school came to the stage. "This party goes back thirty years," she began.

Dylan listened, blanking his mind. When it began to wander, he forced himself to think about the parade that morning—fire trucks decorated with wreaths, Santa waving, horns blowing, the excited faces of the children as soft snowflakes drifted onto their noses and hair. He'd always wished he had kids at Christmas. He could have had one next year.

In spite of his vow not to dwell on it, he glanced at the clock. Ten-thirty. Her appointment had been at nine. There would be no baby next year. The thought turned his stomach, so he focused on the one hundred and fifty active and retired firefighters who'd paraded into the auditorium minutes ago. He glanced toward the kitchen, staffed by Ben Cordaro and some of his old buddies from the line. To the side in the cafeteria, other RFD personnel were setting up for lunch, where each child was assigned his or her own personal firefighter.

"…and every day, we pray to God to keep our firefighters safe." Sister Sara ended her talk.

Be safe, Dylan.

His hand went to the spot over his heart where he wore his St. Luke medal. Funny, he'd lost Beth, but he'd be safer now than he was before he met her—he'd learned the preciousness of life.

Dylan took the stage again and called the Shriner clowns.

Dressed in turnout gear, they mimicked firefighters with hoses that didn't work and turnout pants that kept falling down. He was heading out to change into his Santa costume when he saw Francey and Chelsea enter the auditorium.

So it was over. Jagged pain ripped through him unlike any he'd known before. He swallowed hard and strode offstage.

Minutes later he was handing out presents to each child, which took the edge off his anguish. As each young person was escorted by one or two firefighters, Dylan chided himself for not being thankful for what he had. When Francey and Chelsea brought up their child, he smiled at them through his beard.

They didn't look sad. As a matter of fact, they were grinning. Strange. He knew Francey well. She couldn't have gone through that with Beth this morning and come out unscathed.

A child on his lap distracted him. As he asked her what she wanted for Christmas and if she'd been good, and gave her a special gift picked out just for her, his mind went on red alert.

His heart almost stopped when the last child came to the stage. A three-year-old girl named Ellie, wearing a red velvet dress and a big red bow in her hair. She was a favorite of the fire department because her father was a smoke eater who'd died in the line of duty. Dylan was pleased to see Ellie but shocked at the adult who lovingly handed her to him.

It was Beth, dressed as she'd been at graduation, in the navy blue RFD uniform. But it wasn't how she was dressed that snagged his attention; it was her face. For the first time since he'd met her, she looked totally at peace.

What did it mean?

He was ostensibly giving his attention to Ellie, his mind whirled. He didn't want to get his hopes up. But how could she have just erased her own child from her life, then come here to celebrate the birth of the Christ child? How could she bear to look at all these children who were lovingly cared for by their parents despite their disability?

She couldn't.

Finally the gifts were gone, and each firefighter took his child by the hand, accompanied by parents, to the cafeteria. The auditorium emptied.

Beth was gone, too.

He sighed. Maybe it had been wishful thinking. Maybe he'd just wanted to believe it. But he sure as hell was going to hunt her down and find out. He hurried off the stage to the men's faculty bathroom. He'd change in there so no child would accidentally stumble on Santa's transformation into a firefighter.

In a T-shirt, Santa pants and hat, he was teetering on one foot trying to tug off a boot when the door opened.

And there she was. She snicked the lock, and he was reminded of the retirement party when he'd cornered her in the john.

She had committed to him that weekend.

His pulse beat like a thousand drums. "What are you doing here?"

She arched a brow. A mischievous brow. She'd unbuttoned her coat, and a soft white blouse peeked out. "You've been ragging on me for months to participate in this event. You got some complaint now, O'Roarke?"

"Ah, no, Winters. None at all." He looked at her stomach. "How did the…appointment go?"

She stepped closer, her eyes sparkling. "Good. Though Dr. Halladay was really pissed off at you."

"At me?"

"Uh-huh. She wanted to know why the father of my baby missed the first prenatal visit."

His stomach dropped to his knees and he grabbed the edge of the sink. "Beth, are you saying…"

She covered the distance between them. She took his hands

in hers, then brought them to her stomach. "I couldn't do it, Dylan."

He blinked twice and swallowed hard. "Do you mean it?"

"Yes, I do."

Filled with joy, he caressed her abdomen with reverence, then tugged her to him. He just held on to her, tightly, breathing in the scent of her.

After a few moments she drew back. Her eyes were bright with unshed tears. "Forgive me. I was confused, and scared." She gave him a watery smile. "I'll have your baby. I'll try to be the woman you want, the woman you need."

"Oh, Lizzie," he said, gently brushing his knuckles down her cheek. "You are. I just wanted all of you."

"You got all of me." Her hand went to her abdomen. "All of *us*."

"Well," he said, drawing her close again, "Grandma Katie said I could have it all if I had faith."

She nestled her head on his chest. "Then I'll have faith, too."

Outside, the bells of the Immaculate Conception Church chimed out over the school grounds. Dylan took that as a sign from above. He looked heavenward and pictured Grandma Katie and Tim Winters smiling down at all three of them.

*Turn the page
for a preview of the final book
in Kathryn Shay's exciting trilogy—*
AMERICA'S BRAVEST

CODE OF HONOR

*Harlequin Superromance #882
Coming next month*

"YOU'RE THE PERFECT one to deal with Chelsea Whitmore, Scarlatta. There's already a woman in your firehouse on another shift—and you fought tooth and nail for Francey Cordaro's rights—so the setup is ideal. With Fuller's retirement, there's room on your group right now."

Jake Scarlatta stared at Chief Talbot, the Rockford Fire Department's top man, whom he'd always respected, and tried to keep from objecting immediately. There had to be *some* way to convince the chief that moving Whitmore to his fire station wasn't wise. Damned if he could think of one, though. "I wish you'd reconsider," he said lamely.

Talbot stroked his graying mustache and studied Jake. "This have anything to do with that incident with DeLuca years ago?"

Jake kept himself from flinching at the mention of his one past, very public mistake. "In a way. I like to run a tight ship now."

"And Whitmore will rock the boat?"

More like cause major flooding. But he knew she was a good firefighter, and no matter what his personal feelings were, it wasn't fair to smudge her reputation. "It won't be easy. My men aren't as...liberated as Ed Knight's group. Francey was an easy fit there."

Talbot said, "Well, Whitmore's not going to be an easy fit anywhere. You're the best choice. She didn't make a stink about what happened over at Engine Four, but she could sue the pants off us if she wanted to. We've got to be very careful this time.''

Tales of what had happened to Chelsea Whitmore at her last assignment—she was one of the five females out of five hundred firefighters in the RFD in upstate New York—had swept through the department quicker than brushfire. She'd made the classic mistake—dated a fellow firefighter in her group, broke his heart and then the guy went berserk and endangered himself and his entire crew. The woman would never live that down.

And since Jake knew all about making classic mistakes, and having them haunt you, it looked like his penance was going to be dealing with her.

''When will she start?''

''Her leave is open-ended. She wants to come back as soon as possible.''

Jake sighed heavily. ''Do it, then. We'll manage. Somehow. I just—''

Jake's pager beeped, startling him. He was on edge not only because of the topic of discussion, but because his good buddy's wife, Beth O'Roarke, was expecting their first child any time within the next month and Jake had agreed to be ready to fill in for Dylan on his shift at the firehouse at a moment's notice.

He read the pager note and bolted out of his seat.

Talbot's bushy brows rose. ''O'Roarke?''

''Yep. Beth's in labor. Gotta go.'' Jake was out the door in seconds, and Chelsea Whitmore was the last thing on his mind.

SUPERROMANCE®

Three childhood friends dreamed of becoming firefighters. Now they're members of the same team and every day they put their lives on the line.

They are

An exciting new trilogy by

Kathryn Shay

#871 FEEL THE HEAT
(November 1999)
#877 THE MAN WHO LOVED CHRISTMAS
(December 1999)
#882 CODE OF HONOR
(January 2000)

Available wherever Harlequin books are sold.

Makes any time special ™

3 Stories of Holiday Romance from three bestselling Harlequin® authors

Valentine Babies

by

ANNE STUART

TARA TAYLOR QUINN

JULE McBRIDE

Goddess in Waiting by Anne Stuart
Edward walks into Marika's funky maternity shop to pick up some things for his sister. He doesn't expect to assist in the delivery of a baby and fall for outrageous Marika.

Gabe's Special Delivery by Tara Taylor Quinn
On February 14, Gabe Stone finds a living, breathing valentine on his doorstep—his daughter. Her mother has given Gabe four hours to adjust to fatherhood, resolve custody and win back his ex-wife?

My Man Valentine by Jule McBride
Everyone knows Eloise Hunter and C. D. Valentine are in love. Except Eloise and C. D. Then, one of Eloise's baby-sitting clients leaves her with a baby to mind, and C. D. swings into protector mode.

VALENTINE BABIES

On sale January 2000 at your favorite retail outlet.

HARLEQUIN®
Makes any time special ™

Visit us at www.romance.net

PHVALB

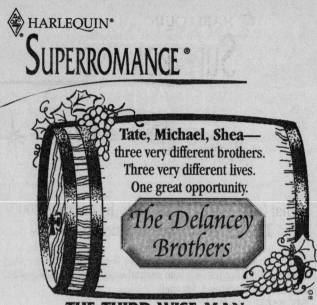

Come escape with Harlequin's new

Series Sampler

Four great full-length Harlequin novels bound together in one fabulous volume and at an unbelievable price.

Be transported back in time with a Harlequin Historical® novel, get caught up in a mystery with Intrigue®, be tempted by a hot, sizzling romance with Harlequin Temptation®, or just enjoy a down-home all-American read with American Romance®.

You won't be able to put this collection down!

On sale February 2000 at your favorite retail outlet.

HARLEQUIN®
Makes any time special ™